THE NEXT
TIME
YOU DIE

Also by Harry Hunsicker

Still River

THE NEXT TIME YOU DIE

HARRY HUNSICKER

THOMAS DUNNE BOOKS
ST. MARTIN'S MINOTAUR
NEW YORK

This is a work of fiction. All of the characters, organizations, and events portrayed
in this novel are either products of the author's imagination or are used fictitiously.

THOMAS DUNNE BOOKS.
An imprint of St. Martin's Press.

www.thomasdunnebooks.com
www.minotaurbooks.com

Library of Congress Cataloging-in-Publication Data

Hunsicker, Harry.
    The next time you die / by Harry Hunsicker.—1st ed.
        p.   cm.
    ISBN-13: 978-0-312-34850-2
    ISBN-10: 0-312-34850-9
        1. Private investigators—Texas—Dallas—Fiction.   2. Clergy—Fiction.
    3. Theft—Fiction.   4. Dallas (Tex.)—Fiction.   I. Title.

PS3608.U566 N48 2006
813'.6—dc22   2006041123

First Edition: July 2006

10 9 8 7 6 5 4 3 2 1

To Scott Broyles
April 13, 1966–October 21, 1993

Acknowledgments

Publishing a book is a team effort, and the final product you now hold is the result of a myriad of professionals. To that end I would like to thank Sean Desmond and everyone at St. Martin's Press, St. Martin's Minotaur, and Thomas Dunne Books for their dedication, professionalism, and support, as well Richard Abate for his help in all parts of the process.

Also, I am proud to be associated with a group of exceptionally talented writers, all of whom contributed to this book in more ways than they can imagine. I owe much to the guidance and support I've received from Erika Barr, Jan Blankenship, Amy Bourret, Victoria Calder, Will Clarke, Alan Duff, Fanchon Knott, David Norman, Brooke Malouf, and Max Wright. Special thanks to Amy Bourret for her last-minute help and to Patti Nunn for all that she does behind the scenes.

Finally, very special thanks to my wife, Alison, for her love, support, and patience, especially during those long days at the end.

THE NEXT
TIME
YOU DIE

CHAPTER ONE

Billy Barringer snapped the guard's neck as if it were a piece of rotten firewood. The noise echoed against the cinder-block walls and tin roof of the maintenance shed. The dead man dropped to the floor and was completely still, the front of his khaki pants darkened with urine.

One down. One to go.

A small-framed man named Charity stood just inside the doorway, wearing regulation prison whites that matched Billy's clothing. Charity gulped several times and stared at the body crumpled on the floor.

Billy snapped his fingers and pointed to the door, indicating for him to keep watch. Charity licked his lips and squinted at Billy, his eyes dull and watery. Sweat dappled his forehead even though the thick walls kept the building relatively cool in the South Texas sunshine.

"Keep your eyes open, for chrissakes." Billy jabbed a finger at the entrance.

Charity blinked and seemed to emerge from his trance. He turned to the door and stared outside.

Billy grabbed the arms of the corpse and dragged the man behind the workbench, near where the lawn mowers were chained together. He tried to control his breathing. The guard had arrived a few minutes ahead of schedule. Although minor, it was the first break in the routine since Billy had started work at the maintenance building eight months earlier, the assignment a result of his good behavior and an assistant warden with a taste for preteen girls that Billy's people on the outside had discovered.

Billy didn't like surprises, not when escaping from a maximum-security unit of the Texas Department of Corrections.

He mentally ran through the next few steps. Lunchtime on court day. The number of guards was lower than at any time during the week. Two sets of noninmate clothing for the two escapees. A key and combination to the employee parking lot, only a few hundred yards from the maintenance shed.

"Billy." Charity's high-pitched voice sounded frightened, as always. The second guard must be approaching. Billy grabbed a short length of two-by-four. He slid from behind the workbench and pressed himself against the wall next to the doorway.

The guard entered. He stopped after a couple of feet and blinked, the light in the dusty building dim after the June sun. He walked a few more paces and swiveled his head from one side to the other.

Billy stepped out of the shadows. The muscles in his shoulders and arms corded and strained against the thin cotton of his jumpsuit as he swung the chunk of pine at the guard's head.

The impact sounded like a cantaloupe hitting a kitchen floor.

The man fell in the exact same spot as the first guard. He started twitching. Billy rushed to pull off his pants in order to avoid the urine problem. Two minutes later he was dressed in the guard's uniform. The length was fine but the clothes hung loose on his frame. Eleven months of weights in the yard had turned him into all sinew and muscle, lean and sleek.

"Put that guy's stuff on." Billy pointed to the other guard.

Charity stared at the fully clothed dead man. "No way. Guy's pissed in his pants."

"Put on the clothes." Billy tried to keep his voice even.

"But—"

"Get changed. Now." Billy grabbed the inmate by his arm and felt the thin muscles, weak and slack like those only a man unfortunate enough to be named Charity would have. The smaller man began slowly pulling the clothes off the corpse.

Billy found the key and a piece of paper with the combination taped on the bottom of a gas can. He wondered how the two items came to be there but decided not to expend too much energy dwelling on such things.

"You didn't have to kill them, did you?" Charity threw his prison whites on the floor.

"Not taking any chances," Billy said. "Don't want to stay on the inside. Do you?"

"No." The smaller man slipped on the guard's shirt and shuddered. "Ain't *never* going back."

Billy chuckled to himself. Prison was a bad place for people like Charity, a cell-block lay preacher following a muddled family tradition of piety and minor criminal activity.

When they were both dressed, the two men stood in the doorway. Billy looked at the parking lot, a shimmering acre of asphalt less than a half mile away. He ran a finger over the teeth of the key as if it were a talisman. Maybe five minutes to walk across the prison yard. Another thirty seconds to open the first gate with the key and then work the push-button combination lock on the second entrance.

The next step was tricky.

A green pickup was supposed to be waiting in the lot, keys on the floorboard. Somewhere in the second row. But how long was that row going to be? And would other guards be in the lot? Odds were in their favor since it wasn't time for a shift change. But there was still a risk, however small.

Billy pulled the shirt tight against his shoulders in an effort to make the garment look like it fit. He swelled his chest and tried to project himself as a prison guard. He stepped into the hot sun, Charity by his side. Together they walked toward the parking lot.

Billy was no stranger to betrayal. Betrayal by one of his closest friends had sent him to prison on a twenty-five-to-life sentence. Betrayal had earned Billy his living before prison. Betrayal was a way of life, a family tradition. Betrayal had also brought Billy a chance to escape.

A man with skin the color of buttermilk, wearing linen pants and a yellow silk shirt, stood with his hands in his pockets, staring at Billy. He said, "It's about time."

His name was Jesus Rundell, and he was a third-string fix-it man in the Houston branch of one of the border cartels. Billy, Charity, and Jesus were standing in the shade of a withered palm tree behind a boarded-up Esso station on a stretch of road ten miles west of Dilley, Texas, about halfway between Laredo and San Antonio.

"I went the speed limit," Billy said. "Didn't want to get stopped."

The plan had worked. They had walked out. Strolled past the towers with the guards, through the gate in the razor wire surrounding the parking lot, and into the waiting pickup. The next car, a four-year-old Crown Victoria, was behind the service station where it was supposed to be, along with new clothes in the backseat.

"You wouldn't had no trouble." Jesus pinched the crease of his pants between a thumb and forefinger. His shaved head gleamed in the sunlight.

Billy pulled on a pair of blue jeans and a white button-down shirt, both new-from-the-store fresh. He wiped the sweat out of his eyes and breathed in the creosote and stale fuel of the old gas station. Nothing was visible anywhere except palm trees and prickly pear cactus and thorny mesquite and the endless South Texas landscape, sandy and flat all the way to the Gulf of Mexico. The cloudless sky was the color of hot chrome.

Billy squinted in the sunlight and stared at the man he had hoped he would never encounter again in this life or any other. Charity was a few feet away, changing also, the scared look still plastered on his face. The man in the linen pants hadn't started in on him. Yet.

"I told you the police wouldn't be a problem." Jesus grabbed his crotch in what appeared to be an unconscious gesture.

"What happens next?" Billy tucked in his shirt.

"I never much liked you." Jesus was massaging his groin now, deep caresses to his genitals through the thin material of the pants. "Fucking Barringers always thought they were better than everybody else."

"Each his own, I suppose." Billy flexed his fingers and kept his hands loose at his sides.

Jesus turned around and faced Charity. He spoke to Billy with his back turned. "So this is your cellmate. Pretty little thing, ain't he?"

Charity's face turned white. His teeth chattered even though the temperature was in the triple digits.

"The plan . . ." Billy said. "Where do we go from here?"

"We're all going to hell." Rundell walked to where Charity stood shivering. "It's just a matter of when."

"I t-t-thought we . . . were gonna go home." Charity's voice quivered.

Rundell placed one hand on the smaller man's shoulder. "What's the going rate for a blow job on the inside these days?"

Billy stepped between the two men. "Let's just get out of here, okay?"

Jesus removed his hand from Charity's shoulder and caressed his cheek before turning to Billy. "What was the guy's name? The one that busted you."

"Oswald. Like the guy that killed Kennedy. Lee *Henry* Oswald." Billy tried not to sound exasperated. This was old news. The bust and all the details had been heavily covered by the media at the time.

"Bet you spent most of the last year thinking about what it would feel like to wrap your hands around Mr. Oswald's throat and give it a big old squeeze."

Billy shrugged.

"Wonder what it would feel like to wrap my hands around *your* throat?"

Billy didn't say anything. Charity's breathing was raspy in the still air.

After a few moments, Jesus relaxed and smiled. "You owe me, in case you forgot. For getting your ass out of the pokey."

"Yeah, I remember." Billy willed his face to remain impassive. He stretched his arms behind him and walked away from Jesus, looking for something to use as a weapon.

Jesus went to the trunk of the Ford and removed a one-gallon gasoline container.

Billy spied an empty quart bottle of Corona.

"Tell me what I need to know." Jesus's voice was low and throaty now, a sure sign he was about to lose control.

Billy scooped up the beer bottle and turned around.

Jesus had a pistol in one hand, the container of fuel in the other.

Billy felt cold. His stomach fluttered. He smelled the gasoline.

Betrayal. Again.

CHAPTER TWO

My workload came from one of several distinct groups, a pattern I figured was typical for any moderately successful private investigator in a major metropolitan area.

Most PIs thought of the first group as their best clients. The business was steady and they paid well and on time. They were lawyers in all their various shades and flavors. What could be more recession-proof than litigation and the ancillary investigations required?

Next came the people missing something of value. An inheritance. A loved one. A spouse's sexual attention. The company's checkbook. Et cetera. This was a diverse group and paid in a diverse manner. Still, work was work.

Finally, there was the miscellaneous category. These were the people who walked on the dark side of the street. The half-bent cops. The occasional call girl with a dead politician stinking up a hotel room somewhere.

And my personal favorites: the dimwit wise guys who had screwed, stolen, or ingested something that didn't exactly belong to them and needed help, off the books and pronto. If they didn't try to kill you, this group always paid, no questions asked.

The tires of my Chevy Tahoe crunched in the gravel parking lot as

I came to a stop in front of a stone and brick building nestled under two old hackberry trees. I slid the gearshift into park, turned off the ignition, and listened to the motor tick. Two guys who looked like out-of-work musicians or maybe the creative team at a small ad agency sat at a picnic table and watched me as they drank from longneck bottles of beer. I watched back for a moment and then opened the door of my truck, steeling myself against the wave of heat and humidity typical of mid-September in Texas.

My concern was that the person who had requested this meeting didn't fall into any of the usual categories, or so it seemed, based on our initial, cryptic phone conversation. He'd said his name was Lucas Linville and he was a preacher of the Baptist persuasion, and wanting to meet in a drinking establishment. If that wasn't enough to give a body pause, I didn't know what was.

I walked across the gravel and dirt yard in front of Lee Harvey's, a bar located a few blocks south of the new Dallas police headquarters in a part of town a friend of mine refers to as the corner of Gun and Knife streets. I pushed open the front door and welcomed the dim light as a relief from the afternoon sun. The air-conditioning was set somewhere between the Arctic Circle and Iceland. The place smelled like beer and burgers and stale smoke.

Originally a house a century or so back, the bar occupied what had once been the living/dining area. It split the room in two, running parallel to the front wall, and had seating on either side. The bedrooms were to the left and had been converted into one big area that now contained a pool table. The kitchen was to the right.

I picked a stool on the opposite side, facing the front door. Nothing behind me except empty room, no other access points. The guy next to me had a portable oxygen tank slung over his shoulder, a cigarette in one hand and a draft beer in the other. He was dressed in a rumpled tuxedo, no tie. He looked to be somewhere between fifty and ninety years old, give or take.

I nodded hello to the bartender, a guy I sort of knew from previous visits, and ordered a Shiner Bock. Across the room the front door opened, and I squinted against the sunlight as the man I took to be Lucas Linville entered.

Five-eight or -nine. Skinny. Late fifties. The pink bow tie was the giveaway, the article of clothing he had mentioned he would be wearing. It was tied tightly around the neck of a beige dress shirt underneath a brown suit. Even from across the room, I could see the outfit was worn at the edges.

He blinked a couple of times against the gloom of the place and then walked to the bar, leaned in, and whispered something to the guy who had just served me a beer. The bartender cut a glance my way without breaking his conversation with Linville.

I nodded.

He pointed to me with an ashtray he'd been polishing.

Linville took a moment to examine his surroundings and then walked around the bar past Mr. Emphysema and took the empty stool next to me. He stuck out a hand and introduced himself. His breath smelled like Wrigley's Doublemint chewing gum, and I caught the faint aroma of drugstore aftershave on my hand where it had pressed against his palm.

Before I could say much of anything other than my name, Linville ordered a shot of Jim Beam with a Budweiser chaser and said, "Did you have any trouble finding the place?"

I didn't reply for a moment as I watched the bartender serve up my newest favorite concoction: a Baptist boilermaker. Might have to start going to church.

"I know my way around town pretty well," I said. A few blocks away a bullet had punched a hole through the side of my new Hugo Boss leather jacket a couple of winters ago. I was still pissed about it.

"I have a small ministry not far from here." He downed the glass of whiskey in one gulp, followed it up with a swig of beer. "This is a troubled part of town, wouldn't you say?"

"No offense." I looked at my watch. "But I didn't come here to talk about urban blight."

Linville leaned back and stared at me, a blank expression on his face. "You find stuff for people, right?"

"Sometimes." Category two: people missing something. I felt a little better. "Depends on what it is."

"A file was stolen from my office yesterday."

I nodded but didn't say anything.

"My ministry helps the people on the fringes." He steepled his fingers underneath his scrawny chin. "Drug addicts. Prostitutes. What society thinks of as the gutter."

He paused for a drink of beer. "Sometimes the people who find themselves on the bottom started out on top."

"Debutantes turned streetwalkers, next on Jerry Springer." I'd been hired once to find the daughter of a social bigwig. It turned out a busboy at the country club had introduced the flaxen-haired lass to the joys of injectable methamphetamines. The situation turned out poorly for all concerned.

Linville nodded. "Yeah. More or less."

"What was in the file?"

"Records on a former employee of mine, a young man named Reese." Linville tugged on an earlobe as he talked. "Came from a prominent family. Mother was involved with all those charity balls. He could have done anything, been anything he wanted."

"What was Reese's problem?"

"He had trouble with opiates, and cocaine, too. Ended up on the streets in a bad way until I gave him a job." Linville clinked the empty shot glass against his beer bottle and asked the bartender for another Jim Beam. "His family has been more than generous to my ministry."

"When did he quit working for you?"

The older man frowned and ran his index finger around the rim of his beer can. "Four or five months ago."

"It's an employment file," I said. "So that means it has his last name."

"Yes." He lowered his voice and looked around the room. "Reese Cunningham."

The name sounded vaguely familiar. It conjured up an image of yacht clubs and cotillion dances. I said, "And Mumsy and Daddy won't be too eager to fund your operation if it gets out that their precious angel was a homeless addict."

"Certain segments of society care about appearances at all costs." He downed his second shot.

"When did you notice it missing?"

"Yesterday, right after lunch."

"Anything else gone?"

He shook his head.

"Who had access—" I stopped and mentally slapped myself on the forehead. The people he ministered to were not exactly pillars of the community.

"I know what you're thinking." Linville's eyes glowed with alcohol, watery yet intense. "Only one other person had keys to my office."

"What's his name?" I got out a pen and grabbed a cocktail napkin from a pile by the beer taps.

"How do you know it was a he?"

I sighed. "Okay. What was *her* name?"

"Oh, never mind. *He* was my assistant." Linville rubbed the bridge of his nose, his voice now sounding distant. "Carlos. He didn't come to work today."

"Last name?"

"Jimenez."

The old guy on the other side of me erupted into a fit of coughing, his chest cavity sounding like a tin can full of gravel. When his wheezing subsided I said, "How long has he worked for you?"

"Must be six months now." Linville drained his beer. "Started as a court-ordered DWI thing. He's been clean ever since."

I fanned away a cloud of smoke from Mr. Emphysema's fresh cigarette. "Where does Carlos live?"

"A boardinghouse. In Oak Cliff." Linville grabbed my pen and scribbled something on the cocktail napkin. His hand trembled as he slid the paper in my direction.

I put the information in my pocket but didn't say anything.

"Discretion is—" Linville covered his mouth with one hand and hiccoughed. "Uh . . . imperative. That's why I didn't call the police."

I mentioned my fee. He produced an already-made-out check. The amount was for a week's worth of my time, a sum of money incongruous with the man's shabby appearance. He described Carlos. Overweight, Hispanic, mid-twenties, a tattoo of the Virgin Mary on his left arm.

A shaft of sunlight penetrated the darkened room as the front door opened and two people entered. Mr. Emphysema coughed a couple of times and spat something on the floor. He ordered an Absolut martini, one hundred proof, straight up. I debated taking up smoking.

"One more question for now," I said. "Why haven't you tried to track down Carlos yourself?"

"My work demands a lot of time. And . . ." Linville stood and looked at two men who had just entered, ". . . I believe certain people mean me harm."

I stood also. The two newcomers flanked out, their attention plainly focused on Linville and me. Their hands were balled into fists. Everything about their demeanor screamed attack.

"Oh, dear." Linville's face drained of color. "Now I've got you involved."

The larger of the two produced a semiautomatic pistol from a pocket. He started toward us.

CHAPTER THREE

The two guys were rednecks. Cowboy hats. One in a Western-style printed shirt; the other, the one with the pistol, wore faded overalls. Lace-up Roper boots. Big, work-callused hands. They were the real thing, not some city cowpokes playacting.

Lee Harvey's was not a redneck bar. It was an urban place. Lee Harvey's was graphic designers with soul patch beards who wanted to pretend they were living on the edge, drinking a few brewskies in a bad neighborhood. Lee Harvey's was the NPR crowd slumming.

Which meant the rednecks weren't randomly looking for a fight. They were here for a reason. And the reason appeared to be Pastor Linville.

Redneck One, the guy in overalls with the gun, moved around the bar toward where we stood. "Are you Lee Oswald?"

"Who wants to know?" I tried to make sense of what was happening, how they knew my name.

"Gonna mess you up, boy." Redneck One spit a stream of tobacco juice on the floor.

"Why?" Not the best of comebacks but all I could manage. I grabbed for the Browning Hi Power on my right hip. Damned if I was going down without a fight.

He laughed and his belly jiggled the denim of his overalls. The bartender reached for the phone.

My hand slid underneath my shirt and rested on the butt of the pistol. Redneck One cocked the hammer of his gun.

I gripped my weapon and began to draw, much too slowly. What the hell was going on? From zero to a gunfight in under five seconds.

The redneck's shoulder and arm erupted in flames. He shrieked. Dropped the gun. Shrieked louder. Hopped from one foot to the other, making the flames bigger.

Somewhere between the first yelp of pain and the dropping of the weapon, I had heard a glass break. Mr. Emphysema cackled. He held a lighter over his head and flicked it, as if he were at a Van Halen concert. His martini glass was gone. I put two and three and four together and realized he had lit the drink on fire and tossed it at Redneck One, who was now rolling around on the floor, getting more flambéed as the seconds ticked by.

That left the second redneck to deal with. I turned his way. He was brandishing a pool cue like a baseball bat. Linville held a beer bottle, arm cocked back as if he was going to throw it.

I racked the slide on my Browning and pointed it at the man. "Who the hell are you?"

"You've got to answer for what you did to Billy." He dropped the pool cue.

I didn't reply. Suddenly the room was cold as a child's grave on Christmas morning. I'd known only one Billy in my life, and I didn't want to think about him ever again.

Sirens wailed in the distance. The man grabbed a pitcher of ice water from the bar and doused his smoldering friend. "Didn't think you could get away with it, didya?"

"You hillbillies are out of your league," I said, "and a long way from home."

"Everything comes back around." He grabbed his friend and pulled him to his feet. Mr. Overalls screamed as his blackened arm hit the side of the bar. Together they walked backward toward the front door. I kept the pistol pointed at them. The sirens grew louder.

Before I could say anything else, they were gone, slipped through the entranceway and into the afternoon sun. I headed after them but stopped when Linville fell over a table and crashed into a chair, ashtrays and glasses clanking to the floor. I holstered my gun and picked him up.

His eyes rolled back in his head. The bourbon and beer on his breath hit me like a wino's wet dream. I turned my head to one side, pulled him into a chair, and felt for a pulse.

"He gets that way," the bartender said. "From time to time."

"He come in here often?"

"When he wants to get shit-faced."

Linville shrugged himself awake. Blinked. Looked around the room.

"Which is how often?" I said.

The bartender didn't answer. The sirens sounded as if they were in the next room. Car doors slammed. The first cop walked through the door.

Two and a half hours. That's how long it took to get everything straightened out. There were reports to complete. Descriptions to give. Questions to answer.

So I sat and told my version of the events to the uniformed officers a half dozen times. The one in charge, an older sergeant, kept staring at my driver's license and asking if my name was for real. I kept saying it was, indeed.

Lee *Henry* Oswald, the gift of a bullheaded father so stubborn he'd insisted on bestowing his name on his only son, even though the words "Lee Oswald" has recently entered the collective consciousness of the world at about the same level of hatred as "Adolf Hitler."

The officer made a bunch of jokes about my name and the bar we were in, Lee Harvey's. I was less amused.

The cops finished with Linville first. While my interview wound down, he ordered one boilermaker after another to the curious stares of the after-work types who ambled inside to get a drink.

The sun had eased behind the trees in the west and the heat of the day had begun to dissipate as we walked out the door. Linville was drunk. He staggered a little and looked as if he was going to vomit.

"You need a ride?" I said.

"Y-y-yeah. I don't . . . uh . . . no car here."

I got him in the passenger side and exited the parking area. The dogs in the junkyard next door were out now. They ran the length of the fence separating them from the outdoor seating of the bar and whined at the smell of food and drink and activity. Linville gave surprisingly lucid directions to an ancient brick structure that might have been a school at one time, a dozen or so blocks south. It had a newish red sign over the front door that read, NEW HOPE SOUP KITCHEN.

The building was on a corner, next to a Quonset hut–looking place called Jimmy Earl's Social Club and a boarded-up house with a handful of people sitting on the porch in the dim evening light, drinking beer from quart bottles. Across the street was a two-story apartment building that looked like a prime target for the city's next tornado. What was either a car backfiring or gunfire rattled in the distance.

As Linville opened the door to my truck and staggered out, a wiry man with brown skin, Filipino, probably, exited the front door of the church, hurried over, and grabbed him by the arm. The man stuck his head inside. "Thank you for taking care of him." I nodded and said sure, no problem, as he half carried the drunken preacher up the sidewalk. Another man had exited the building and was standing on the steps, holding what looked like a shotgun. A sentry, watching for trouble.

I wanted to ask Linville some more questions, but he was incoherent. I wanted to know why the two rednecks had confronted us. I wanted to know why they had invoked the name of a dead man.

That could wait. It was time to leave this part of town. The sun was going down; the night people would be out soon.

I zigged and zagged through the narrow streets past empty lots and tiny wooden houses and cars on blocks. Though only a few blocks south of the central business district, the area might as well have been a hemisphere away from the power and privilege residing in the sleek towers that made up the Chamber of Commerce version of Dallas.

After a few minutes, I hit Ervay Street, a major thoroughfare leading north to downtown. The street was originally a bustling commercial district, the storefronts housing whatever businesses had been popular a hundred years earlier, haberdasheries and milliners, maybe, or small dry-goods merchants and pharmacies, the Gaps and Starbucks of another era.

But the economy and the population had shifted, leaving South Ervay boarded up and decaying like so many parts of the city.

The street wasn't empty of people, though. There were dozens of figures milling about on the corners. Small knots of young men in two-hundred-dollar sneakers and oversized, low-slung jeans. Children were on the curbs, runners the police wouldn't arrest for delivering a glass vial of crack cocaine to the eager hands of the living dead who scurried in and out of doorways like cockroaches, looking to score.

I locked the doors of my truck and headed north.

CHAPTER FOUR

I drove through downtown Dallas, under the long shadows cast by the concrete-and-glass towers forming the skyline, past the new bars and stores and clubs lining the narrow streets, the latest attempt at pretending a suburban city could have a thriving downtown. I drove by churches and a couple of old buildings where I had been told several nice brothels and opium dens had operated in the early part of the twentieth century, when Dallas had been an open city, the vices of its frontier heritage still evident along the cobblestone streets. This was during the same era that the Ku Klux Klan ran the city, and a Dallas dentist named Hiram Wesley Evans was elected as the national Imperial Wizard.

Now the century-old gingerbread structures housed small law firms and real estate offices, and I wondered if maybe we might not have been better off with the brothels and opium dens, minus the Klan, of course.

Ten minutes later I was in my neighborhood in old East Dallas, an eclectic chunk of town devoid of the strip malls, swaggering real estate developers, and big-haired, Neiman Marcus–ized woman that make up so much of the city's stereotype.

I stopped at a taqueria on Gaston Avenue and bought a to-go plate of carne asada and a six-pack of beer. I made small talk with an acquaintance of mine named Hector, a sometimes bookie and full-time owner of a bar a few blocks away.

Last stop was home, a snug little brick Tudor on Sycamore Street, a few blocks north of Baylor Hospital. Except for a Caucasian assistant DA with a topless bar addiction who lived one street over, half my neighbors were Hispanic, the other half Asians from perhaps a dozen different countries.

I got out of my car with dinner and the beer. The air smelled like charcoal fires, fresh-cut lawn, and livestock, the latter the result of the goats my neighbor next door, a retiree named Mr. Martinez, sometimes kept in his backyard. I didn't live in a fancy part of town, and the city officials didn't enforce the codes about such things. That was fine with me since every so often Mr. Martinez would ask me over for a plate of slow-barbecued *cabrito*.

Inside my house, I ate the carne asada and drank two beers. I played fetch for a few minutes with my elderly chocolate Lab, Glenda. At eight-thirty I put the dirty plate in the dishwasher.

Then I puttered. Or tried to. I took apart a shotgun in my basement workroom and began to clean it, stopping halfway through with a rod still in the barrel. I made a grocery list but tore it up. I started the latest Lee Child thriller, anxious to see what troubles had befallen Jack Reacher this time. I raced through the first twenty pages, two lifetimes' worth of adventure for a normal person, just a typical day for Reacher. At the end of the second chapter, I put the novel down.

The name of a man, dead for many months now, kept swirling through my head, interfering with my concentration.

Billy Barringer.

My best friend.

After the ten o'clock news, I went to bed. I slept fitfully, Billy making an uninvited guest appearance in my dreams.

We were on a beach. I recognized the place as South Padre, the Texas Riviera, a barrier island only a few miles from Brownsville and the border. I smelled the sea and suntan lotion. A freighter was barely visible in the distance, a dark wedge of iron slicing through the glassy ocean.

All around me were the gringo snowbirds from the north, with varicose veins and pinched Midwest accents, and affluent Mexicans holidaying in their high-rise condos lining the beach.

Billy walked around a pair of Mexican girls, tanned and oiled, sitting in beach chairs and chattering on cell phones. He tried to tell me something but I couldn't understand the words. Finally he pulled a knife from his pocket and made a deep cut in the palm of his hand. The blood turned black as it hit the sand. Thunderclouds rolled in, and the air grew cold. The two girls were no longer talking on their phones. Their throats had been slit. The blood from their wounds was black, too.

Then I woke up. Heart pounding, coated in sweat. Sleep would not come again. At seven I showered, fixed breakfast, and left the house.

Carlos lived in a boardinghouse on Tyler Street in the Oak Cliff section of Dallas, south across the Trinity River from downtown and the polished concrete facade of the northern half of the city.

Originally a separate town before the turn of the last century, the area possessed some of the only natural beauty in this part of Texas—hills and valleys, creeks and massive old live oak trees. It was where the business and civic elite of the era made their homes in block after block of stately mansions and quaint stucco cottages.

But then things changed.

The wealth and development grew north across the river, leaving Oak Cliff a shell of its former self. Potholes. Crime. Immigrants with mahogany-colored skin and little command of the English language. Benign neglect from City Hall.

In other words, the perfect place for a guy named Carlos who worked in a soup kitchen to live.

I crossed the Trinity River on the Continental Street Viaduct, passing the site where I had almost died during a firefight with a drug crew a couple of years back. On the other side, I bottomed out in a pothole big enough to serve as a wading pool.

The houses and buildings were small and faded: peeling paint, overgrown yards, cracked windows. At Sylvan Avenue I turned south and drove through the sporadic traffic heading to downtown. After a few minutes, the road jogged left and became Tyler Street.

A dozen blocks later I found the correct address. The place had obviously been a single-family home years ago, before being converted to its current use as a boardinghouse. It looked like it had been painted as recently as the Carter administration. The yard was dirt and weeds and empty beer cans.

I pulled to the curb behind a midseventies Monte Carlo. I guessed it was originally green but it was hard to tell with all the rust. A black woman wearing a pink miniskirt, six-inch heels, and a blond wig was leaning against the back of the car, smoking a cigarette.

It was eight o'clock on a Friday morning.

I got out, chirped the alarm, and stepped onto what passed for a sidewalk, a mishmash of broken concrete and packed earth.

The woman blew a cloud of smoke into the humid morning air. "Looking for a date?"

"Nope."

"You a cop?"

"Uh-uh." I pointed to the ramshackle structure where Lucas Linville's assistant supposedly stayed. "You live there?"

"What do you care, if you ain't looking for a date?" She flipped the cigarette butt into the street and adjusted her left breast within the red bra she wore as her only top.

"Know a guy named Carlos?" I removed a twenty from my wallet.

"Maybe." She put one foot on the bumper of the elderly Chevy and scratched the inside of her thigh.

I pulled another twenty out. Waved them at her.

"Second floor. Room Two-C." She grabbed the money and stuck it in her bra.

"Thanks." I walked toward the entrance of the boardinghouse.

"Another ten and I'll suck you off," she said. "Nobody in Dallas gives better head."

I ignored her, though I did admire the direct marketing aspect of her sales pitch.

"Screw you, whitey." She was shouting now. "Bet you're a faggot, anyways."

I pushed open the front door. What was once the foyer and living room now served as a communal area, with several worn sofas and what looked like outdoor carpeting, dark green and filthy. The room smelled like sweat and urine. A small person of indeterminate gender and race was huddled in a ball on one of the sofas, snoring loudly.

The stairs were to the right. I took them two at a time. Halfway up I brushed past a man in a seersucker suit and a white button-down shirt. He was completely bald, his skin the color of vanilla ice cream. The odor of Old Spice aftershave trailed after him.

"Good morning to you, suh," he said as we passed. His accent was thick, elongated vowels that made me think of grubby little bars with names like the Dew Drop Inn along the farm-to-market roads of East Texas.

I nodded hello as my pulse quickened. I felt for the Browning on my hip, hidden beneath an untucked denim shirt. At the top of the stairs, I leaned against a wall and waited, straining to hear any sounds from downstairs. I had no idea what the man in the seersucker suit was about, but I wanted no part of it.

After a long twenty count, I could discern no activity from below. The only thing audible was a radio or TV tuned to a Spanish-language station, coming from somewhere on this floor.

The second story was one narrow hallway with rooms on either side.

Two-C was to the right, at the end. The Spanish broadcast grew louder the closer I got to Carlos's unit.

The door was ajar about an inch. The heightened awareness brought on by the man in the suit returned. Senses focused, mouth dry.

I grabbed the Browning. Chambered a round. Pressed myself against the wall to the right of the entrance. Pushed open the door with my foot.

The air smelled metallic. Copper. Salty. I led with the muzzle of the pistol, followed by my head. Peered into the room.

A twenty-inch black-and-white television was tuned to a Mexican soap opera, volume turned all the way up.

A shirtless and overweight Hispanic man lay on a twin bed, an ear-to-ear scarlet smile where his throat should have been. The blood was still seeping from the wound. He'd been dead only a few minutes. I could see a tattoo of the Virgin Mary on his shoulder. The fingers on his right hand were twisted at odd angles, obviously broken.

I stepped inside, shut the door, and turned off the TV. The room was small and contained very little besides the corpse, a dresser, and a couple of lawn chairs. What possessions the young man owned appeared to have been thoroughly searched. At the end of the bed was a small pile of broken glass and picture frames. I picked up several of the photographs that were scattered among the debris. All of them were snapshots of the dead man and a matronly looking woman. In all the shots, the older figure had her arm around the man, a loving gaze on her face.

On the dresser were several envelopes addressed to Carlos Jimenez. I rifled through them and saw most were bills. The last one had a return address a few miles north of here, from Maria, same last name. I opened it and saw another picture of the same woman and Carlos. I stuffed the envelope in my pocket.

Between the bed and the wall I found a large manila file folder on the floor. I picked it up. There was no label. The only markings were on the bottom corner where someone had pressed a rubber address stamp.

The words were faded but legible: "Pastor Lucas Linville, Church of the Harvest, Pleasant Grove."

The folder was empty. I creased it in two and stuck it in my pocket next to the envelope and searched the rest of place. In the bathroom a ripped pile of magazines lay on the dirty floor. I grabbed a handful of glossy paper. All of Carlos's reading material seemed to have a similar theme: sports and betting. I wondered if the young man had traded drinking for gambling.

I went back into the bedroom, heard voices in the hallway, and decided to wait a moment before leaving.

The solitary window in the room faced the street. I pulled the dirty shade to one side about a half inch and peered out.

Seersucker Suit and the woman in the miniskirt stood next to the elderly Monte Carlo, talking. A chartreuse Mercedes-Benz with gold wheels was double-parked by the Chevy. I could just make out a figure in the driver's seat.

The streetwalker waved her arms a lot when she spoke, hands moving one way and then the other. She paused to light a cigarette. Seersucker Suit pulled what looked like a wad of currency from a pocket. He gave it to her. She pointed to my Tahoe, then the second floor of the boardinghouse.

Seersucker Suit looked at the window from where I was watching his little gray-market economic exchange. He waved like an old friend, turned, and walked down the sidewalk, hands behind his back.

I let the shade drop and moved to the door leading to the hallway.

I strained to hear anything. Witnesses would be bad at this point.

Only silence in front of me, Carlos's silent body to my rear.

I eased open the door and stepped out of the room. The aroma of morning wafted through the corridor: bacon, coffee, cigarettes. A toilet flushed nearby.

I walked as quickly and quietly as possible along the hallway and down the stairs. When I got to the bottom, the figure asleep on the sofa had awoken.

It was a woman, I think. She was leaning against the wall by the stairs. Bloodshot eyes. Body shaking. She squinted at me and started to say something, but the words wouldn't come. Instead she closed her eyes and slid down to the floor, a tiny string of spittle drooling out of the corner of her mouth.

I crossed the foyer and threw open the front door. Dashed down the torn-up sidewalk. Made it about twenty feet before I was stopped by a figure so large his bulk blotted out the sun.

He wore a purple suit, double-breasted with eight buttons on either side, over a shiny gold shirt and black tie. His shoes were as big as some foreign cars and made of a synthetic material that resembled orange leopard skin.

He held a baseball bat in one hand. "Whatchoo doing messin' wit' my hoes?"

CHAPTER FIVE

The pimp was about ten feet away. The bat looked like a billy club in his oversized grasp. His suit had a reflective material woven into it, and the sun made it shimmer and shine like a humongous violet diamond. He looked like Huggy Bear updated for the new millennium.

I could run but he would catch me in two strides.

I could shoot him but that would entail too much paperwork.

"What?" I said.

"My bitch." He swung the bat at nothing, as if it were a flyswatter. "Said you was asking after Carlos."

A marked police unit passed. The driver and passenger paid no mind to the baseball bat–brandishing pimp.

"Don't know what you're talking about." I reached for the sap in my hip pocket, the one I decided to carry today on a hunch.

"Don't be fuckin' wit' me, cracker." He took a very slow and ponderous step in my direction. He looked as spry and agile as a statue. He swung the bat once more, again very slowly, aiming at air and connecting.

When the bat had cleared my head, I went in low, left elbow to his gut, the leather sap in my right hand going for a joint shot.

My elbow sank into a couple of feet of purple dough. The sap connected with a *thwack* on the side of his knee.

Huggy Bear grunted and fell over on one side. The ground shook. I dropped on top of him and bonked both his legs with the sap, a double tap to each kneecap. He squealed and curled into a very large, purple ball.

I stuck the sap in my pocket and pulled out the Benchmade automatic knife I kept tucked in my waistband. I held the knife in front of the pimp's face and pressed the recessed button in the handle.

The three-inch blade sprang into action like a Viagra-snorting used-car salesman at the Playboy Mansion.

I stuck the tip in Huggy's nose. "Carlos is dead. Suppose you tell me about it."

Huggy growled. Spit flecked his lips.

"Gonna have to do better than that." I exerted another quarter ounce of pressure on the blade, pressing against the outside of his nostril.

"Screw you, whitey." He spoke through clenched teeth. "You are a dead muthafucka."

I didn't say anything. Just slid the blade up his nose a few more millimeters.

He yowled.

I eased back a micron.

"All right all right all right." He seemed scared now. I figured he had been busting up six-plus-feet deadbeats for a long time. Probably the first time one had fought back.

"Tell me about Carlos," I said. "Who killed him?"

"I-I-I didn't know he was dead." His breath was ragged. "No shit, okay?"

"Who would want to kill him?"

No response. The man chewed on his bottom lip, sweating. I rotated the blade inside his nostril an eighth of a revolution.

"*Noooo.*" He tried to move but his knees probably wouldn't work right yet and I was sitting on his arms. "T-t-they gonna get me, if I tell you."

"Consider yourself already got."

"You don't understand—"

I was sweating now, too, not just from the heat and exertion required to keep a 350-pound pimp under control, but also from the fact that we were on a city street in broad daylight. The cops might drive by again and decide to stop this time. There was also the other one, the man with the shaved head who'd passed me on the stairs.

"Tell me about the white guy in the seersucker suit."

Huggy's eyes got wide as his pupils narrowed. "That's what I'm trying to get across to your dumb white ass. You are dead, see what I'm saying?"

I heard a car door slam, looked up, and saw a late-model Cadillac across the street. Three more very large men in neon-colored suits stood beside it, watching the traffic go by, apparently waiting for a break to cross.

"Who is he?" I pressed the tip of the knife against the flesh on the inside of his nose.

"Listen up, cat." The man's voice trembled. His coffee-colored skin seemed to pale. "If you have to ask then you ain't in the game. And you are seriously fucked."

I rolled off the man. Picked up his baseball bat and threw it as far away as possible.

"What's his name?"

"Go on. Get out of here. If that crazy muthafucka don't get you, I will." Huggy Bear wobbled himself upright, legs shaky. He mopped at a tiny trickle of blood coming from his nose.

One of the men from across the street stepped into traffic. Brakes screeched. Horns honked. I hightailed it to my truck, using the confusion as an opportunity to get the hell away from the dead man's boardinghouse and the pissed-off pimp in the purple suit.

I set the air conditioner in the Tahoe to ex-wife cold. My breath fogged. Ice formed on the inside of the windshield. By the time I got downtown, my core temperature felt as if it had dropped below one hundred, just in time for the stop-and-go traffic that inexplicably materialized right after morning rush hour.

It was ten o'clock when I found myself in front of Old Red, the historic, nineteenth-century courthouse on the east side of downtown, overlooking the Kennedy Memorial, the Texas School Book Depository, and the infamous grassy knoll.

The terra-cotta building was five stories of ornate brick, Victorian style, almost as red as a good Cabernet. The turrets on each corner seemed to reach for the sun, a slap in the face to the dullness of modern municipal buildings elsewhere in the city.

Twenty minutes yielded a half block of forward travel, an inch-by-inch visit with Old Red. Ninety seconds after that, the unseen clog dissolved and I continued on toward the converted prairie-style house in East Dallas where I officed with three other people: a lawyer suffering from Napoleon syndrome, a real estate appraiser with a gambling problem, and my partner, a former profiler with the San Antonio Police Department, who made so many bad choices when it came to relationships, she could have her own season on the Dr. Phil show.

The office was on Rieger Street, not far from my home, in a residential area slowly going commercial. Eclectic was one way to describe the neighborhood. Dangerous-after-dark was another. The rent was cheap, the location good. Who was I to complain?

I parked in the rear on the gravel driveway, underneath a dying hackberry tree. I went in the back door. My office was one of the two rear bedrooms. My partner, Nolan O'Connor, occupied the second.

I managed to get to my desk without anybody noticing. I turned the window AC to high and grabbed a half-liter bottle of water from the dorm-sized refrigerator in the corner. I fired up the computer and did a phone number search for Reese Cunningham.

There were a half dozen R. Cunninghams in the Dallas/Fort Worth area. I printed out the info. Next I did a property search on various county databases looking for evidence of home ownership, either for Reese or his parents. Again, a number of possibilities materialized on the screen, but none was in the locales where a family of means might reside. I printed that information also.

I leafed through the hard-copy results of my searches and drank the rest of the water. After a few minutes a plan formulated in my overheated brain: Go see Lucas Linville and ask him what the hell was going on.

Before I could leave, Nolan O'Connor appeared at my door. She wore a pair of skintight faded Levi's that accentuated her long legs and the curve of her hips, a plain white T-shirt, and a pair of low-heeled cowboy boots. And very little makeup, which she didn't need anyway, since her high cheekbones and thin nose belonged more on a model than a PI partnered with a low-end wiseass like myself.

Her dark hair was shoulder length and loose, thick bangs dangling in front of a pair of blue eyes that never missed a thing. Unless it was about her own personal life.

"Hey, Hank."

"Morning."

Silence. She twisted a lock of hair around her index finger, a blank look on her face.

"What's up?"

"I dumped Larry last night."

"That's good." I raised my eyebrows slightly. "Right?"

"Damn straight."

"What about the church and the caterer?"

"Canceled it all." She waved her hand in a dismissive gesture. "To think I was gonna marry that guy."

"To think."

"What's the workload like right now?" she asked.

"We've got a new case." I tossed the empty bottle in the trash. "So far it's about a pimp and a preacher."

"Good," she said. "I wanna kick somebody in the balls today."

CHAPTER SIX

We talked as I drove to the building where I had dropped off the preacher less than twenty-four hours before.

I explained everything so far. The pimp and the streetwalker and the dead guy in the boardinghouse that morning. The strange man in the seersucker suit. Linville and the request to find the missing folder, followed by the two rednecks at the bar the previous afternoon.

Nolan asked me why I hadn't taken her along yesterday. I mentioned the meeting she was supposed to have had at that same time with her future sister-in-law and Larry's only sibling, a woman named Brandi who had just got out of prison after doing eighteen months for passing bad checks.

After a few blocks, Nolan broke her silence. "What are you leaving out?"

"What do you mean?"

"You were evasive," she said. "When you were talking about the two guys at the bar."

Nolan could spot a hustle from across a pool hall. It must have been the psych background. Not much got by her, including me, whenever I tried.

"They mentioned Billy."

Nolan sucked in a mouthful of air.

"Said I had to answer for him."

She banged her hand on the dash. "Why the hell didn't you tell me?"

"It's not your problem."

"Don't be a dumbass, Hank."

The crack dealers weren't out yet on Ervay Street. My guess was they probably worked different corners during the morning hours. I turned right on a side street and soon we were back in the interior, the houses and cars on blocks appearing even more dismal in the bright light of day.

A block from Linville's place two guys in ragged sweatpants and sleeveless T-shirts shared a quart bottle of Schlitz malt liquor. As we passed, one shot us the finger and the other grabbed his crotch.

I made a couple of drive-bys and checked for surveillance of the redneck variety. Except for the occasional emaciated wino and the two guys drinking beer, the street was dead. No other people visible. No discernible activity in or around any of the houses. Nobody at the Quonset hut that housed the bar.

"Here we are." I stopped the truck across from the building Linville used for his ministry.

"Think it could be a setup?" Nolan pulled a Para-Ordnance .45 automatic from the gym bag she had brought.

"By who?"

"This Linville guy. Or his people."

"Kinda doubt it." I tried to keep the sarcasm out of my voice. "They could have done it last night. Plus, we're dropping in unannounced."

"I dunno. Can't be too careful." She rammed a sixteen-round clip in the butt of the pistol. Then she pulled out a pair of matching Glock .40-calibers and began loading them.

When I had first met Nolan a couple of years ago, her interest in firepower had been minimal: a snub-nose .38 stuck in her back pocket and she was good to go. As time passed and the quality of her dating choices declined, her interest in weaponry grew.

Her last boyfriend, the one before Larry, had been a mobile home salesman a couple of counties south of Dallas. When she had caught him in the sack with a cocktail waitress from the local VFW lounge, she had gone out and bought a fully automatic M-16. I was more than a little worried about what she would acquire after the Larry fiasco.

"Leave the Glocks in the truck," I said.

"But—"

"Guy's a preacher." I opened the door and stepped onto the hot asphalt. "Not some gun nut."

"Like David Koresh?" Nolan hopped out, too.

"Okay, maybe you've got a point." I paused in the middle of the street. "Take a walk around back. See if anybody's there who shouldn't be."

She reached inside the truck and grabbed one of the Glocks.

I chirped the alarm, and together we headed to the building where I'd dropped off Lucas Linville the day before. Nolan went to the left, to circle around back and meet me in front. I waited for her on one side of the main entrance. Three minutes later she emerged from the other side, sweaty and dirty and brushing leaves from her hair. She positioned herself on the opposite side of the doorway, nodded an okay. I knocked on the door.

An intercom buzzed. "Who is it?" The voice sounded like the Filipino man from the evening before.

"Hank Oswald."

"Please. Go away."

Nolan and I looked at each other.

"Need to talk to Linville," I said.

"He's sick. Please leave."

"I found the file."

Silence for a few long moments. Then, "Stick it in the mail slot."

"No can do." I banged on the door. "Open up or I go find the rich kid's parents and tell them what's going on."

"You don't understand."

"Amen, brother." I slapped the door again. "Now open up."

The intercom clicked off. A long silence followed. I started to sweat again. The two guys drinking beer wandered down the sidewalk and peered at us. One of them looked as if he was going to say something until Nolan pulled out the big Para .45 and pointed it at his crotch. He dropped the beer bottle, and they both turned and ran the other way.

After what seemed like a long time, I heard the crackle of deadbolts. The thick wooden door opened a fraction. The face of the man from the previous evening appeared. I could see his features more clearly now. His hair, close-cropped all the way around, had horizontal hash marks every few centimeters on the sides, leading up to the top of his head, where it had been allowed to grow thicker. He looked like a rapper circa 1992.

He said, "Give me the folder."

"Where's Linville?"

"He is, uhh . . . like . . . sick."

"Hangovers will do that to a body." I put a hand on the door. "But we really need to talk to him. About Carlos."

That was the magic word. The man hesitated a moment and then stepped aside and let us in.

I was nine years old when I began to understand Billy Barringer's family business for the first time.

Billy's people lived on a farm a few miles east of my family's place just outside Waco. The Barringers were as pure country as Hank Williams, John Deere tractors, and chicken-fried steak. Taciturn and tough. Windburned and hard drinking. Good workers, but at what I was never sure. Until later.

One thing for certain, though, they never lacked for material possessions. The pickup trucks were always new and shiny. Billy's toys were always the latest and coolest, as if they'd come straight from the Sears catalog. Billy's mother drove a black Lincoln. She got a new one each year; that summer's model had an eight-track tape player. She always gave a lot of money to the church, too, and to help foreign missions and stuff. Billy said his daddy got mad at her for sending his cash to all those damn gooks, but at least it kept her off his ass. His mother and father got mad at each other a lot, it seemed to me, even more than my parents. I had the hazy impression that Billy was at the center of their arguments, more often than not, but as a child these things were hard to understand.

Because Billy was my best friend and because he had all that cool stuff, it was always fun to go visit. In addition to the toys, there were horses and cows and barns and acres of pastureland, all sorts of things for nine-year-old boys to enjoy. We swam in the stock tanks and played in the pecan orchard behind the white clapboard house where Billy lived with his parents and three brothers.

I was spending the Fourth of July weekend with them. After dinner Billy and I shot off Roman candles and bundles of Black Cat firecrackers in the back pasture. When all the fireworks were gone, Mr. Barringer asked us if we wanted to go for a little ride. His eyes were loopy and his words slurred. The whiskey in the mason jar he carried slopped out on his overalls when he walked.

Billy and I climbed into the bed of his father's pickup. Billy's uncle sat up front with Mr. Barringer. We took a dirt road leading to the back of the farm and pretty soon we were deep in the woodlands growing next to the Brazos River. I still remember the sound of the water and the smell of tilled earth and cane pole.

We came to a tin shack in a clearing. Ten or twelve pickups were parked on the packed dirt around the structure. I heard men laughing and shouting. Mr. Barringer got out and went to the front door. He talked to one of his other brothers, the one with the bum leg who had gone away for a while after his wife had disappeared.

Billy grew quiet, not his usual boisterous self. I asked him where we were and what was going on. He didn't reply.

A man dressed in a worn denim work shirt and faded jeans came through the door, almost as if he'd been pushed. He stood in front of Mr. Barringer. They talked for a while, the man raising his hands a lot, Billy's father nodding with his arms crossed in front of him.

The punch came unexpectedly. One minute the man in the denim shirt was talking, gesturing with his hands. The next he was on the ground, holding his stomach. Mr. Barringer stepped back and rubbed his knuckles. He kneeled down and spoke to the man.

The noise inside the shack got louder, a rising tide of male voices, yelling like when my father and his friends watched football. From a long way off, I heard the *woomph* of a fireworks show; a few seconds later a starburst of red and blue sparkled faintly through the tops of the trees, followed by another muffled *boom*. Mr. Barringer reached into the man's pockets and removed something. He stuffed it inside the front of his overalls and returned to the truck.

The noise from the shack grew louder. Billy's dad leaned into the back of the truck, where we sat, and looked at me. "Don't you mind none of this, Hank."

I nodded slowly.

"Just trying to collect what's owed to me, you unnerstand, don'tcha?" He smiled and tousled my hair. "Tell your daddy I said hello."

CHAPTER SEVEN

We stepped into the vestibule of Linville's building. Concrete floor, rough, exposed-brick walls. The room was lit only by a single, buzzing fluorescent light and was empty except for a Remington shotgun resting on a metal chair. A plain wooden door was on the far wall, leading to the rest of the building.

The Filipino man wore a pair of baggy shorts, barely resting on his skinny hips. They were long, stopping about midcalf, a few inches above a pair of sneakers made out of what looked like smooth white plastic, not a lace visible anywhere. An iPod hung on his waistband, the ear buds dangling around his neck.

"Yo, homey." The man moved his shoulders from side to side in a rough approximation of a street strut. "What'sup?"

"Vanilla Ice called," I said. "He wants his haircut back."

"Huh?" The man frowned.

"Where's Linville?"

"He's sick, like I told you."

"We need to see him."

"Look, homey. I'll give him the file." The man quit wiggling his torso and folded his arms across his chest. "You mentioned Carlos?"

"What's your name?" Nolan asked.

"Arthur." The man seemed to notice her for the first time. "Who are you?"

"What's with the scattergun?" Nolan pointed to the Remington.

"What?"

"The shotgun." She tapped the chair with her boot. "Why do you have one?"

Arthur started to say something but I interrupted. "Don't you want to know about Carlos?"

"No . . . I mean, yes." Arthur shook his head and blinked several times. "Why y'all messin' with me, huh?"

"It's what we do when people are trying to scam us." I smiled. "Now can we see Linville?"

The Filipino man took a deep breath and put the earpieces from his music player in place. He turned and walked toward the door leading to the interior of the building. We followed.

The first room was a large common area with groups of worn tables and Salvation Army chairs, a few bookcases, and an elderly television set in one corner.

A half dozen people of varying ages, genders, and ethnicities were busy arranging a serving line on two folding tables set end to end. The group glanced up as we walked by, faces blank, eyes hollow and distant, with a look similar to that of soldiers I had seen suffering from combat fatigue.

Arthur walked to a side door, opened it, and motioned for us to follow.

We did so and found ourselves in a narrow hallway, our navigator hurrying along the poorly lit passageway. A metal door with a deadbolt blocked the end of the hallway. Arthur knocked once, fished a key out of his pocket, and turned the lock. He pushed it open and stood to one side. We walked in, and the door closed behind us.

The wood-paneled chamber was dimly lit, illumination coming from a low-wattage bulb in an open closet and a desk lamp resting on a milk crate. The floor was covered with a brown shag carpet, circa *The Brady Bunch* with their highest ratings. Debris was everywhere: pizza boxes, soft drink cans, beer bottles, old newspapers, and other unidentifiable crap. The odor of rotting food and the sour stench of unwashed clothing filled the space.

A bed was in one corner, tangled linens in a pile. A worn sofa and coffee table flanked the opposite wall. Pastor Lucas Linville sat in the middle of the swayback divan, elbows on his knees, head in his hands. He wore a pair of sweatpants and a dingy wife-beater undershirt. He was completely still. He didn't move or say a word, just sat there. For an instant I wondered if he was breathing.

"Linville." I snapped my fingers.

No response.

"This place smells like ass." Nolan waved a hand in front of her face.

Lucas Linville looked up, his face cadaver pale except for the greenish tint around his eyes. He blinked several times and looked at Nolan. "Who are you?"

"Carlos is dead." I knocked a pizza box out of a high-back chair and sat down.

"What?" More blinks.

"Somebody slit his throat." I nudged away the moldy remains of what looked like a bologna sandwich with one foot. "This is Nolan, by the way. We work together."

"Ever thought of hiring a cleaning lady?" my partner said.

"What happened? Who . . . how . . . ?" Linville's face got paler.

I pulled out the folder that was supposed to contain the case file for Reese Cunningham and placed it on the coffee table. The preacher grabbed it and looked inside. He stared at the empty pocket for a few moments before dropping it on the table.

"Where can we find Reese?" Nolan said.

"You don't get it, do you?" Linville stood unsteadily. He staggered to a cardboard box by the bed, reached down, and pulled out a quart bottle of Jim Beam.

"Don't drink that." I stood also.

Linville took a long pull of whiskey.

"I meant for you to do that," I said. "Reverse psychology."

He tipped the drink to his lips again, a four-second swig this time.

I walked to where he stood and took the bottle from his hands. "Where is Reese?"

"How the hell should I know?"

"A man of the cloth shouldn't swear," Nolan said.

"Reese won't be able to help you." He eyed the bottle in my hand.

"Something in his case file was worth killing over." I walked back to the coffee table and put the whiskey down. "There's also a connection somehow to a dead man named Billy Barringer."

"You're a piece of shit, Oswald." The preacher's face purpled with rage. "Just find the file. I paid you good money."

I didn't reply, more confused than ever by his sudden anger.

"Get out," Linville said.

"What do you know about Billy?"

"He was a piece of shit, too." Linville's voice was slurred as he wobbled his way to the bottle of booze on the coffee table.

He didn't have much more time left in the land of sober-minded folk. I sat down on the sofa, removed the bottle from his hands yet again, and said, "I saw a man at Carlos's place this morning. White, late forties."

Linville's eyes rattled in their sockets like marbles in an ashtray. He didn't say anything.

"Guy was a clothes hound. Wore a seersucker suit, pressed just so. Shaved head."

The preacher took a deep breath. It sounded like a hiccup.

"I've run across people like him before." I placed the bottle on the coffee table, out of his reach. "The kind you get a bad feeling off of without them doing a thing."

"M-m-may God have mercy on your soul." Linville was trembling now. "He'll be the death of us all."

Nolan put one foot on the coffee table and leaned over. "What's his name?"

"It doesn't matter. Nothing does anymore." Linville's voice was hoarse with emotion or whiskey. "This is a journey. And the road is fraught with many perils."

"Maybe you should quit stopping at the roadside taverns."

The older man's torso spasmed, like a sigh gone wrong. He grabbed his stomach.

I stood up. Cryptic, drunk preachers I'd had enough of. Nolan moved to the door. Linville's face turned from cadaver cream to lemon yellow. He put a hand over his mouth.

"The two guys at the bar yesterday." I walked to where my partner stood. "Were they after you? Or me?"

"Or both?" Nolan said.

Linville didn't reply. His faced shined with sweat. He swallowed repeatedly. *Vomitus Preacherus* was about to occur. Nolan and I left the room to the sound of retching.

Arthur and another man stood in the hallway, whispering to each other and watching the door.

"Where can I find Reese Cunningham?" I said.

The new guy was white, pudgy, midthirties. He wore camouflage fatigues. He had what looked like a Winchester 30-30 carbine slung over one shoulder. "Who the hell do you think you are?" He swelled up like a tough guy.

I walked over to where he stood, put one hand on his chest, and pressed until he stepped back. The sneer left his mouth. I kept pressure up until the metal of the rifle clanked against the brick wall.

"What's it to you, GI Joe?" I said.

"Don't be rad, dude." Arthur pulled out his earpieces and stepped between us. "Shit, dawg, I'll give you the address of Reese's family."

"Thank you, Arthur." I removed my hand from the other man's chest.

The Filipino scurried down the hall.

"Why all the firepower?" Nolan pointed to Camo Guy's rifle.

"It's a war zone out there," he said.

"Amen, brother." I turned and walked down the hall after Arthur.

CHAPTER EIGHT

We walked back through the common area. The serving line was set up. Cooking smells wafted through the room, greasy meat boiling somewhere close by, bread warming in an oven. The man in the camo fatigues followed closely behind, muttering under his breath. Once we were in the entryway to the building, Arthur handed me a piece of paper with an address on it.

"You never told us about why you've got a shotgun by the front door." I pointed to the weapon. "Or why GI Joe is running around acting like he's getting ready for a firefight."

"There are some people out there want to put a cap in Pastor Linville."

"Who are they?"

"If I knew, don't you think I might try to stop them?" He sighed, betraying the faintest hint of impatience.

I didn't reply, more than a little worried that Arthur, the hip-hop impersonator, and the overweight man in the camouflage clothing couldn't stop a Boy Scout, much less a halfway-pissed-off thug. Nolan and I moved to the door.

Arthur spoke again. "He does good work here, you know. He saves lives."

"Everybody's but his own." I stepped outside. Nolan followed. The door to Lucas Linville's ministry slammed shut behind us. As we walked back to the truck, I watched for any threats, but the street was empty except for the heat of the day and the buzz of cicadas in the humid air.

We got in the car. Nolan pulled off her armaments and placed them back in the gym bag as I turned on the air-conditioning.

"We're not going to track down Reese right now?" Nolan's voice was unusually monotone.

I shook my head.

"We're gonna go help Olson with something, aren't we?"

"He doesn't ask for favors very often." I turned onto Ervay. The two beer-drinking guys were sitting on a stoop in the shade, smoking cigarettes. They ignored us as we drove by.

"He's your best friend," she said. "Guess we have no choice."

"You need to get over the whole thing." I turned the AC up a notch. "Larry was way out of line."

"Shut the hell up, Hank."

O lson still bore a scar on his neck from the encounter with an enemy bayonet not far from the city of Al-Busayyah in southern Iraq in 1991. The wound earned him a Purple Heart and a secret commendation from the CIA. It would have garnered him a trip back home to Fort Worth in a body bag if I hadn't managed to reload in time.

All I got out of the deal was sand lice and the undying friendship of a six-foot-six quasi-psychopathic homosexual shit kicker.

Nowadays, in addition to taking the odd assignment that I found a tad too gray market for my taste, Olson made his living as an arms merchant, a purveyor of fine military weapons and ammunition. Occasionally he entered into a transaction that was almost legal. But only occasionally.

He'd called yesterday morning. Asked if I could meet him at his new shop over on Ross Avenue. Needed a favor, a little help with a problem.

Also a chance for some work for the Oswald and O'Connor Investigative Agency.

New shop? I'd asked. Uh-huh. Finally found somebody to hold a federal firearms license, he'd said. The Bureau of Alcohol, Tobacco and Firearms was so darn picky these days. I'd started to say something else but stopped. It's better not to ask too many questions. He told me the location of his store, between a we-tote-the-note used-car lot and a check-cashing place. Noonish, if you please.

A job would be good, especially one not involving drunken preachers intoning the name of a dead wise guy. On the other hand, a request from Olson had the potential to be bad. The last one involved seventy cases of fragmentation grenades and two handcuffed Guatemalans.

I turned onto Ross Avenue, past a Mexican supermarket and video store.

"If he mentions Larry, I'll shoot him," Nolan said.

"He won't. It's all forgotten."

Larry, an ex-cop turned used-car salesman, skewed toward the homophobic side of the fence. Someone had an ill-conceived idea to get everybody together: Olson and his partner, me and date du jour, Nolan and Larry. The evening would have been all right except Larry ordered a round of shots called Dick Lickers. Things went downhill from there.

The owner of the restaurant dinged us two grand for the damage. Mr. Fiancé needed seven stitches in his forehead. And crutches, but only for a couple of weeks.

"Larry hasn't forgotten," Nolan said.

"You don't care about him anymore, remember?"

She didn't reply, instead pulling a Spyderco lock-back knife from her pocket and opening and closing it repeatedly.

The downtown part of Ross Avenue was all skyscrapers and concrete canyons, a glass-and-stone testament to the city's economic power. As we headed east, the street changed from multistoried office buildings to bars with blackout windows and dice games in the back, working-class diners serving blue plate specials, and burglar-barred convenience stores run by men with names like Abdul or Achmed.

I found the shop without any trouble. Wyatt's House of Guns was a few blocks down from the Cesar Chavez Learning Center and a used-tire store, and across the street from a bar called Los Tres Hermanos. The gun shop had steel posts embedded in the concrete in front to keep thieves from crashing through the cinder-block walls and plate-glass windows.

Olson's Suburban was parked in front, next to a Lincoln with gold rims and a layer of red dust. Nolan and I hopped out of the Tahoe.

The driver's-side door of the Lincoln opened and a heavy-set man with red hair exited. He was in his midtwenties and wore a white-dude-trying-to-look-hip-hop gangster outfit: oversized athletic jersey, baggy jeans, and shiny Nikes. He moved in, blocking the front door, arms folded across his chest. All in all he was doing a pretty good job of looking like a tough guy.

When we were a few feet away, he said, "Sorry, store's closed for a while."

"Why?" I stopped and raised an eyebrow.

"They're . . . um . . . doing whatycallit . . . inventory." He was clearly the lowest on the pecking order of whatever organization he belonged to. For his own sake I hoped he was street smart because he sure wasn't any other kind.

"That's too bad." Nolan pulled the big Para-Ordnance from her waistband. "I need to get more bullets. Down to my last fifty."

"Whoa." He raised one hand. "You're jacking with stuff you shouldn't be."

"If you play nice, we can do this without you having to go to the hospital." I moved to one side of the entrance and placed a hand on the butt of my Browning Hi-Power.

Red Hair reached under the tail of his shirt.

I lunged, one hand going for his arm, the other going for his throat.

By the time I got to his gun hand, he had a small semiautomatic out. With my left arm I pressed the gun against his thigh but knew that couldn't last too long. Using my other arm, I pressed his neck against the metal door.

His free hand was in my face, fingers and thumbs searching for an eye socket.

"A little help would be nice about now." I rotated my head until I thought my neck would pop. Two of his fingers found an earlobe and began to pull.

"You're in the way," Nolan said. "Can't get a clear shot."

My ear felt like it was ripping from my head. *"Shoot me then."*

Nolan moved into my peripheral vision. She raised the big .45 and walloped Red Hair on the top his head.

He let go of my ear, found my nose, and twisted.

"Uuuhh." Tears flooded my eyes. Vision gone. I heard another metal-on-flesh impact, louder this time. My nose was free again. Sight returned.

Red Hair slumped on the ground, bleeding from a laceration on his scalp.

I probed the flesh of my nose. Then I pulled out the Browning and racked the slide back.

Two shots rang out from the other side of the front door, big, heavy booms so close together that they sounded almost like one.

"Shit," Nolan said.

CHAPTER NINE

My partner stood on one side of the door, the Para-Ordnance held in a two-handed grip. I was on the other side in a replay of this morning's activities at Lucas Linville's place.

"How do you want to do this?" Nolan said.

"Go in low and hit the ground." I placed my free hand on the metal door. The two shots had occurred only seconds before. Loud noises and bright flashes in an enclosed area meant disorientation, ringing ears, and temporarily blinded eyes.

I twisted the handle. Pushed open the door. Dived in. Rolled over to the right, came to rest on my knees next to a glass display counter. I swept the room with my pistol.

My friend Olson was to the right, sitting on another display counter, an ugly black shotgun resting across his knees, a pair of earmuffs over his blond hair. Rows and rows of rifles and other long guns were lined up behind him.

"Hey, Hank." He removed the muffs and tossed them on the counter.

I didn't reply. Instead I looked across the room to where two men were curled up, shaking. They were about three feet apart and the display case behind them was a pile of broken glass and twisted metal.

Blood seeped from a handful of double-aught buckshot holes in the gray pants of the man on the right. The face of the one on the left was stark white, drained of all color. He was shivering even though it was warm in the room.

Nolan appeared to my left. She holstered her weapon, as did I.

"Fucking shakedown." Olson slid off the counter. He was dressed like a Corpus Christi coke dealer: lizard-skin boots, faded jeans, and a Pepto-Bismol-pink Hawaiian shirt.

"Somebody's trying to get their hooks into you?" I felt my nose again. It hurt but didn't seem to be broken.

"The bleeding one's in charge. Says I'm gonna have to pay ten percent off the top from now on to stay in business."

"Must be from out of town." Telling Olson he *had* to do anything was tantamount to a death wish. Also, Dallas was an open city. Except for some of the sex industry and a little gambling, there was no one group controlling anything, especially not the gun trade.

"What happened to the retard outside?" Olson said.

"I asked him if he wanted one lump or two." Nolan patted the big automatic on her hip.

"Thanks." Olson addressed her for the first time since her fiancé had caused the fight over the unfortunately named drinks. Then he turned to me. "That's why I called yesterday. Knew I could handle these two, but anything outside was gonna be tough."

"You could've told me," I said. "A little intel up front is always good."

"Eh." He waved one hand in a dismissive gesture. "You handled it okay, didn't you? Got another job for you anyway."

"What are you gonna do with the three of them?" Nolan said.

Olson laughed until tears came to his eyes. Then he told us.

Nolan shook her head. "You're an animal, you know that?"

I didn't say anything, instead mouthing a silent prayer, thanking God that Olson was my friend, not my enemy.

After we bolted shut the steel transport container loaded with a half dozen liters of bottled water, a carton of beef jerky, and the three men, Olson drilled some air holes in the sides. Then we waited until the man with the flatbed truck and crane arrived and hoisted the container aboard.

"How do you know they are actually going to end up more or less in one piece?" I wiped the sweat out of my eyes.

"Nothing in life is certain, is it?" Olson said.

"Matamoros?" Nolan shook her head.

"Nobody checks trucks headed *south*." Olson put the drill away and suggested lunch.

We piled into my truck and drove to a Vietnamese restaurant near Baylor Hospital. The place served food buffet-style all day long and was located between a secondhand store and a homeless shelter. The clientele was a mix of Asians, blue-collar workers, guys in suits, and young people with dyed hair and body piercings.

We ate in silence. After a few minutes Olson spoke to Nolan. "How is . . . uh . . . Larry?"

"We broke up." She chewed for a moment. "Last night."

"That's too bad." Olson beamed. "You know, I've got some new Rugers in. There's a sweet little .458 Magnum I bet you'd like."

"I'm not buying another one of your overpriced guns just because I'm single again."

"A .458'll stop a Cape buffalo dead in its tracks." Olson dumped a packet of artificial sweetener into his iced tea.

"A Cape buffalo? Those are big suckers." Nolan chewed on her lip, eyes narrowed. "How much—"

"For Pete's sake, Olson. She's not buying an African big-game rifle." I banged a fork on my plate. "Tell me about the job."

Olson covered his mouth with one hand and stage-whispered to Nolan, "We'll talk later." To me he said, "Remember Vernon Black?"

"Yeah."

"Saw him night before last at a Human Rights Commission fundraiser."

"Who are we talking about?" Nolan said.

"Senator Vernon Black." I eyed the last pile of moo shoo pork on my plate. "That rich guy from East Texas. Remember the article in yesterday's paper about the Caddo Lake deal?"

Nolan nodded and went back to her food.

"Said he needed to hire you." Olson dumped some cachemira sauce on his remaining egg roll.

"Me?" I speared a piece of pork. "Why not you?"

"I'd rather let him explain." Olson busied himself with his food.

A Vietnamese man with a pockmarked face and eyes hard enough to crack steel stepped outside and lit a cigarette. Through the plate-glass window, I could see a bruise on his cheek. I tried to remember his name but couldn't. He ran a string of brothels masquerading as Asian modeling studios in the western part of the city.

The three of us finished at the same time. Olson threw some money on the table and stood up. "Let's go."

We cut over on Henderson Avenue, past the trendy restaurants and nightclubs with no names, places available only to the those young or rich or pretty enough to know the secrets to navigating the velvet ropes.

At Central Expressway, Olson told me to go north to LBJ Freeway, the inner loop of the city. Traffic was heavy but moving.

This part of town was glass towers and a couple billion tons of concrete. Cars and trucks everywhere, blue-gray exhaust making the windshield look like it needed cleaning. At LBJ we headed west toward the airport and Texas Stadium.

We stopped well before we saw any airplanes or football players, at a shiny black-windowed office building not too far past the Dallas Tollway, the highway that split the northern half of the city in two. I parked in the visitor-designated area by the front door and we all got out. It seemed hotter in this part of town, with all the concrete and asphalt. The roar of automobiles in the background made conversation difficult.

The lobby of the building was two stories tall, all dark marble and polished hardwood, dominated by a fountain and a half dozen potted ficus trees so big they looked fresh off the boat from the rain forest.

The three of us got on the elevator. Olson pressed the button for the top floor, number fifteen. The air in the confined space smelled like lemon oil and money.

The lift opened onto a set of frosted-glass doors. The lettering above them read, BLACK ENTERPRISES.

"They let the help go in the front way?" Nolan said.

"Let's find out." I pushed open the door.

We walked into a wood-paneled reception area that opened up to a glass-walled conference room. An attractive young woman sat behind a small desk to the right. She smiled when she saw us.

Olson walked over to her desk. "We're here to see Senator Black."

She smiled more, dimples dotting each cheek. "Do you have an appointment?"

"Yes, we do." Olson smiled back. "Would you tell him that Lee Oswald is here?"

"I sure will." She picked up the telephone, a finger poised over the keypad. "Wait a minute . . . that name's familiar. Didn't you used to play for the Cowboys?"

Olson, who played next to Ed "Too Tall" Jones under Coach Landry, winked and cocked a finger at the girl. "Can't fool anybody who knows their Dallas history. I was All-Pro, linebacker, 1989."

"Oh, yeah. I remember now. That is so cool." The girl's eyes got big, her voice high-pitched. "Can I get your autograph? Roger Staubach was here the other day. *He* signed one for me."

"Sure thing, darlin'." Olson grabbed a pen and a piece of paper from her desk. "Next time he's here, tell Roger I haven't forgotten about the money he owes me. From when we got those hookers in Houston."

The girl gulped.

I stepped up to the desk. "Lee's just making a joke. Could you tell the Senator that *Hank* Oswald is here?"

A young man in khakis arrived a few minutes later and escorted us down the hall to a corner office. The windows offered a view of downtown to the south and Texas Stadium in the hazy distance to the west.

The other two walls were dominated by bookcases, and various plaques and trophies. The largest was from the Environmental League of Texas, awarding Senator Black their Outstanding Environmentalist Award for 2001. Next to that was a picture of Black and former Eagles drummer, Don Henley, at Caddo Lake, the only non-man-made body of water in the state. Vernon Black, scion of a wealthy East Texas oil and timber family, had turned into a rabid tree hugger upon election to political office.

Black sat behind his desk, facing the window. He had a phone pressed to his ear and a pen in one hand. He clicked the pen repeatedly as he talked.

After a few moments, he turned and noticed us. He waved and pointed to the leather chairs arranged in front of his desk.

We sat. He talked. About a Senate bill that some dipshit from Amarillo was gonna screw up. One minute stretched to two and then three. Nolan shifted in her seat and shot me a look. I turned and stared at Olson. He shrugged.

A moment later the senator ended his call, turned to us, and stood up. He was as I remembered. Early fifties, slim build. A full head of slowly-going-gray hair bracketed a thin face and pointed jaw. Craggy but handsome. An urbane Marlboro Man.

"Hank, how the hell are you, buddy?" He flashed a thousand-watt smile as his hand reached for mine.

We shook. I told him I was great, super, fantastic. He was the kind of guy who brought that out in you. He exchanged greetings with Olson and then with Nolan.

The senator sat down, steepled his fingers, and stared at Nolan's chest. "Hank, you got any family?"

"Yeah." The Oswalds weren't exactly a close-knit bunch, but I did have relatives here and there.

"Bet you wouldn't like it if somebody was messing with 'em, would you?"

I shook my head but didn't say anything.

"Me? I'm just a good old boy from East Texas. All I got is family and friends."

And an MBA from Wharton and a Texas-sized trust fund. I kept that thought to myself.

"Gets my dander up when somebody messes with my people, you follow?" His accent seemed forced, as if he were speaking to the Lufkin, Texas, Rotary Club.

I nodded.

"One of my oldest friends and first business partners was a guy named Jimmy McPherson."

He paused. Olson shifted in his chair, causing a squeaking noise in the otherwise quiet office.

"His daughter's in Dallas now. Works here part time." His voice sounded hoarse all of a sudden. It took me a moment to realize he was trying not to let his emotions get the better of him. "I remember bouncing her on my knee as a child. . . ."

Nobody spoke for a few moments.

"This is real important." Black cleared his throat, coughed a couple of times. "I want somebody to look after her."

"Like a bodyguard?" I said.

He nodded.

"What's the threat?" Nolan said.

The senator ignored her and spoke to me. "Things are never quite what they seem, you know what I mean?"

I shrugged.

"She needs to stay out of East Texas especially."

"Why?" I said.

The senator pursed his lips and positioned his shoulders and head as if the cameras were rolling. "There are forces that are aligned against us."

"Huh?"

"Good people make bad choices sometimes, you know?" He shook his head slowly.

"Now's not a good time." I shot a glance at Nolan. "Got a full plate right—"

"We'll take the case."

Senator Black looked at me and then at Nolan.

Olson said, "You two want to get on the same page?"

"We're busy at the moment." I shook my head, thinking of Lucas Linville and a dead man named Billy Barringer.

"The rent's due in a week," Nolan said. "And we need to make another payment on that bionic ear thing you just had to have."

I sighed and rolled my eyes.

Nolan smiled. "Beats the hell out of chasing ghosts."

"That's great." Black grabbed a tablet and a pen.

"Ghosts?" Olson said.

"Yeah." Nolan chuckled, a mischievous look on her face. "Didn't Hank tell you? Billy Barringer is back."

CHAPTER TEN

The room was silent. After a few moments Senator Black laughed.

"That's funny," he said. "You had me going there for a minute."

"Billy Barringer is dead." Olson spoke to Nolan but looked at me. "Dental records proved it."

"He burned up, didn't he?" Black put on a pair of reading glasses and scribbled something on a tablet.

"It's hard to kill a legend," I said.

"Here's Tess McPherson's address." He handed me a piece of paper. "She's in Lubbock right now, plane lands about six. Why don't you meet her at her apartment a little later."

"Will do." Nolan plucked the paper from my hand.

"Billy. Barringer." Olson spoke the two words slowly, distinctly.

"His name came up in a case I'm working on." I stood.

"Even though I'm against capital punishment, I'm damn glad that guy is dead," Black said. "The last thing this state needs is any more of that redneck mafia. Makes us look bad to the rest of the world. Bonnie and Clyde and John Gotti rolled into one, living in a dinky trailer park in the woods. No more bodies need turn up . . . that way."

Ruthless enforcement had been a Barringers trademark. The typical hit attributed to Billy was a .22-caliber bullet in the belly button, the victim left in a remote location for a long, painful death.

"But the family's still around." Olson looked at me.

"Billy was the brains," I said. "The rest of them came from the muddy end of the gene pool. The only thing they could organize to take out would be Chinese food."

The phone on the desk buzzed and a woman's voice filled the air. "Senator Black, your three o'clock is early."

Olson leaned over the desk. "If it's Roger Staubach, tell him he better have his checkbook."

The young man in khakis entered a few seconds later and hustled us out the door. In the hallway we passed a couple of lawyer-looking types. We rode down alone in the elegant wood-paneled elevator. Halfway to the bottom Olson said, "You didn't tell me somebody mentioned Billy to you."

"Doesn't matter one way or the other," I said.

Nolan gave him the nickel version of events, including the dead body at the boardinghouse this morning, Lucas Linville and the redneck thugs the evening before, and the missing case file for a trust-fund lapdog named Reese Cunningham.

"Retards or not, don't you think the family might be looking for a little payback?" Olson said.

I didn't reply.

Nolan said, "Makes sense to me."

"I would have mentioned it but we were a little busy with those clowns trying to shake you down."

The doors dinged open. We exited the building into the heat of the afternoon. The air felt grimy and oppressive, like wearing a dirty wool coat in the jungle.

I cranked up the truck's AC to high. After several blocks, the air cooled enough that I stopped sweating. We were back on the LBJ Freeway, heading east along with a hundred thousand other cars, traveling at a velocity between five and ten miles per hour. The air shimmered in front of us.

"There was a guy this morning at the boardinghouse," I said, "coming down the stairs as I was going up. Made me want to shoot him in the back of the head just so I'd feel safe."

"What did he look like?" Olson said.

I described the man with the shaved head. "He sure as hell didn't live there. And then I find the preacher's assistant, a slit throat and dead only a couple of minutes."

Olson nodded thoughtfully. "Let me do a little research."

I dropped Olson off at the gun store. It was five o'clock. Nolan and I were near the center of town, the tiny office we shared, and our respective homes. I headed east with no particular destination in mind. The traffic was heavy as the workers from downtown headed to the snug bungalows and remodeled cottages of the Lakewood area, so named because it wrapped around White Rock Lake, one of the city's prettiest locales.

"Let's eat." I parked in front of a bar called the Lakewood Landing, a misnomer since the only body of water visible was a pool of oily liquid in the parking lot. The building itself was low-slung wood, painted white but gone frayed at the edges. They served pretty good food but the primary emphasis was on cocktails.

Nolan shrugged but didn't say anything.

We walked through to the back and sat at a booth by the jukebox. The place was dim and smoky and loud, people standing three deep at the bar, the happy hour crowd mixing with the spillover day drinkers.

A waitress drifted by. We ordered cheeseburgers and a pitcher of Miller Lite. Halfway through the first mug of beer I said, "We've got about an hour before we're supposed to babysit the girl. You want me to take the first shift and you can pick it up tomorrow?"

"I'll go with you. I don't have any plans." She wiped a foam mustache off her lip. "People who have significant others have plans."

I ignored her pity party invitation. "Why did you mention Billy back there?"

"You put the redneck Don Corleone in prison. Then he dies trying to get out," she said. "Didn't it cross your mind that his people might be looking for a little payback?"

The waitress brought our food. We ate, finished the pitcher, and paid the tab. By the time we got in the truck, it was six o'clock and the heat had eased a little, maybe now in the midnineties.

Nolan squinted at the paper we'd gotten from Black. "Looks like she lives in an apartment near the American Airlines Center. Makes sense. She's young and probably single. Lots of nightlife, people to go out with . . ."

I recognized this as my cue. "Don't worry, you'll meet somebody else. Maybe this time you can look somewhere other than a VFW hall or a tractor pull."

"Shut up, Hank." She crossed her arms and sulked.

"Just a thought."

"I wonder if Olson has any new machine guns in stock?"

Tess McPherson lived in some bourbon-swilling-developer's idea of what an urban environment would look like stuffed on the Texas plains.

Her home was part of a brand-new half-dozen-block conglomeration of four-story buildings designed to look like turn-of-the-century brownstones in a hip section of some unnamed East Coast city. All of the structures orbited around the most important feature of the project, a six-story parking garage. The buildings all housed chain retail stores and expensive, trendy restaurants on the ground floor, with apartments on the upper stories. Dallas does Manhattan.

The place was called the Chelsea Tribeca Meadow.

We got lucky and found a parking space in front of a Gap and a T-Mobile store, avoiding the long valet lines at the watering holes a hundred yards away. I checked the address again. Tess lived on the fourth floor of the building where the cars were congregating.

Nolan and I made our way through the throngs of twenty-somethings milling about on the streets, hopping from one bar to the next. Everybody looked the same. The men all had gelled hair and shirts like something David Cassidy would have worn during his *Partridge Family* days. The girls wore midriff-baring tight T-shirts and had hair done like Paris Hilton's or Lindsey's or whoever the It Girl of the moment was.

I smiled and nodded at a group of three particularly toothsome women, the leader a statuesque blonde whose black T-shirt stopped about four inches above her navel.

She smiled back. "Hey."

Nolan elbowed me in the ribs. "We're working. Remember?"

I turned away from the blonde and kept going.

The entrance to Tess's building was to the left of a restaurant. It didn't have a doorman, only a glass-and-wrought-iron door with a key-pad access. As we approached, two women were leaving. We stepped inside before the entrance shut. So much for security.

I was aware of it as we waited for the elevator. The barest trace of cologne. I tried to remember where I had smelled it last, but the odor was too faint. It was stronger when we got inside the lift. When the doors pinged for the fourth floor, I remembered the man from the stairs at the boardinghouse that morning.

I put a hand on Nolan's arm. "I think he's here."

The doors started to open.

"Who?"

The bullet-headed man stepped into the narrow chamber and pushed the down button. "Why you following me, huh?" As he spoke he threw a right into my stomach. His fist punched a hole in my gut all the way through to my spine. On the way to the floor I saw him backhand Nolan. Her skull bounced off the side of the elevator.

The aroma of Old Spice aftershave filled my head.

CHAPTER ELEVEN

I opened my eyes because I couldn't breathe.

Drowning in a room full of air. Diaphragm mangled around my spleen. Lungs struggling. Mouth wheezing. I looked up and saw Bullet Head in the corner of the elevator. He had Nolan's throat squeezed in the crook of his elbow. She was bleeding from her head and a cut lip. Her face was purple. I looked at the control panel. The STOP button had been pushed.

"Oh, yeah, that feels good." With his free hand, Bullet Head massaged Nolan's left breast. He looked at me. "How you doing, buddy boy?"

"Uuggh." I shook my head and tried to relax my chest to get some air.

He stuck his tongue in Nolan's ear and moved his hand to her other breast. She fought until he increased pressure on her throat and her eyes started to bug out.

"Retribution is nigh upon you, Mr. Oswald." His voice had a singsong quality to it. His skin glistened with perspiration.

He smiled and kicked my kneecap. I screamed and curled into a ball.

I barely heard him speak over the din of my pain. He said, "Three of my men paid a visit to your fudge-packing gun dealer today. Can't find any of 'em now. Tell the faggot I'm coming after him next."

"Your guys aren't that good then." I spoke through clenched teeth. "Look for 'em south of the border." I braced for another blow.

Bullet Head laughed as if I were Stand-Up Comic of the Year. "Billy used to tell me you was a tough guy. He wasn't fooling, no sir."

In one motion he hit the START button, released Nolan, and threw her against the wall. He pressed his face against hers, his mouth to her lips, one hand on a breast, the other maintaining pressure on her throat. After a few seconds, or an eternity, depending on your point of view, he released her and stepped out of the elevator. She fell to the floor beside me.

I tried standing. My knee still hurt like hell and felt like it was made of rubber, but it worked, more or less. Nolan was on her hands and knees, spitting repeatedly in a corner. The doors were closed; we were on the ground floor.

"You okay?" I tried to quash the nausea that came from getting a heavy shot to the gut.

My partner looked up. Her face was white, eyes blinking repeatedly. "Nolan?"

Sweat dotted her face. She clutched her stomach and heaved but nothing came out.

"Don't know why he's here." A fresh wave of pain swept across my kneecap. "I'm sorry."

Nolan wiped her mouth. "I will kill that Yul Brynner–looking motherfucker if it's the last thing I do."

I remembered why we were there. We looked at each other and spoke at the same time. *"Oh, shit."*

"What's the number?" I hit the button for the top floor.

"Four-eleven."

The ride up took an eternity. The doors opened, and we spilled out into a narrow carpeted hallway. The sign across from the elevator indicated 411 was to the right. I limped that way as fast as possible. Nolan followed with her gun drawn.

The door was cracked open about an inch. I didn't waste time knocking or crouching or being careful. I kicked it open with my good leg. My bad one went south and I fell into Tess McPherson's apartment on my face.

Nolan hopped over me. I pushed myself up on my good knee. A dark-haired young woman sat on a sofa underneath a framed print advertising a French Impressionist show at the Dallas Museum of Art.

She appeared to be in her late twenties. A look of stark terror marred her otherwise attractive features. She wore a white terry-cloth bathrobe and her hair was damp. She was shivering, her arms crossed. It took me a moment to realize she wasn't looking at us but rather at the door.

Two people busting into her living room with weapons drawn wasn't very scary after a visit from the bullet-headed man.

"He's gone." I holstered the Browning.

The woman didn't say anything.

"Are you okay?" Nolan sat beside her on the sofa.

The woman looked at her but still didn't say a word. I made a quick inspection of the apartment. It was a one-bedroom unit. Kitchen to the right, sleeping chamber to the left. The living/dining area was in the middle. Nobody else was in the place. The bedroom had a balcony overlooking the street scene. The same people were still there, going from one place to another, laughing and having a good time, unaware of who or what walked among them.

Something brushed against my leg. I reached down and picked up a large Siamese cat and carried it into the living room.

The woman watched me walk toward her, cat cuddled up in the crook of my arm. I handed the pet to her. She clutched the animal to her chest and shivered.

————

After a few minutes Tess McPherson put the cat down. "Why are you here?"

"Your family's friend. Senator Black was worried." I gestured to the door. "With good reason." I decided not to mention anything else. Hysteria wouldn't do at this point.

"Who was that guy?" Tess shivered again.

"We don't know." Nolan rubbed the back of one hand across her mouth for the tenth time at least. "He's not long for Planet Earth if I have anything to say about it."

Tess asked if we wanted some green tea. Nolan nodded. I said, sure, tea would be nice. Tess went to the kitchen and brought us back three steaming mugs in less than a minute. It was an instant-hot-water thing on her sink, she explained. The domestic activity seemed to calm her.

We drank tea. Nobody spoke for three or four minutes.

"How do you know he's gone?" Tess placed her mug on the coffee table next to a crystal bowl of potpourri.

"We don't," I said. "It's an assumption. He's not here at the moment, though."

"What happened to your head?" She squinted at my partner's lacerated scalp.

"Hank was being a wuss, rolling on the ground." Nolan smiled. "Baldy got the better of me."

"I'm sorry," Tess said.

"It's not your fault," I said.

Nolan put a sympathetic hand on the woman's shoulder. "What did he do to you?"

No response.

"We need to know everything about that guy so we can get him." I put my mug down. "That's what we do. Stop people like him."

"You can't stop him." Her voice was soft, a struggle to hear. She pulled her robe tighter. "Please excuse me for a moment." Tess jumped up and went into her bedroom, closing the door behind her.

"Now what are we gonna do?" Nolan stood up and took her tea mug into the kitchen.

"I'd like to get a big glass of Glenlivet and a Vicodin." My knee was stiffening. I massaged it gently.

"No, dumbass." Nolan came back to the living room and sat down. "I mean about her. She's a basket case. We can't just leave her here." Occasionally my partner makes sense.

"You're right." I stood up pressed my ear against the bedroom door. "Maybe she's got some friends she could stay with."

Nolan walked to where I stood. She pulled me away from the door. "That guy is beyond bad. If there was an Olympic Fuckstain Team, he'd be captain."

"What about that duplex on Washington?" I said. "We could put her there."

Nolan cocked one eye. "The place next to the crack house?"

I ignored her and hobbled back to the middle of the room.

The bedroom door opened. Tess McPherson came out wearing a pair of jeans, tennis shoes that looked like hiking boots, and a denim jacket over a white shirt. She carried a leather overnight bag. She looked at both of us. "What? You think I'm spending the night here?"

"No." I smiled for an instant. "We'll find some place safe for you."

"Thanks. I don't really know that many people in town." She went to a polished-wood breakfront, fished a key from her pocket, and unlocked one of the bottom doors. She pulled a green canvas pistol case out, unzipped it, and removed a small black semiautomatic pistol. She racked the slide back, let it fall, and then stuffed a magazine in the grip of the weapon.

"Daddy didn't feel right, me not having a gun in the big city." She stuffed the firearm in her overnight bag.

"Daddy sounds like a smart guy." I opened the door to the hallway and peered out. It was empty. I turned and motioned to the two women standing in the living room. We left.

The trip to my truck was uneventful. The party atmosphere had grown. More people were outside now, walking, talking, enjoying themselves. I backed the Tahoe carefully, splitting the crowd so they flowed around me as if I were a branch stuck in a swift-moving creek. Bullet Head could be anywhere among them, watching.

I exited the Chelsea Tribeca Meadow as fast as possible and soon we were heading north of downtown on McKinney Avenue, past galleries, restaurants, and high-rise apartments. We decided that Tess would spend the night with Nolan, at the house she rented a block away from a strip of bars on Greenville Avenue. I headed that way and crossed over Central Expressway at Knox Street.

"Is there a place to get a drink near your house?" Tess said.

"Uh-huh." Nolan flicked her knife open and shut in the front of the truck. "One or two. You feel like a drink?"

The woman nodded.

At Nolan's house, I pulled into the driveway and parked in back.

The Greenville Avenue Bar and Grill, formerly a gritty live music club now converted into a semi-respectable restaurant and drinking establishment, was a couple of hundred yards to the east. The three of us hopped out of the truck and walked that way.

The bar and grill had been there for probably seventy-five years and the building it occupied had housed similar endeavors for another fifty before that. According to some old drunks I knew, the place had reached its zenith in the late seventies as a fixture on the regional music scene.

The reason: a smart-ass kid from South Dallas who could play a guitar like the unholy offspring of Jimi Hendrix and Eric Clapton. To this day they still mourn the premature curtain falling on hometown favorite Stevie Ray Vaughan.

We managed to find three stools at the bar. Tess ordered a Bombay Sapphire martini straight up. Nolan got a Shiner Bock while I indulged in a single-malt scotch only a few years younger than our guest. The place was crowded, which seemed to act as a balm on our new friend. Safety in numbers, I guess. The bartender placed our drinks in front of us along with a bowl of salted nuts.

"There's no way he could have followed us, is there?" Tess downed half her drink in one swallow, her eyes restlessly surveying the crowd. "And he couldn't do anything with all these people, right?"

"We're okay." I tossed a peanut in my mouth. In fact, I had made several false runs and double-backs on the way to Nolan's house. We were in the clear. Our respective homes were also untraceable; the utilities and ownership records were under aliases.

"Tell us what happened." Nolan made circles on the bar top with her beer bottle.

Tess was quiet for a moment. "He didn't hurt me, if that's what you mean. Didn't even touch me . . ."

"Start at the beginning." I ran a finger around the rim of my glass.

"I had just taken a shower. I was going out for drinks; my friend wanted to set me up with this lawyer." As she talked she kept her gaze locked on the half-empty martini glass in front of her. "I went to get something out of the kitchen. And there he was, holding my cat."

"How did he get in?" Nolan said.

Tess shook her head. "I have no idea. The door was locked."

"What did he do?" I rubbed my knee. It was still tender.

"Nothing. I mean, he never touched me or anything like that." Tess shuddered. "He just talked."

I didn't reply.

"He said he knew a hooker in Houston that looked just like me. Till he had to beat her to death with a baseball bat because she ripped off his boss."

"Yeah, he's a real sweetheart, that one." Nolan signaled for another round of drinks. "What else?"

"He said bad things about my father."

"What?" Nolan and I spoke in unison.

Tess closed her eyes. "He said he was going to kill him, after he raped me and my mother and made Daddy watch."

Nolan patted her on the shoulder as glasses clinked and laughter tinkled around us.

"Nobody's going to do anything like that." I hoped my tone of voice conveyed a sense of confidence that I definitely did not feel.

The second round of drinks arrived. Tess finished the last bit of number one and slid the glass across the bar.

"What was it he wanted?" I said.

She shook her head again. "He never told me. It was like he didn't care about the goal, only the chance to hurt somebody."

"Sociopath." Nolan's voice was a mutter.

Tess nodded. "Yeah. A real-life one."

"Anything more?" I knocked back half a shot of scotch.

Tess shook her head and then said, "No. . . . Wait. He did say something else." She frowned. "It didn't really make sense, though."

"What was it?" I motioned to the bartender for the check.

She bit her lip, obviously thinking. "He said things were gonna be different in Dallas. What do you think he meant?"

CHAPTER TWELVE

We got back to Nolan's house at about nine. I checked all the windows and doors while Nolan showed Tess the spare bedroom. We made plans for tomorrow. Tess had said she had never heard of Linville or his ministry, so first up was another visit with the good reverend, hopefully a come-to-Jesus talk from which we could get a solid lead on our assailant. After that I wanted to find Reese Cunningham and learn about his connection to Billy Barringer.

I drove home and thought about the events of the past day, trying to piece together the who and the why of it all.

Tess's story about hookers in Houston made me think Bullet Head might be mobbed up. But what was he doing here in Dallas?

At one time the Barringer crime clan had planned to infiltrate the urban areas of the state from their base of operations in the piney woods of East Texas. Mostly it was all talk, and Billy's incarceration and subsequent death ended their plans. While the Barringers had connections in Louisiana and among South Texas border families, they were tenuous at best, sometimes overlapping ventures that in the interest of the mutual good were ignored in the fringe areas. But maybe there was a link I couldn't see.

Nothing had resolved itself by the next morning. I fed the dog and limped around the kitchen for a few minutes, stretching and working my knee. It hurt at first but gradually eased to a dull ache. To clear my head I wandered the streets of my neighborhood for thirty minutes, moving a at a fast walk rather than the usual jog, in deference to my knee.

At a convenience store on Gaston Avenue, I passed the day laborers hoping for a contractor or two to come by and hire them on a Saturday. The work was backbreaking, the pay only a few dollars an hour, most of which would be sent home to Mexico by next weekend. I passed a new Thai restaurant next to an old pool hall and across the street from a typewriter repair store. The new and the not so new and the buggy-whip maker.

At the abandoned doughnut shop, I gave the legless man in the wheelchair a five-dollar bill like I did most mornings when he was around. We talked about the happenings in our little section of Big D, mostly who got arrested for vagrancy and how the price of discount-brand beer kept going up. I asked him if he still had my phone number in case he ever wanted to get off the streets for a while. He nodded and said yeah, maybe when it got cold. I told him he was always welcome and that I still had his Purple Heart and two Silver Stars locked up in my safe whenever he wanted them back. He said thanks and rolled away. I wondered again for the hundredth time where I might be if a Viet Cong mine had taken my legs off in some nameless rice paddy.

At home, I hit the weights in the basement and worked a little on the body bag hanging from the rafters. I turned on the coffeepot before taking a shower. Afterward, I plunked a piece of ham in a cast-iron skillet. When it was warm, I fried two eggs. Everything went on a plate. The eggs got a good soaking with Tabasco, and breakfast was ready. I ate, watched the morning news shows, and skimmed the paper.

By eight-thirty, I was in my truck headed to the office. A few minutes later, I parked in my spot behind the office. An unmarked police car and a cherry red late-model Mercedes sat in front, the latter out of place in the neighborhood.

For some reason I decided to go in the front door.

The first thing I saw was Bullet Head, sitting on our one good sofa and drinking coffee from my favorite cup, the one I got from the softball league a couple of years earlier.

I reached for my gun but stopped when I saw the two cops sitting in the easy chairs in the corner. The first one was about nine feet tall and wore a uniform, corporal bars on his shoulders.

The second one was a black man in a three-button, dark gray suit named Franklin Delano Jessup, a homicide sergeant I'd had a run-in with a while back. He was in his early fifties, salt starting to weave its way through his close-cropped hair.

Bullet Head placed *my* mug on *my* wagon-wheel coffee table, on a two-year-old copy of *D Magazine*. He crossed one leg and ran a finger down the crease of his pants. "That's him, Sergeant."

The black detective and the nine-foot-tall uniformed officer stood up.

"He's the one that killed that poor Messican boy." Bullet Head remained seated.

"Lee Oswald. Again in trouble. Who would believe it." Jessup took a step toward me, hands by his sides.

"What the hell is going on?" I looked from Jessup to the bald man and back again.

"We got a dead gangbanger and two people who put you at the scene," Jessup said.

"And who the hell is he?" I pointed to the man on the sofa. "You always let civilians ride along for this kind of stuff?"

"This is Mr. Jesus Rundell." Jessup jerked his head at the man in the cream-colored linen suit and terra-cotta T-shirt. "Mr. Rundell is a . . . uh . . . fellow law enforcement officer."

"For who, *Miami Vice*?"

Nobody laughed.

"We need to go downtown," Jessup said. "Clear some things up."

"That guy assaulted me last night." I pointed to the man on the couch.

Rundell made a *tssk*ing sound and stood up. "They're all the same, aren't they? It's always somebody else's fault."

"Let's make this easy," Jessup said. "You're not under arrest, so there's no need for handcuffs and all that."

"Check him for weapons." Rundell brushed the wrinkles from his jacket. "His type is always armed."

"Thanks." Jessup's voice betrayed a hint of irritation. "I was just getting to that."

"He's from South Texas." I pulled up my denim shirt, displaying the butt of my Browning. "Probably working for one of the border cartels. Have you checked him out at all?"

The uniformed officer moved behind me and pulled my pistol from its holster. He did a quick pat-down and took the Seecamp .32 off my ankle and the Benchmade lock-back knife from my waistband. He also pocketed my cell phone.

"I am insulted." Rundell puffed up. "I am an honorary member of the Houston Police Auxiliary."

"Where's your decoder ring?" I balled my fist.

Rundell's face clouded for just a moment. Jessup opened the front door and said, "Let's go."

They put me in the backseat of the unmarked unit. Rundell got in the red Mercedes. He followed us to the Jack Evans Police Headquarters, a shiny new building just south of downtown, not too far from Lucas Linville's place.

During the ten-minute ride, I tried to initiate conversation with Jessup, but he wouldn't respond.

They stuck me in a windowless room on the third floor. It could have been a conference area for a midlevel company. A large mirror dominated the wall on one side of the room. A framed NO SMOKING sign hung on the opposite wall. The place smelled like fresh paint. The carpet looked brand-new, and the seats around the lacquered wooden table were upholstered leather.

Interview rooms had come a long way. I tried to recall the last one I had seen. Albuquerque, maybe. Something to do with a former high school buddy and a redheaded call girl.

Ten minutes stretched to twenty and then forty-five. Almost an hour after leaving me there, three people entered. Jessup and two guys in blue suits. He introduced them as assistant district attorneys. They looked as if they were about twelve. They sat on either side of the detective.

"You need anything?" Jessup smiled. "A cup of coffee?"

"Am I charged with a crime?"

Blue Suit One scribbled something on a yellow pad.

"Not at the moment, no." Jessup kept the pleasant expression on his face, trying for the good cop effect. It might have worked if I hadn't been aware of how big a hard-ass he could be.

Blue Suit One pushed the pad in front of Jessup. He ignored it. "Yesterday morning a Mr. Carlos Jimenez was found in his room with his throat cut. Guy been worked over pretty bad. Fingers broken. Real messy."

"I want a lawyer."

"You think you need one for some reason?"

I didn't reply.

The two blue suits leaned behind Jessup and had a whispered conversation. When they were finished, Blue Suit Two jotted something on his yellow pad. He paused, squinted at me, and wrote some more stuff.

"Let's be reasonable here." Jessup leaned back in his chair. "We've got two people who can place you at the scene."

"My lawyer. Here. Now." I spoke softly so there would be no misunderstanding. One of the witnesses had to be the purple-suit-wearing pimp, not the most reliable of testimony.

"Hank, this is just a friendly visit." Jessup smiled again. "Let's run through the whole thing and see if we can make sense of what all happened."

"There's nothing to run through," I said. "Are you denying me the right to counsel?"

Blue Suit Two tapped his notepad and looked at Jessup.

"We can get your lawyer." Jessup quit smiling and waved a dismissive hand at the suit. "That's the hard way. And that will make me want to fuck with you when we're through. You don't want that, now do you?"

The room grew very quiet. He was right: A homicide detective at a big-city police force could make my life very unhappy if he so chose.

I shrugged but didn't say anything.

Jessup leaned forward and placed his forearms on the table. "Where were you yesterday morning?"

I told him. Everything except finding Carlos's still-steaming corpse. I was sure that not reporting a dead body was against the law and would cause the suits to get acne or something. I told him I had knocked on the door but no one answered. Then I told them who I saw on the stairway. Bullet Head, now identified as one Jesus Rundell.

"What was he doing there?" I said.

"You're not the one asking questions." Jessup steepled his fingers and looked at me.

"The guy is a professional creep. He leaves a trail of slime wherever he goes."

"He's a cop."

"He's in the police *auxiliary*." I slammed the table. "There's a slight difference."

Nobody spoke for a few moments. Finally Jessup said, "Let's go through it again."

A half hour later, Jessup left and another investigator entered. He was younger and fatter and wore a lime green sport coat with western yokes on the shoulders. He asked the same questions. The suits scribbled more notes. After another thirty minutes, he left.

Jessup returned. He handed me an evidence box containing my guns, pocketknife, and cell phone.

"Don't take any trips for a while, okay?"

"Or what?" I turned on the cell phone. The voice mail indicator flashed.

"How about trying to not be an asswipe, huh?" He left the room; the two suits followed.

I stuffed my weapons where they belonged and checked my voice mail. Nolan twice. *Where the hell are you.* Olson once. *Call me.* I left a minute or so later. Nobody I recognized was in the hallway, only a handful of uniformed officers and several clerical types.

I took the elevator down to the ground floor, a huge expanse of marble giving way to a commendation wall honoring officers killed in the line of duty. I walked outside. It was a little before noon on a Saturday, and the walkway in front of the building bustled with cops moving about.

The air was thick with humidity and the buzz of the freeway a few blocks north. I started to sweat within a few seconds. As I pulled out my cell phone to call Nolan for a ride, I smelled Old Spice aftershave. I turned around. Jesus Rundell stood a few feet behind me. The bright sun illuminated a series of old injuries on his bald head, one a jagged scar two inches long above his ear, next to a shallow indentation.

"That nigger cop don't think you killed the greaseball," he said.

"That's because I didn't. You did." I pointed to the concave place on his skull. "How did you get the hole in your head?"

"That's from Daddy." Rundell touched the spot. "South Texas boys got hard heads, let me tell you what."

I thought of a joke about postnatal birth control but decided against telling it.

"Used to fuck an old girl from Lufkin, what looked a lot like your partner." Rundell pulled a pack of Juicy Fruit gum from his coat pocket. " 'Cept she had one leg shorter than the other."

"What do you want from me?" I reached for my Browning but didn't draw it. It would be so easy at this range. One shot, right where the eyebrows met. But my course in life was not a suicide mission.

"She tried to stiff me on her weeklies one time." He pushed a stick of gum in his mouth and let the foil wrapper drift away in the smoggy breeze. "Till I started playing on her nipples with a pair of pliers. Then she remembered where my money was."

"What's so important about the file Carlos stole?"

"You give it to me, an' I'll tell you." He winked. I felt unclean, icky, like accidentally seeing Great-Aunt Mildred getting out of the shower.

"I don't have the file. You know that."

"Don't lie to your buddy Jesus." Two uniformed officers stood close by, lighting cigarettes. He lowered his voice. "That'd just make me angry."

CHAPTER THIRTEEN

Nolan picked me up fifteen minutes later in the two-year-old Mitsubishi that had been a gift from her ex-fiancé, Larry. It had a leaky valve and spit out blue smoke whenever she accelerated. I filled her in on the last few hours, including the name of our assailant from the previous evening. She had a knot on her forehead the size of a grape from her impact with the elevator wall the night before and a faint bruise on one cheek that was undoubtedly much worse without the makeup.

"How's our houseguest doing?" I pulled out my cell phone and dialed Olson. No answer. I left a one-word message: *Call.*

Nolan honked at a slow-moving minivan. "As a personal favor to me, do you think you could try to *not* sleep with her?"

"Where did that come from?"

She sighed dramatically.

"I liked it better when you were still taking Wellbutrin," I said.

"That was just to quit smoking." Nolan banged her hand on the steering wheel. "I thought we all agreed on that."

"Gotcha." I watched the city drift by.

"She called somebody this morning," Nolan said.

"Who?"

"No idea. She's unhappy since."

"So naturally you thought I would want to have sex with her?"

"You need to be careful with this one. Something's off about her." Nolan sighed again, signaled to change lanes, and turned onto Greenville Avenue. "Plus you know how you are with the whole damsel-in-distress thing."

"Whatever." We passed an Irish pub called the Tipperary Inn, and I imagined how good a pint of Guinness would taste in a dark bar, away from psychopathic South Texas whack jobs.

Nolan seemed to read my mind. "We need to check on her before anything else."

I nodded.

A few minutes later we turned left at the Greenville Avenue Bar and Grill, and a few seconds after that we pulled into the driveway of Nolan's rental. The grass was yellow and about a foot high, making the snug brick house appear shabbier than it really was.

"Want me to come over and mow sometime?"

"That was what Larry used to do." Nolan slammed her car door shut. "Every Sunday afternoon."

"Looks like it's been a lot of Sundays since he broke a sweat on it."

"Larry took care of me." She sniffled once and kicked a beer can off the sidewalk and into the jungle that was her front yard.

"Like the time he threw the bottle of gin at you?"

She made an obscene gesture with one hand as she unlocked the front door and stepped into her living room, a plaster-walled area with a fake fireplace at one end and a worn leather sofa at the other. I followed her into the empty room.

"Tess?" I walked toward the kitchen.

Nolan went to the guest bedroom to the left of the front door. "Hey. We're back."

We both ended up in Nolan's room at the rear of the house. Her dresser was all pictures, a shrine to her ex-fiancé: Larry at a shuffleboard tournament; Larry in a sleeveless T-shirt, holding up a twenty-inch striper bass in one hand, a can of Old Milwaukee in the other; Larry getting the Salesman of the Year award from his employer, Don of Don's Used Cars.

"Was she going anywhere?" I said.

"Uh-uh." Nolan picked up a picture of Larry wearing a Dale Earnhardt number-three jersey and eating sausage on a stick.

"What was the last thing she said?"

Nolan sighed and stared at the framed image.

"Maybe if you got rid of all those pictures, you wouldn't feel so down."

"I had so much invested." She put the picture back on the dresser and picked up another. "I don't want to end up alone."

"You're thirty-three. Plenty of time to find somebody." I headed to the door. "I'm gonna look around some more."

Five minutes later we had scoured every crevice of Nolan O'Connor's two-bedroom house. Tess's leather overnight bag was at the foot of her bed. Other than that, nothing. We ended up back in Nolan's room.

"This is not good." I paced in the narrow area between her bed and the far wall. "How about the garage?"

Nolan followed me through her kitchen and into the overgrown backyard. We passed the Weber kettle grill that Larry used to cook burgers on and the lawn chair where he used to sit and drink beer.

The garage was old, like the house, and had a sliding door rather than an overhead one. I pulled it open and stepped inside.

"Tess? You in here? It's me, Hank."

No reply. I fumbled for the light cord dangling overhead. The bulb flickered on.

She was in the far corner, wedged between the wall and a seldom-used workbench. She was sitting on a wooden crate.

"Tess?" I kneeled in front of her.

She rubbed her eyes and cleared her throat several times.

"What's wrong?"

She looked at me. "Never let them see you cry."

CHAPTER FOURTEEN

I should go home." Tess took a sip of her three-dollar coffee drink and shivered.

"I don't think your apartment is a good place to be." I dialed Olson again. The call went straight to voice mail.

"No. I mean home where my family is." She cupped the mug of coffee. "They need me."

"Tess." Nolan leaned forward. "Tell us what's going on."

"What if that guy from last night goes after my family?"

I didn't say anything because there wasn't a good response to that scenario.

We were at Legal Grounds, a small coffee shop by White Rock Lake, a quasi-bohemian section of the city a few miles south of where Nolan lived. The place was a daylong hangout for graphic artists and other creative types, guys with ponytails and portfolios tucked under one arm, banging on laptops or whispering into tiny cell phones while scribbling on yellow pads.

"We've got to get a handle on what's happening." I rolled a glass of iced tea across my forehead.

"Look. You don't owe me anything." Tess pushed her chair back from the table. It scraped on the tile floor. "Thanks for all you've done. But I'm not looking for your help. I just need to go home."

"You want us to leave you here, by yourself?" I slid my chair back, too. No reply.

"Tess." Nolan kept her voice low. "This is the major leagues, the big bad nasty."

"Shit." Tess pulled her chair back to the table. "What am I gonna do?"

I took a look around the shop, trying to find the right words, something that would offer her a modicum of comfort. The room we were in was long and skinny, old law books lining one wall, scarred wooden tables dotting the open area. Two easy chairs were next to each other in the front window. We were sitting in the middle of the room. I had my back to the books, keeping watch on both entrances.

"We need more intelligence on the situation." I spoke softly. "We need to find out who Jesus Rundell is and how he fits in with Black. And where Lucas Linville ties in with everything."

A waitress came by and refilled Tess's coffee cup.

"You work for Black," I said. "Who would benefit if the Caddo Lake bill didn't pass?"

"Nobody." Tess took a drink. "Except for a couple of rednecks who want to hunt out there, most people are in favor of it."

"The Barringers," Nolan said.

"Who?" Tess frowned. "You mean like those East Texas mafia guys?"

"Yeah," I said. "The cowboy Cosa Nostra."

"What's the connection?"

My cell phone chirped before I could respond. Olson's number popped up on the screen.

"Yeah."

"Where the hell are you?" His voice sounded muffled and angry at the same time.

I told him.

"Don't go anywhere. I'm two minutes away." A horn honked in the background.

Ninety seconds later, Olson shoved open the door of the coffee shop and stepped inside. He stopped in front of a stocky young man with close-cropped hair, wearing camo cargo shorts and an Olds 97 T-shirt. The young man was tapping away on an Apple notebook, head bobbing to the music from his MP3 player. He looked up, mouth open, hands frozen over the keyboard, as Olson stood there, swaying.

I could understand his apparent shock. I'd seen my friend worse off, but not by much. One eye was almost swollen shut. His silk shirt was torn in two places and a patch of skin was missing from an elbow. He staggered a little as he stepped into the room.

Mr. Apple swallowed once and continued to stare.

"What the hell are you looking at?" Olson bumped against the man's table as he made his way to where we were sitting.

He sat down in the open chair between Tess and Nolan, facing me. He reached in his hip pocket, pulled out a silver flask, and took a long pull.

"What's the other guy look like?" Nolan said.

"Worse." Olson capped the flask and stuck it back in his pocket. "At least he's not in pain anymore."

"How many?" I said.

"Three total. Two meatheads plus the head-weirdo-in-charge."

"His name is Jesus Rundell." I relayed his warning about Olson's arms business, given to me only an hour or so before.

"Jesus. Rundell." Olson nodded slowly as if committing the information to longterm memory. "He is one mean motherfucker." He squinted at Tess with his good eye. "Who are you?"

"This is Tess McPherson." I made the introductions and filled him in on the last eighteen hours, starting with our encounter with Rundell in the elevator at Tess's apartment, followed by my interrogation by the police about the dead body.

"These guys were friends of the three from yesterday?" I said.

"Looks that way." Olson probed the corner of his eye socket with two fingers.

"You ever heard of this guy Rundell?" Nolan said.

"Nope. Looks like he's a newbie on the local douche-bag circuit."

"It's like he's an evil spirit or something." Nolan rubbed her mouth again.

"No, he's not," Olson said. "Evil spirits don't bleed. At least the ones I've tangled with."

"Did you get a shot at him?" I said.

Olson didn't reply. He pulled a lock-back knife from his waistband and dropped it on the table. The sunlight streaming into the coffee shop highlighted the blood on the handle.

Tess stared at the blade and trembled. "Is he dead?"

Olson shook his head.

"Then I bet he's pissed off," she said.

"Oh, yeah." Olson took another drink from his flask. "Just a little bit."

CHAPTER FIFTEEN

Because it was past lunchtime and I was hungry, I ordered a sandwich. Nolan got a bowl of soup. Tess drummed her fingers and looked pissed off.

"You're just gonna eat?" she said.

"Yep." I dumped another packet of Sweet'N Low in my iced tea.

"You need to get some food in you," Nolan said. "No telling when the next opportunity will be."

Olson went to his truck. He returned a minute later with a second flask.

He took another long pull, wiped his mouth. "I need to tell you the interesting part."

I raised my eyebrows. "You mean it gets better?"

Olson was outside the storeroom behind his new gun shop, unloading cases of shotgun shells with one of his employees, when they arrived. Three of them in the cherry red Mercedes. Jesus Rundell, decked out in the immaculately pressed linen outfit, exited first, followed by two goons in tracksuits and sneakers.

"I just trick-fucked your boy Oswald," Rundell said. "Now it's your turn."

The two goons advanced, one pulling out a length of chain, the other producing a piece of metal pipe. They didn't waste time. They almost covered the twenty feet from the Mercedes to the storeroom in a few seconds, about as long as it took Olson to drop the case of shells he was holding and pull the .45 automatic from its holster underneath his shirt.

When they were five feet away Olson fired a 185-grain jacketed hollow point into the chest of the one on the right.

The one on the left swung his bike chain at the same time, catching Olson on the side of the head.

If Olson had been a mere mortal, that would have been it, game over. But he was not. He was Olson, a former Dallas Cowboys linebacker who once got into such a fierce fight with a teammate that they demolished the back third of a house in Plano. (Olson liked to say afterward that Sheetrock is really underrated as a weapon.)

He went down to his knees. Dropped his .45. Shook his head. Put his hands on the ground to get up.

That's when the guy hit him the second time with the chain, striking him across the shoulders and back of the head. Because the soft tissue cushioned the blow somewhat, the second impact to the brain wasn't as severe.

The goon started to pull the weapon back for another shot.

Olson grabbed it. Wrapped the chain around his fist. Pulled. The guy in the tracksuit was cannon fodder, not the most polished piece of silver in Jesus Rundell's crime outfit.

He held on, fell on top of Olson, whom he had just whipped over the head with a piece of chain.

Olson went to work, making his way from top to bottom. Elbow to the man's nose. Two quick blows to the stomach and ribs. Fist to the crotch. On the second pass, he gave the barely conscious man a fast one-two punch to the windpipe.

He grabbed his Colt, looked around for Rundell.

The bullet-headed man was to the right, well away from his Mercedes, where he'd last been seen. He had the unconscious gun store employee by the neck. He yanked the man's shirt up, stuck a small-caliber handgun in his belly button, and pulled the trigger.

The sound was muffled by the flesh of the employee's abdomen and the low power of the cartridge.

Olson passed out.

When he opened his eyes, Rundell stood over him. He said, "You're pretty tough for a pole smoker."

"You're pretty lively for a dead man." Olson's gun was nowhere in sight. He sighed deeply, grimaced with pain, and let his right hand brush up against his waistband, where a Microtech SOCOM four-inch switchblade was hidden by a belt buckle.

"Big talk coming from somebody in your position." Rundell squatted by Olson and pulled a small billy club from inside his jacket.

"Listen to my advice, Shit-For-Brains." Olson eased the small knife out and palmed it. "Go back to whatever trailer park your whore of a mother spit you out in. You have no idea what you're getting into."

"There was this little blond boy on my cell block in Raiford." Rundell ran the fingers of his free hand through Olson's fair hair. "His bunkmate was a big ole nigger named Mon-roe."

"You're not getting the picture, are you, Freak Boy?" Olson coughed once to hide the sound of the blade popping open. His left hand covered his right, keeping the weapon out of sight.

"Mon-roe used to tie that boy up in the shower, sell a ride for a pack of Camels or a shot of pruno." Rundell ran a callused finger down Olson's cheek. "You'd a liked that, wouldn't you?"

"I ain't that little." Olson moved his right hand.

Rundell swung the billy club at his face. Olson twisted, taking the impact as a glancing blow to the corner of one eye. He kicked a foot toward his attacker, connected. Heard a gasp.

He lashed out with the knife. Felt the blade plunge into flesh. He heard a howl. Felt blood on his hand.

Olson may have passed out; he wasn't sure. A few minutes later he pulled himself up, tried to clear his vision. The bloody knife was still in his hand. The man with the shaved head was gone, a small pool of blood marking where he had stood. The gun store employee had died relatively quickly, for which his boss was grateful. He looked for his .45 and found it in the bushes behind the store before staggering to the Suburban.

We left Legal Grounds. Nolan volunteered to bandage Olson's arm and head. They went to Olson's truck to look for a first aid kit. Tess and I wandered down the sidewalk, past a Chinese restaurant and a used bookstore. We stopped in front of my Tahoe.

Tess leaned against the hood and crossed her arms under her breasts. "They looked at you funny, when Olson talked about his guy getting shot in the stomach."

"There was a guy that used to do that, to send a message." I stared at the display window of the bookstore. They were having a special on Michael Connelly novels.

"What was his name?" Tess came and stood beside me.

"Billy Barringer."

"He was part of that family, right?" She leaned in and stared at a book. "But he died."

"Yeah." I turned away from the window and looked across the parking lot.

"What does he have to do with any of this?"

"He was somebody I knew a long time ago. Beyond that, I have no idea."

Nolan had finished patching up Olson. They laughed at something as he pulled a wooden crate halfway out of the back of his Suburban. Probably selling her a surface-to-air missile.

"You don't strike me as the kind of guy who's friends with the Tony Soprano of East Texas."

"We'd known each other since we were kids," I said.

"Yeah?"

"It's hard to explain."

Nolan and Olson walked our way.

"I hear you." Tess ran her fingers through her hair and turned to face the sun, eyes closed. "A lot of things are."

I rubbed my ear where the fat hood from yesterday had almost pulled it off.

"Hank." Tess put a hand on my shoulder. "I need to get home. I'm worried."

"Do you trust me?"

"Why should I?"

"Your father's best friend hired me. Other than that, no particular reason."

She paused for a few moments. "Go on."

"You're safer here. If it gets really rough, we've got a half dozen places to hide. Lots of different people to keep an eye on you." I neglected to mention the quality of the people or places.

She crossed her arms again, a distant look on her face. "Okay. We'll do it your way."

"Good."

Nolan and Olson stopped in front of us. We discussed the situation for a few moments and decided Nolan and Tess would take my truck and look for Reese Cunningham while Olson and I would pay a visit to Carlos Jimenez's mother and then hit the street to try to get a handle on Jesus Rundell.

CHAPTER SIXTEEN

I headed north on Abrams Road. Maria Jimenez lived in an apartment near Park Lane and Greenville Avenue, in an area that had once been a hot spot for the swinging-singles scene of the 1970s. Now the low-rise buildings provided housing for the city's most recent immigrants.

Her complex was behind a small shopping center where men sat on the curb drinking beer from cans hidden in paper bags. They ignored me when I drove into the parking lot of Shady Acres Apartments.

The woman I presumed to be Carlos's mother lived on the second floor of the first building. Olson was looking a little woozy, so I told him to stay put. He nodded and leaned back against the headrest.

Several children were playing in the patch of grass in front, two women who looked barely out of their teens watching them. I nodded hello but they ignored me, continuing to visit with each other in Spanish.

Jimenez's unit was in the middle of the walkway, overlooking where the kids were playing. I knocked and stood to one side. The blinds on the window moved. After a minute or so, I knocked again. More movement, then the door opened a crack.

"Whatchoo want?" A man's voice.

"Senora Jimenez."

"Ella no está aquí."

"When will she be back?"

The door shut.

I knocked again, harder this time.

It opened further, displaying the face of a young man in his twenties. He looked a little like the pictures of Carlos. A brother or cousin maybe. "Go away, *por favor.*"

"No can do, amigo." I shook my head. "Just need to ask her a few questions."

The man was clearly agitated, breathing heavily, trying to find the right words in English.

"I mean no harm." I raised my hands.

"All you gringos say that." His face hardened. "They've already been here. Go way."

"Who's . . . *quien*?" I really needed to listen to those Spanish-language tapes I'd bought a couple of years ago.

"*El chino, el hombre loco, todos.*" He spat on the ground at my feet. "Go away." He slammed the door.

I tried to translate what he'd said. A Chinese crazy guy didn't make any sense. I started to knock again but heard a noise from the end of the walkway. I turned and saw three young men, all wearing matching denim jackets with the sleeves ripped off.

"*Hola.*" I smiled and tried to look like a nonthreatening gringo.

"Why you bothering Senora Jiminez?" The one in front pulled a sawed-off pool cue from behind his back.

"Just asking her a few questions." I started moving backward.

"You need to ask us first." He bounced the business end of the stick against his palm a couple of times and started toward me. "Show some respect, understand. This is our complex."

One of the other guys produced a length of steel pipe.

I pulled out my Hi Power and pointed it at the first one. "I'm leaving now. No need for this to get messy."

The three of them stopped and whispered to one another. I kept moving backward until I reached the end of the walkway. Then I took the stairs three at a time and raced back to Olson's Suburban. He blinked his eyes open when I hopped in.

"What happened?"

"Oh, not too much." I put the truck in gear and got us out of there as fast as possible.

Connie the crack whore gave blow jobs for twenty bucks a pop in an alley behind Jefferson Avenue in South Dallas. To say Connie was plugged into the latest news of the street was something of an understatement. After the unproductive visit to Carlos's mother, she seemed like a logical place to start gathering information on Rundell.

Also, she owed me a favor or two since I had stopped a one-legged speed freak from almost beating her to death with his prosthetic limb a couple of months before.

Not too many years ago Jefferson Avenue had been mostly vacant, boarded-up buildings punctuated here and there by a used furniture store. Lately, however, the main commercial street in the southern sector of the city had taken on a distinctly Hispanic flavor, dominated now by Mexican bridal shops and storefronts that specialized in arranging bus charters to visit relatives south of the border.

I slowed as we passed the Texas Theater, a minor footnote in Dallas's history, where the police had arrested Lee Harvey in the aftermath of the events on that fateful November day so many years before.

Olson sat in the passenger seat and drank from his flask. I knew from experience that, when angry, he grew very quiet, nursing the rage and focusing his attention on revenge.

He hadn't said a word since we'd left Senora Jimenez's apartment complex.

A few hundred yards past the theater, I turned right on a side street and drove past the alley running behind Jefferson, where a panel truck blocked the narrow access point.

I turned right again and stopped across from a Honda Accord with deep tinted windows and skinny after-market tires. Two tough-looking guys were leaning against the hood, staring down the street. I parked behind a Toyota pickup resting on its axles, the wheels missing.

We got out. I locked the doors.

"Do you know how pissed off I'll be if my wheels get boosted?" Olson wobbled a little as he spoke.

"We won't be long." I headed toward the alley, Olson staggering behind me, flask still in hand. Connie had a particular Dumpster behind which she liked to ply her trade. I moved past the panel truck and saw it belonged to a plumber.

The rest of the alley was empty, except for a grocery cart resting on its side and a large metal trash receptacle about halfway down. I made my way toward the Dumpster but stopped after a hundred yards when Olson leaned over and vomited.

"You okay?"

He wiped his mouth. "Damn this cheap scotch."

I stared at him for a few moments.

"Keep going." He waved me away. "I'll be all right."

I headed toward the Dumpster, turning around every few feet to check on my friend. He was back to swilling from the flask so I figured he was going to make it.

I stopped a few feet from the Dumpster. "Hey, Connie, you back there?"

A burly guy in a work shirt with a name tag sewn on the chest jumped out from behind the trash receptacle, zipping his pants. He had that weasel-caught-in-the-headlights look in his eyes. He stared at me for half a second and then ran in the opposite direction.

A few moments later Connie appeared, wiping her mouth with the back of her hand. She wore a sleeveless T-shirt knotted across her belly and a dirty denim skirt that stopped about ten inches above her knees. The effect was to make her scrawny legs appear even skinnier. I knew she was in her late twenties, but life on the streets and the drugs made her look twice that age.

She squinted at me. I waved. She took a hesitant step forward and then seemed to recognize me. She frowned and walked warily to where I stood.

"Heya, Hank."

"Hi, Connie."

"I was in the middle of a date."

"Sorry."

"He hadn't paid me yet."

I sighed and pulled out my wallet. I was getting tired of giving out Andy Jacksons to hookers.

"Thanks." She took the twenty. "Who's he?" She pointed to Olson, who was swaying in the still air of the alley, an empty flask dangling from one hand.

"Try not to pay attention to him. It's better that way."

"Okay." Connie placed a hand on my forearm and dragged her nails along my skin. "You want to go behind the Dumpster?"

"Uh . . . no. Thanks." I moved my arm. "Anything new happening I need to know about?"

She frowned but didn't say anything.

Olson started to snore.

I decided to try a different tactic. "You got a pimp?"

"Hell, no." She shook her head. "I'm a free agent."

"Anybody tried to recruit you lately?"

She gave me an blank look. The cocoa leaves had fried one too many circuits.

"Some new guys might be coming into town," I said, "trying to take over."

"Whoa." A hint of comprehension appeared in her eyes.

"Yeah?"

"These guys from East Texas." She looked over her shoulder, peering down the empty alley. "It's never been this way in Dallas."

"Talk to me." I placed a hand on her shoulder.

"My friend Becky." Connie tugged at an earlobe. "She's like upscale and shit. Got her own Web site."

"Uh-huh."

"These dudes. They want a cut off the top."

"I'm looking for info on the head cat. Guy with a shaved head, dresses like a *GQ* model."

Her face blanched.

"You know who I'm talking about?"

She gulped and nodded once.

"Where's he hang?"

"That titty bar over on Industrial Boulevard." She squinted at me and bit her lower lip. "Your last name is Oswald, right? Like the guy that killed Lincoln."

"Kennedy."

"You . . ." She shook her head as if to clear the dust away.

"What?"

She brushed my arm off her shoulder and started walking. When she was about ten feet away she turned around. "Remember at the end of *The Godfather*, when Michael has all the bad guys killed?"

I nodded.

"Dawg, get out of town." She turned and ran down the alley.

The summer after high school graduation, I punched my father in the mouth and told him never to lay a finger on my mother again. Then I drove to Waco to see some old friends, got drunk, and enlisted in the army.

At about the same time I was signing the papers that put me under Uncle Sam's benevolent control for the next few years, Billy got his first craps game to run, a weekly affair held in the back room of a Barringer-owned roadhouse on Highway 6.

When my hangover had abated, I took a drive east and stopped by the cinder-block shack one hot July afternoon. Since my family had moved to Dallas a few years before, I hadn't seen my friend in a while.

Mr. Barringer was in the front, sitting at a table by the jukebox with a pouch of Redman chewing tobacco and a can of Falstaff beer in front of him. One of the black whores who worked in the trailers behind the bar sat on his lap. He pushed her off when I walked in.

"If it ain't Hank Oswald." He leaned back and adjusted the battered straw hat perched on his head. "What brings a city boy back to the country?"

"I came to talk to Billy."

"He's in the back. Working." Mr. Barringer jerked a thumb toward the rear. "Ever had any brown sugar, Hank?"

I didn't reply.

"Ain't nothing like it." He laughed and grabbed the girl's buttocks, giving one cheek a good squeeze through the tight pair of Daisy Dukes she wore.

"Can I see Billy?"

"You like to gamble, Hank?"

I shook my head.

"Go on." He opened the packet of chewing tobacco and stuck a wad in his mouth. "Just don't stay too long."

I headed toward the back room, past the bar where Billy's brother sat reading a week-old copy of the *Waco Tribune Herald*. He moved his mouth silently as his finger traced the words on the page. I had always wondered if he had been born slow or his father had hit him on the head one too many times during his formative years.

I went down a narrow hallway that smelled of sweat and beer. A plain wooden door, guarded by a large black man in overalls and no shirt, was at the end. As I approached, he moved out of the way and opened the door.

The room was small and filled with smoke and people, all of them appearing to be local farmers and tradesmen.

Billy stood at the head of the table, collecting money and working the stick. He hadn't changed much, hair still thick and dirty blond. His nose was long, his face angular and handsome like that of a B-grade movie actor whose name seems to be on the tip of your tongue.

He nodded once at me and then handed the stick to one of his other brothers, the mean one a few years older than us. He motioned me outside. I followed him out onto the packed earth behind the bar, where an oil drum converted into a cooker sat underneath a live oak tree, pouring out smoke.

We shook hands and exchanged small talk for a few moments. He asked me what it was like, living in Dallas with all the girls and things to do. His tone was wistful until I told him to come on up and see. His voice got hard then.

"Did like we always talked about," I said. "I joined the army."

"I was going to. . . ." Billy turned away. He kicked an empty beer can across the dirt.

"Why didn't you?"

"A man's got to do what a man's got to do."

"You *like* fleecing farmers?"

"You don't get it, do you?"

I shrugged.

"I read this book one time." He stuck a cigarette in his mouth. "It was about destiny."

"Huh?" I shook my head.

"Just bought a brand-new pickup. Paid cash for it."

I didn't say anything.

"Go back to Dallas." Billy put an arm around my shoulders. "The Barringers're kicking ass and taking names. You don't want to get hurt."

CHAPTER SEVENTEEN

After one more furtive glance, Connie darted between two buildings and disappeared.

We headed back. The Honda was gone as were the rims on Olson's Suburban.

"My wheels." Olson pointed to the vehicle. "They stole my wheels."

"Guess we shouldn't have left it by the other one." I pointed to the Toyota. "At least they didn't break in."

Olson leaned against the wall of the building at the corner of the side street and the alley. "I'll add it to your bill."

We walked down Jefferson Avenue, trying to look as inconspicuous as possible. Under the circumstances, that was pretty tough. Olson was six-six with blond hair and a full-size .45 automatic barely hidden under his shirt. He looked like he'd been dragged for a couple of miles down a bumpy road. I was about three inches shorter and limping. We were the only Anglos on the street.

A few blocks past the Texas Theater, we stopped at a steakhouse with a twenty-foot papier-mâché cow on the roof. The Chinese guy working behind the bar paid no attention to our condition. He poured us two cups of coffee like I asked and went back to polishing glasses.

I pulled out my cell phone to call Nolan and find out if she'd learned anything about Reese Cunningham.

The phone rang before I could call.

"Yeah."

"Where are you?" Nolan said.

"Remember Connie the crack whore?"

"I don't want to hear about your love life."

"How about this then? I'm in Oak Cliff without a ride."

"You need to get to North Dallas. No sign of Reese Cunningham but you're gonna want to check this out."

"What do you mean?"

"I'll explain later." She recited the address and hung up. We finished the coffee and left.

CHAPTER EIGHTEEN

Dallas was a car town, L.A. without the mountains or movie stars. The mass transit system consisted of a couple thousand diesel-belching buses and a barely there, bewildering light-rail system. The buses operated on schedules designed to get people in the southern section to their North Dallas domestic servant jobs, while the trains moved empty cars around the city.

Olson phoned his partner, sat down on a curb, and produced yet another flask, this one from his boot. He took a long swig and passed out. I debated whether to call 911. I dragged him off the street and into the alcove of a bakery, checking his pulse and vitals as best I could. The problem appeared to be based more on the alcohol and less on his injuries.

Twenty minutes later, a brand-new Bentley drove up and stopped.

The hazard lights came on.

The door opened.

Delmar, my friend's same-sex life partner and the meanest man in this hemisphere, stepped out.

He wore a perfectly tailored dark blue three-button suit over a cream silk shirt with a pair of woven leather loafers. The outfit probably cost more than my last three house payments. Delmar did very well in the buying and selling of investment-grade firearms.

I waved hello.

He frowned and crossed his arms.

Because his partner and I shared a blood bond forged in the heat of battle, Delmar had to put up with me. He didn't like it and didn't particularly care if I knew it or not.

He walked to where we were huddled in the shade of the old building, looked down at the unconscious Olson and then at me. "What the hell did you do to him this time?"

"New guys in town were trying a shakedown." I stood up. "Didn't have anything to do with me."

"Sell it somewhere else." Delmar looked at his partner.

"Business good?" I nodded toward the quarter-million-dollar automobile.

"Where's his Suburban?"

"Somebody stole the wheels." A Ford pickup painted neon metallic green drove by, the front bumper about a half inch above the pavement. The ground shook from the Tejano rap blaring from behind its darkened windows.

Delmar waited until the truck passed before speaking. "I try to put up with the bad shit you get him involved in. I really do."

"Me?" I tried not to sound too incredulous.

"The thing last month? With the guys from Miami?" Delmar waved his hands in the smoggy air of Jefferson Avenue. "That was so unnecessary."

"It was Olson's deal. *He* asked me to ride along." I tried to control my anger. "The last thing I said before it went to shit was to quit doing business with Cubans."

"Let's not get bogged down in the details, okay?" Delmar walked to where his partner lay. He grabbed one arm.

Olson's eyes rolled open. "Where am I?"

"What happened to his face?" Delmar said. "And his shirt?"

"A bad guy named Jesus Rundell." I grabbed Olson's other arm. Together we pulled him to his feet.

"What the hell . . . is he drunk?" Delmar looped an arm over his shoulders. "It's the middle of the afternoon, for God's sake."

"It's my fault. Everything. Made him drink a bottle of scotch at lunch." I helped walk Olson to the rear passenger door of the Bentley. "Then I registered him as a Democrat."

"Fuck off, Hank." Delmar eased his partner's legs inside the plush automobile and shut the door.

"After that he gave a big donation to Handgun Control, Inc." I opened the front passenger-side door and sat down on the smooth leather seat. "Expect to get a real nice letter from Sarah Brady next week."

Delmar got behind the steering wheel but didn't respond. Despite their sexual orientation, both he and Olson possessed political views somewhere to the right of Pat Buchanan. Then there was the whole Second Amendment thing.

I laughed to myself and reclined the seat.

Twenty minutes later, we pulled into the driveway of their converted duplex on Hershel Street in the Oak Lawn section of central Dallas. Delmar stopped the car in the shade of the magnolia tree that dominated the front yard.

Their home looked unassuming, but I knew that it was fortified only slightly less than the White House. It sat directly across the street from the local office of the Gay and Lesbian Anti-Defamation League.

Olson woke up, looked around, and got out of the car like nothing had happened. His partner and I followed. Olson ignored us and went inside. Delmar and I stared at each other, the Bentley forming a barrier between us. The leaves of the magnolia dappled the afternoon sun across the hood. A dog barked from a long way off.

"He'll be all right," I said.

"What was the guy's name?"

"Rundell."

"What's he look like?"

I told him.

Delmar chewed his lip.

"If he shows up, don't waste time talking," I said.

He looked at me as if I were simple-minded but didn't say anything.

"I need a car. Got anything to spare?"

"Pepe has the Mercedes," he said. "Won't be back for an hour or so."

I didn't want to know who Pepe was or why he had the Benz. I didn't say anything.

Delmar stared at me for a few moments. "You're not taking my new Bentley. That's all there is to it."

"I don't think I'm classy enough to drive it, anyway."

"Shit."

"What?" I raised my hands.

"You really piss me off sometimes, you know that?" He tossed me the keys.

CHAPTER NINETEEN

The Bentley handled like a sports car half its size, reminding me of the black Trans Am I'd owned briefly in high school before wrecking it on the way home from a Belinda Carlisle concert. The English vehicle also had a powerful motor like my old Pontiac, as evidenced by the strip of rubber I accidentally left on the driveway as I was backing up.

Delmar chased me for half a block, yelling. I couldn't understand what he was saying, which was probably just as well.

By the time I had gotten to the corner of Oak Lawn, I was pretty comfortable with all the switches and buttons, except for the creepy British voice that kept telling me to fasten my seatbelt.

I headed away from downtown. Reese Cunningham's parents lived in the Preston Hollow section of North Dallas, a tony area of multiacre lots and gigantic homes designed to look like French chateaus and English castles. The Bentley would fit in perfectly.

From Inwood Road I turned right onto Deloache. Pretty soon the busy city disappeared, replaced with a narrow tree-covered avenue, both sides lined by massive stone walls and wrought-iron gates. I made a couple of more turns until I found the correct street.

Casa Cunningham was nestled behind an ivy-covered brick wall that stretched for three or four hundred yards in either direction from the massive carved wooden doors that formed the entrance to the estate.

I called Nolan. She didn't answer. I inched forward to an intercom on a steel pole protruding from the driveway surface. The intercom was old and weathered and had only one button and a single speaker, no dialing pad or anything else.

I pressed the button and leaned out the window, waiting to answer whoever spoke to me.

Nothing happened. After a long ten seconds, the wooden doors began to swing slowly inward. I put the Bentley in gear and eased down the driveway into the Cunningham grounds.

Bradford pear trees lined the curving asphalt; beyond them lay sloping hills of grass and trees leading downward to the center of the estate. In the distance, a redbrick mansion sprawled next to a small creek. The house looked like an English manor glistening in the hot Texas sun, a set location from *Masterpiece Theater*.

But the grounds on either side of the driveway were unkempt, grass too long in places, too withered and brown in others. The trees needed trimming; the ruts and grooves in the driveway ached for a patching.

As I got closer, the disrepair of the main house became more apparent: peeling paint, gap-toothed shutters, empty flower beds. My truck was parked in the middle of the circular drive, by the front door. I stopped behind it, got out, and walked to the entrance.

The air felt cooler in this part of town, the vegetation soaking up some of the heat. Robins warbled from the live oaks in front of the home as water trickled over the rocks in the creek. I smelled leaves composting to dirt, oily residue on the asphalt, and the moldy aroma of a house not properly cared for.

The front door opened. Tess McPherson stood in the entryway. We walked through a two-story foyer, the floors marble, the staircase wide and twirling upward into a chintz-covered hallway.

"Welcome to Weirdville." She pointed to the right. "We're in the sunroom."

I followed her into a long, narrow chamber off the entryway. The walls were bright yellow. The furniture was green and lemony, plush and angular at the same time, as if it had been new around the time of the Watergate scandal. The place smelled like mothballs and dust.

Tess motioned to the far side of the room where a woman sat in the corner in a low-slung chair next to a glass-topped table. The chair was covered in a flower-patterned fabric, yellow and orange. The table was empty except for a lamp, a rotary telephone, a Rubik's Cube, and an autographed picture of Larry Hagman during his J. R. Ewing days.

"Hi," I said.

"You must be Lee Oswald." She held up a mottled hand, palm down. "The girls have been telling me all about you."

She could have been fifty or eighty; it was hard to tell. The plastic surgeries had stretched her face so much her cheeks looked like drum skins; her lips were frozen in a perpetual half grin, half grimace. The most startling feature, however, was her hair. The platinum locks were Panhandle big, teased wider than her shoulders, held in place by who knows how much hairspray.

"Call me Hank." I sat down next to Tess on a terra-cotta velour love seat.

"Call me Bunny." She wore gold-sequined house shoes and a loose-fitting warm-up suit on her bony frame. A diamond the size of a peach pit was on her right middle finger. On her left wrist was a gold Rolex, the secret decoder device for women of a certain age in particular Dallas zip codes.

I turned to Tess. "Where's Nolan?"

"Upstairs," Bunny answered for her. "Doing research on your problem."

"Research?" I cocked an eyebrow.

"She's in Reese's room," Tess said. "I'm keeping our, uh . . . hostess company."

"My late husband knew Jack Ruby." Bunny Cunningham touched

one strand of her immense hairdo as if to see if everything was in place.

"That's nice." I crossed my legs and tried to look casual. "We need to talk to your son."

"You're not any relation to the other Oswald, are you?"

"Where is Reese at the moment?" I picked up the Rubik's Cube, looked at it for a second, and then put it back down.

"Mrs. Cunningham was just about to tell me when you came in," Tess said.

"That was my son's." Bunny pointed to the cube, a vacant look on her face. "My husband gave it to him right before he died."

"About Reese . . ." I tried not to sound impatient.

"He was a good man, my husband. They named a building after him at SMU."

"Why don't you tell us a little about him, Bunny." I sighed. This was going to take longer than originally planned.

"Mort was one of the last wildcatters." Bunny dabbed a piece of tissue at the corner of one eye. "He died on a rig, doing what he loved."

The name finally clicked in my head. Mortimer Cunningham, a legendary Texas oilman. A hard-partying roustabout who made and lost hundreds of millions of dollars over the course of his career. His death had involved a waitress at the Elks Lodge in Buda, Texas, and a jealous husband, not an oil rig.

"When did he pass away?" Tess said.

Bunny sniffled. "Nineteen eighty-five. Reese was a freshman in high school."

I did the math. Her son was around thirty-five now, a little younger than I was. I got a mental image of the man. Three and a half decades on this planet, looking for an identity in the shadow of a boisterous and grandiose rich man, doomed forever to be The-Son-of instead of his own person.

"We met in Waco," she said.

I nodded and tried to look as if I cared.

"You see, I was from a little town east of there."

"Where?" Tess frowned.

I perked up. East of Waco would be Barringer country.

"What's the name of the town?" I said.

Bunny looked as if she were going to speak again but stopped when my partner entered the room.

"We're too late." Nolan's face was blanched, eyes wide. She looked sick to her stomach.

Nobody made a sound. Bunny Cunningham fanned herself with one hand.

Nolan walked out of the room. I heard the front door open and close.

I jumped up. "Where's Reese's room?"

"At the end of the hall." Bunny stood also. "What on earth was she talking about? He said he was going to take a nap."

I ran out of the Cunningham sunroom. Took the stairs two at a time, Tess on my heels. At the top to the right was a long hallway leading to the back of the house. To the left was an open door that obviously went to the master suite. Tess and I slowed when we got to the hall.

Another dead body, judging by Nolan's reaction. Jesus Rundell had beaten us here somehow.

At the end of the hallway was a partially closed door, a rolled-up towel lying on the floor. I stepped into Reese's part of the house, and the cloying stench of perfume swept over me. The room was a sitting area, a sofa and two easy chairs on one side, a desk with a computer on the other. A crack pipe sat on the desk next to several rolled-up balls of foil and a dozen or so pills scattered haphazardly across the surface. A half-empty jug of grocery-store wine was on the floor.

There were four or five overflowing ashtrays on the coffee table by the sofa. I kept waiting to smell the stale cigarette smoke but couldn't because of the perfume. Dust was everywhere.

"Reese sure was a party animal." Tess pointed to the pipe and wine on the desk.

On the far side of the room was another door, leading into a bedroom, I was willing to bet.

Tess placed her hand on the knob.

I ran across the room and grabbed her arm. "Don't go in there."

CHAPTER TWENTY

Reese Cunningham was dead.

I looked at the condition of his body, thought about the drugs and cigarettes in the other room, and figured his heart had blown a main seal a year or so before.

The skin on his face was still intact, though now desiccated and loose on his skull. The lips had curled back, exposing his teeth, and the bedspread covering what was left of his body was stained where the gasses had finally erupted from his midsection.

"Holy shit." Tess stood at the foot of the bed. "Is that him? H-he's been there for . . ."

"A long-ass time." I looked around the room and saw nothing much of interest, a big-screen TV on one wall, a door leading to the bathroom on the other. The still air was a weird mix of smells, fetid earth and perfume and dust. "I'm guessing Bunny has a problem with reality."

"W-w-what do we do now?" Tess was shivering, her face pale like Nolan's had been.

"I don't know."

"She's been living here. With that." Tess placed one hand on her stomach, the other in front of her mouth. Her shoulders hunched forward as if she were going to be sick. She dashed out of the bedroom.

I mentally ran through everything. Linville had lied; Reese had checked out at least a year ago. What was in the file of a dead man that was so important? And why would a mobster from South Texas care about it?

I went into the other room.

"Here's a reminder of an appointment with a doctor." Tess was at the desk, holding a slip of paper. "A cardiologist."

I opened a drawer at random and found a bong.

"What exactly are we looking for, anyway?" Tess shuffled through more papers, her voice becoming shrill.

"I don't know." I walked out of the room and down the hall.

At the head of the stairs, I turned left and entered the master suite. Another desk was in the sitting area. I sat down and started looking through paperwork. After a while, the picture became a little clearer.

Reese Cunningham had been an only child. His mother had no one left except for a second cousin in Houston. No husband, no son, and from the looks of things, not a lot of money, either. Mortimer the wildcatter had checked out on the downswing. I found a delinquent notice for the property taxes on the estate. I found statements from brokerage houses and banks, all the figures declining. The charade was about over for one-time society bigwig Bunny Cunningham.

What I did not find was anything that would help me understand the connection among the players involved. Tess walked into the room and stood beside me. I briefly explained what I had learned. She told me about her hurried examination of Reese's room. Nada.

We went downstairs. Bunny hadn't moved. She held the Rubik's Cube in her lap. Her eyes were moist. I sat in the velour love seat and placed one hand on hers.

"Bunny. This is really important." I squeezed her fingers gently. "Do you know anything about the Barringer family, from East Texas?"

"Reese is still asleep?"

I nodded.

"The Barringers?" She frowned. "I don't get out much anymore, you know."

"What about a man named Lucas Linville or Jesus Rundell?"

She shook her head.

I looked at Tess. She shrugged.

Bunny gripped my hand. "When do you think Reese is gonna wake up?"

"Real soon." I stood and walked out of the room.

Tess followed me into the cavernous marble foyer. I looked out the peephole and could see Nolan sitting in my truck. I pulled out my cell phone and scrolled through the address book, looking for the entry of a woman I had dated a few months earlier.

"We can't just leave her here," Tess said.

"We're not." I found the name. Cyndy, with two Y's. A caseworker for the Dallas County Council on Mental Health. I pushed SEND and hoped she had gotten past all the bitterness and anger of our breakup. I tended to get that moving-on feeling when women started talking about bridesmaid dresses and wedding receptions on the third date.

Cyndy was over it. She was now dating a former priest turned psychologist. I explained the situation to her. She said she would be up there within the hour. I hung up.

"Now what?" Tess moved to the front door.

"Lucas Linville gets a visit." I stepped outside just as a yellow cab rolled to a stop behind the Bentley. Nobody but tourists or drunks took cabs in Dallas. Who would be arriving at the Cunningham estate in a taxi?

The rear door opened and Larry Chaloupka, my partner's ex-fiancé, stepped out. He wore the clothes of a successful used car salesman working the Saturday shift: a pair of lime green Sansabelt pants, a yellow short-sleeve dress shirt, and a burgundy tie.

He pulled what looked like a small aerosol container from his pocket and squirted it in his mouth. The cab maneuvered around the Bentley and drove away.

"Hi, Larry." I waved at him from the front doorway of the mansion.

He frowned, hitched his thumbs in the waistband of his beltless pants, and took a couple of steps toward me.

I walked to the driveway. "What are you doing here?"

"Nolan called me." He smoothed back his thinning hair with one hand. He was in his late thirties. His face was ruddy from twenty years of beer and bourbon.

As if on cue, my partner stepped out of my truck, ran to her ex-fiancé, and embraced him.

"We're working," I said. "On a case."

"Playing at being a cop again, huh?" Larry said.

"How long were you on the force before getting fired?"

"You can't keep us apart." He ignored my comment and rubbed Nolan's shoulders.

I didn't say anything.

"That shit upstairs." Nolan turned to where I stood. "It got to me."

"You've seen dead bodies before."

"You don't get it, do you?" She stamped her foot. "I'm not cut out for this. I need some time away."

"With him?" I tried not to sound too harsh.

Larry pushed Nolan away and balled his fists. "You got the drop on me last time. Won't happen again."

"Don't be stupid." I took a couple of steps toward him until we were only a few feet apart.

"Hank, please." Nolan put a hand on my arm. The sun hit her face at just the right angle, making her blue eyes sparkle. Her hair was shiny, her features those of a model. I asked myself for the hundredth time what she saw in a mutt like Larry Chaloupka.

"Her leg still hurts sometimes." Larry stuck his chin out.

I didn't reply. Everything was on the table now. During our first time working together, through my own stupidity, I had caused my partner to suffer a grievous injury, a bullet wound to the thigh.

"Don't go there." Nolan turned to her boyfriend. "That's ancient history."

"If I'd been around back then, Mr. Lee Oswald wouldn't be such a tough guy." Larry balled his fists again.

I walked toward the Bentley.

"I'll leave your truck at the office," Nolan said.

I opened the driver's-side door of the expensive automobile.

"Hank, I'm sorry."

I sat behind the wheel. Tess was already in the passenger seat. "It seemed a little awkward out there," she said. "I thought it was best if I waited here."

"Let's go find Lucas Linville." I turned on the motor.

B illy Barringer and I were ten years old when we went to the state fair in Dallas for the first time. My mother drove us up from Waco in our wood-paneled station wagon.

Like a lot of stereotypes, the old cliché about everything being bigger in Texas was rooted in truth. The saying certainly applied to the state fair, the largest such festival in the country.

Carnies and cops, schoolkids and old people, bankers and plumbers; everybody came to the State Fair of Texas. The fair was loud. The fair was crowded. The fair was glorious. The fair was an assault on the senses; the dusty air under the steel-colored autumn clouds stunk from fried food and sweat and diesel engines used to power the rides.

To my young eyes, the massive art deco buildings seemed like something out of an old-time Roman chariot movie, the front of each structure dominated by exotic statues. One had a bull that looked like a pagan god I'd once seen in a history book. Another had a twenty-foot-tall, muscled warrior drawing back on a bow, aiming an arrow skyward.

In case you forgot and thought you were in some exotic land like Egypt, or maybe New Jersey, a five-story talking doll named Big Tex stood in the exact center of the fairgrounds, next to the Cotton Bowl. Tex wore mega-XL jeans and boots and a cowboy hat big enough to sleep a family of ten. Every half hour or so, his hinged jaw would drop and he would boom out the latest happenings for that particular day.

To a couple of kids from the country, the state fair was as cool as Fonzie and mood rings. I arranged a meeting time and left Mom at the beer tent. Billy and I raced to the midway and gorged on Fletcher corn dogs, cotton candy, and Dr Pepper.

We rode the Kamikaze and the Paraglider. We went to the House of Mirrors. We visited the freak show, which still had freaks in those days. We laughed and horsed around as the sugar high kicked in.

At the Hammer Ride, the one that swung you in a big arc, up and down, the carny working the gate dropped his cigarette. When he bent to retrieve it, Billy coughed and leaned against the man's high-top table as if he were dizzy. The spell passed after a second and we continued on.

After they buckled us in, Billy prodded my knee with his and cupped his hand, displaying a wad of cash.

I licked my lips. "Where'd you get all that dough?"

"Shit-For-Brains shoulda been watching closer."

"You stole it?"

"Yeah."

"But that's . . . wrong."

"Don't be a faggot, Hank. It's a man's right," Billy said. "Take what you need."

We stopped talking as the ride cranked up. Afterward we walked down the midway to a bench. Billy sat down, counted out the money, and stuffed a portion in his back pocket and the rest in his front.

"What are you doing?" I said.

"Gotta give Daddy a cut."

I didn't reply since I didn't know what he was talking about. We continued walking. I stopped near a black girl sitting on the steps in front of the automobile building. She held the remnants of a grape snow cone; the sticky water dripping on her hand seemed to balance the tears running down her cheeks. She looked like she was in the first or second grade, about my sister's age. No one else was near her.

"Hey," I said. "What's wrong with you?"

She didn't reply, just kept on crying.

"Shit, Hank." My friend pulled me to one side. "What the hell you doing talking to some pickaninny?"

I shrugged out of his grasp and turned to the child. "You okay?"

The girl looked at me and stopped sobbing for a moment. She didn't say anything. Billy walked to her side. He removed a twenty from his front pocket and gave it to her. "Go on. Get yourself a corny dog and anuther snow cone."

The girl sniffled once more and scampered away.

"There. That make you feel better?"

"Guess so." I nodded slowly.

"Can't do too much shit like that." Billy shook his head. "These city folks gonna think we're a couple of pussies just cuz we're from the country."

"No, they won't."

"Daddy says country boys need to stay in the country."

"I thought you wanted to live in the city sometime."

"Want's a funny thing, ain't it?" He turned and walked back to the midway.

I followed. We rode some more rides, ate more cotton candy, but it wasn't the same. Then it was time to go. We trudged back to meet my mother.

"Why'd you give a shit about that little girl, anyway?" Billy said.

"That's like something my mama would do." He said the last with a trace of disdain for his churchgoing mother.

"I dunno. Guess I didn't, really." My stomach began to ache. I tasted corn and caramel and licorice. "We're still friends, right?"

"Yeah," Billy said. "We're still amigos."

CHAPTER TWENTY-ONE

Tess opened the glove compartment of the Bentley and looked inside. She pulled out a stainless-steel revolver with a snub-nose barrel and placed it on the console. The weapon was the size of a thirty-ounce T-bone.

"That's a big-ass piece," she said.

"It's one of Delmar's car guns. He likes forty-four Magnums. Says they make a big hole."

"And who is Delmar?"

"Olson's . . . partner," I said.

"What does he do for a living?" She swiveled her head, taking in the plush leather and polished wood of the automobile.

"If you don't know, then you can truthfully say under oath that you have no knowledge of his business activities."

Tess stared at me for a moment and then returned to rummaging. A few minutes later she placed a pint bottle of Courvoisier XO cognac next to the stainless revolver. After more digging she produced a small package of waxed paper. She unwrapped it and held up a wad of grayish material, about the size of a golf ball.

"What's this? Play-Doh?"

"Semtex. If I had to guess."

"Huh?"

"Plastique. TNT. You might want to put that down, okay?"

She carefully put the explosive back in the glove compartment and shut the door. "All I wanted was some gum."

We were on the Dallas Tollway, headed south to Lucas Linville's place, my third visit in two days. As we passed the American Airlines Center on the northwest side of downtown, Tess pulled out her cell. She dialed a number, held the phone to her ear until we were south of the city center, and hung up.

"No one's at home," she said.

"What's that mean?"

"There are no easy answers, are there?" She sighed and tugged on her hair. "If you could be anything in the world, what would it be?"

I frowned for a moment. "Hugh Hefner."

She laughed. "Not who. What."

I shrugged.

"I'd be a ballerina. In a country where the music never stops."

I didn't reply.

"What was your family like, growing up?" she said.

"Like most, I suppose." I exited the highway at Ervay Street.

"Are you still close to them?"

"No."

"Why?"

I didn't say anything. I thought about the man who sired me.

"My dad worked all the time when I was growing up," Tess said.

"My dad gambled. And drank."

"Oh."

I turned off Ervay toward the worn brick building that housed the Linville ministry. More people than usual milled about, some standing in the middle of the narrow streets, moving reluctantly as we approached. They stared at the Bentley as it rattled over the potholes.

The door to Lucas Linville's building was open. I stopped the English automobile in front and got out. Tess followed me. I chirped the locks shut and pulled out my Browning.

"Stay out here." I racked the slide back.

"No."

I ignored her and stepped inside the building. The next door, leading into the common room, was open, too. The area was empty, the furniture where I remembered it but no people sat there. The bookshelves had been overturned, drawers emptied. Papers littered the floor, most ripped into pieces as if to exert the maximum damage.

Together we explored the remainder of the structure. Each room was empty. The door leading to Lucas Linville's living area was open, too. The room appeared as I remembered it: tangled linens on the bed, empty pizza containers and beer bottles on the floor. With all the debris it was hard to tell, but it appeared to have been thoroughly searched, too.

"What kind of preacher is this guy?" Tess picked up a quart bottle of Jim Beam with a half inch of amber liquid sloshing around the bottom.

"Baptist." I dug through a pile of papers sitting on the coffee table.

"Really."

I heard footsteps from the hall and pushed Tess against the wall to one side of the entrance. I stood between her and the open door and waited.

The footsteps got louder. I raised the Browning.

The door moved toward us. Brown fingers grasped the edge of the wood. With my left hand I reached around and grabbed the wrist attached to the fingers and yanked, pulling the owner of the digits into the room.

I twisted the wrist up and into the back of Arthur, Lucas Linville's Filipino assistant. With my free hand I ripped the ear buds from the iPod out of his ears.

"My arm," he said. "You're breaking it."

"Not really." I raised his forearm a fraction of an inch. "This is what it feels like when it starts to break."

"Don't go post office on me, homey." Arthur stood on his tiptoes to relieve the pressure. "What do you want?"

"The truth." I let go and shoved him across the room. He tripped over the coffee table and fell between it and the stained sofa. He pulled himself up and sat on the worn divan.

"Pastor Linville is gone," he said.

"No kidding." I holstered the Browning. "Where'd he go?"

Arthur pointed to Tess. "Who is she?"

"I'm asking the questions here." I sat down in a kitchen chair that was resting by the coffee table.

"My name is Tess McPherson. That mean anything to you?" Tess found another chair and sat down, too.

Arthur stared at her but didn't respond.

"Hey." I snapped my fingers to get his attention. "What happened here?"

"The bald man came." Arthur rubbed the arm I had shoved into his back.

"And . . ." I leaned forward.

"He beat up Gary."

"Who?"

"The man in the army uniform."

"GI Joe." I remembered his show of bravado earlier. Jesus Rundell would have made mincemeat out of him.

"Yeah. That's the one."

"Where is everybody else?" I said.

"The bald dude and his friends threw them out." Arthur stared at the floor and fingered the thin white wire running across his chest from the music player attached to his waist. "They play for keeps, said they're gonna put the hurt on anybody that comes back around."

"Linville?"

"I haven't seen him." Arthur shook his head. "He wasn't here when they came."

I stood up, grabbed the Filipino by his sore arm, and pulled him to his feet. I squeezed his bicep. "What's in the file on Reese Cunningham?"

"I don't know. Linville never told me." He wrenched free of my grasp and took a step back.

I moved toward him.

"I grew up on the streets of Manila. You really think you can do anything to me that hasn't already been done?" He placed the buds from the player in his ears and did the shoulder-wiggle thing like a rapper in training. "You ain't no better than Baldie."

I didn't say anything.

Tess stood up. "How is your friend? Will he be okay?"

Arthur shrugged. "The man in the ambulance thought he would probably lose his eye." He turned to me. "Pastor Linville used to preach at a place south of here."

"The Church of the Harvest?"

"Yeah. In Pleasant Grove," he said. "You might try there."

"What about you?" Tess said. "What are you gonna do now?"

"Shit, bee-yotch." He moved his shoulders from side to side and held one hand out, ring finger and pinkie pointed downward in a generic gang signal. "Quit acting like you care."

CHAPTER TWENTY-TWO

We left the empty building and stepped into the late afternoon heat. Arthur stayed inside.

Outside, three young men were making a big show of being very visible, standing in front of the Bentley. The oldest one appeared to be the leader. He wore a pair of baggy jeans with two inches of red boxer shorts visible above the waistband, a sleeveless basketball jersey over a white T-shirt, and a dozen or so heavy gold chains around his neck.

I walked toward them and stopped about five feet away.

Mr. Jewelry pulled a Beretta nine-millimeter from under his shirt and held it in front of his groin, muzzle pointing to the ground. "Clean ride, cracker."

I nodded and took a step closer.

"Whatchoo doing here, anyway?

I shrugged.

"You lookin' for some rock?"

I shook my head.

"Holmes here don't chitchat too much, does he?" Jewelry spoke to his friends. They laughed. He looked over my shoulder to where I knew Tess was standing.

"Juicy white girl you got there," he said.

I looked down like I was scared, raised my hands in a gesture of appeasement.

He laughed. "I'm gonna fuck you up, white boy."

I kicked the Beretta straight into his crotch, aiming for a spot a foot or two behind his buttocks.

He went down, mewing like a tabby caught in a garbage disposal. His friend on the left was quick. He had a pistol almost out from under his shirt when my foot connected with his head. He fell backward, his skull bouncing off the hood of the Bentley and leaving a dent. Delmar was going to be pissed about that.

The third guy hadn't reacted at all. He stared at his two fallen friends and swallowed repeatedly. I punched him twice in the stomach because it felt like the thing to do. He went to his knees.

I grabbed him by the back of the head and stuck the muzzle of my Browning under one eye. "You tell the guy running your crew that Hank Oswald is coming after Rundell."

The man blinked but didn't say anything.

I pulled him up by the hair and made him assume the search position, hands on top of the Bentley. A pat-down yielded a plastic bag full of tinfoil pouches, each about the size of a book of matches. He also had a short-barreled Glock semiauto in his back pocket.

"Don't move." I left him leaning against the car.

Mr. Jewelry groaned when I rolled him over. There was a wad of hundred-dollar bills in his front pocket and not much else. I took that and his Beretta, and placed them next to the drugs and weapon of his friend. Gangsta Number Two was still out cold. I removed a pistol and a wad of cash from him, too.

"What are you gonna do?" Tess said.

I popped open the locks of the Bentley. In the glove compartment I found a butane cigarette lighter. A week-old copy of the *Dallas Observer* sat on the backseat. On the sidewalk I made a nest of crumpled newspaper and placed the drugs in the middle.

I lit the paper, pulled the conscious hood away from the car, and made him watch.

"That's an assload of merchandise you're burning up," he said.

I hit him in the gut again. He went down on his knees next to Mr. Jewelry.

"Tell whoever you got to tell that Oswald has got the file. Rundell will understand." The lie rolled easily off my tongue. I slapped him twice across the face and shoved him to the ground. Tess ran to the passenger side as I picked up the three pistols and the cash, and got in the Bentley.

I dropped the guns on the floor underneath Tess's feet and told her to buckle up. She asked where we were going. I ignored her and aimed the big British car south on Corinth Street toward the bridge into lower Dallas. There was very little traffic.

As rivers go, the Trinity was not going to be on anybody's top-ten list. The thin stream of dirty water flowed not quite diagonally across the city from the west to the east, effectively cutting Dallas in half, in more ways than one.

Fifty years earlier, the city fathers had built a series of levees on either side of the river, forming a half-mile-wide flood channel to handle the spring rains as well as creating a painfully obvious moat between the rich whiteness of the north and the poverty-stricken darker hues of the south.

I stopped in the exact center of the bridge, turned on the blinkers, and waited while a Dallas Area Rapid Transit bus whizzed by, carrying working people home from their jobs in the north.

I scooped up the pistols and hopped out of the car. The setting sun hit the wisps of clouds and smog just right, making the twilight sky to the west appear a dazzling shade of lavender and orange. At the railing overlooking the trickle of water that was the Trinity River, I dropped the guns in one by one. They hit with a muffled splash.

I stood there for a minute and thought about Billy Barringer, Jesus Rundell, and the hard-to-fit pieces in the jigsaw puzzle that was my life. I got back in the car and continued on south.

Tess said, "Where'd you learn to do that stuff back there, with those three guys?"

"The army."

"Yeah?"

"I taught hand-to-hand. For the Rangers."

"I like it," she said. "The way you moved."

We passed over the river and reentered South Dallas. I turned right on Eighth Street and stopped in front of a homeless shelter and soup kitchen. Together, they'd had a couple of grand on them. I peeled off a hundred and stuck it in my pocket. The three would be buying me and Tess dinner.

The rest went to an earnest young man named Jonathan who ran the place. He shook my hand repeatedly as his eyes welled up with tears. It had been a lean fund-raising year for the shelter.

I got back in the car. "Want to get something to eat?"

Tess cocked her head. "You asking me out?"

"On a date?"

"Yeah."

"No."

"Why not?"

"I was just asking if you were hungry."

"So it's not a date?"

"Nope." I put the car in gear. "That's against the private investigator's canon of ethics."

"Technically speaking, I'm not a client, though." She smiled and shifted in her seat, legs crossing at the knees in a relaxed fashion.

"Okay, call it a date." I was keenly aware of her physical presence now, the way her breasts filled her T-shirt, the line of her hip against the tight denim of her jeans. And the no-nonsense way she handled herself, confident and demure at the same time.

"Nah. Let's not. I always make bad choices when it comes to men."

CHAPTER TWENTY-THREE

Twenty minutes later we pulled into the valet line at Javier's, just north of the Uptown area. Tuxedo-clad waiters scurried around a series of rooms decorated in early hacienda hunting lodge as we made our way through the crowds of patrons.

The wait for a table, as always, was long, so we went to the cigar room in the back and ordered at the bar, drinking margaritas and eating chips while the kitchen worked its magic.

As we ate, the bar filled up with young, pretty women, coiffed and tanned and implanted to perfection, and men with slick-backed hair and silk shirts. In the corner, the new Cowboys wide receiver, a Heisman Trophy winner, chatted with a forward for the Dallas Stars. The women hovering about the pair of athletes were three deep, a fleshy fence of lip gloss and estrogen, all clamoring for attention.

"Do you come here a lot?" Tess stirred her drink with a straw.

Before I could answer, the bartender greeted me by name and placed a fresh margarita on the bar.

"Uh . . . occasionally."

"A single guy like you could meet a lot of interesting people in a place like this." She nodded toward a throng of women in the corner, underneath a stuffed elk.

"It is a target-rich environment." I paused for a sip of the icy drink. "Not really my crowd, though."

"What is your crowd?" She licked a bit of salt off the rim of her glass and shifted on her bar stool. Our legs brushed together.

"People like me tend to operate better alone."

"Does alone mean lonely?" Her leg moved against mine again.

"Sometimes." I paid the bill with the confiscated C-note, and we left, walking out past the stuffed grizzly bear guarding the middle room and the eight-foot-long swordfish dominating the wall in the main dining area.

The Bentley was parked by the front door, next to a black Ferrari 360. I gave the valet guy a ten-spot, the remainder of the hundred, and we drove away.

I said, "Under the circumstances, I don't think you should stay at Nolan's tonight."

Tess nodded.

"There's an extra room at my house." I crossed Central Expressway at Monticello. "Or you can get a hotel."

"Did you and Nolan have a thing going?"

"Huh?"

"Did you ever date?"

"We work together." I shook my head. "And we're friends."

"Relationships are funny things, aren't they?"

Talking about the *R*-word with women had never been my strong suit. I ignored her comment. "What about the lawyer? The guy your friend was gonna set you up with last night."

"It wouldn't have worked out. I know his type," she said. "I need somebody with an edge." She smiled.

I nodded.

"Think I'll skip the hotel." Tess eased her seat back and crossed her legs. "Take me to your place."

Ten minutes later I pulled into my driveway, parking in the rear so the Bentley wouldn't be too much of a target. We went through the back door into the kitchen, a room I had only recently finished remodeling by myself. Several of the halogen lights underneath the cabinets were set with timers and were already on, providing just enough illumination to make the granite countertops and flagstone floor look like an ad from *Architectural Digest*, if you didn't examine anything too closely.

The room smelled like cinnamon. The week before, a flight attendant I slept with on an occasional basis had left some spicy smell-good stuff in a bowl on the table in the breakfast nook.

"Nice place." Tess looked around. "Never know this was here from the outside. Or the neighborhood."

Glenda padded into the room, looked at Tess, and passed gas.

"Don't mind her." I shooshed the dog out the pet door. "Want a beer?" I opened the refrigerator and grabbed two Dos Equis darks.

She accepted the mahogany-colored lager and followed me to the spare bedroom, a place I used as an office. The room was pretty spartan, no decorations on the walls, not much furniture. A twin bed sat in the corner, a desk with a computer in the middle, a case of NATO 5.56 mm rifle ammunition next to the desk.

"I sleep in the back," I said. "The bathroom is in the hall."

"Nolan has my bag." Tess sat on the bed and bounced a couple of times.

"I've got a toothbrush for you. You want a T-shirt or something?"

An awkward silence ensued.

"Yeah," she said. "That would be great."

"If you want to take a shower, there're some clean towels in the cabinet. I'll leave you a shirt on the bed."

Tess nodded but didn't say anything. She smiled. I smiled back and left to make sure the house was locked and secure. By the time I was finished I could hear water running in the shower. In my closet, I dug out an extra-large T-shirt advertising a long-defunct bar. The garment was in pretty good shape, with only a few holes in it. I left it on the spare bed and went to my room.

After a few minutes I heard the bathroom door open, followed by the closing of the guest bedroom's. I headed to the shower and washed off the day's grime, dried, and wrapped a towel around my waist.

I opened the door. Steam billowed out.

Tess stood in the hallway, arms at her sides. The borrowed shirt stopped a little above midthigh. Her legs were tanned, her hair damp, eyes sparkling and vulnerable and alluring all at the same time in the dim light of the hall.

"I don't want to sleep alone," she said.

I kissed her.

She kissed back. Her breath tasted like beer and toothpaste.

We stood in the hallway for a long few moments, locked in an embrace. She put one hand behind my head, the other in the small of my back, and pressed our bodies together. After a bit we pulled apart and came up for air.

"Show me your room," she said.

I took her by the hand and led her to the back. The only light came from the television on the dresser, tuned to the ten o'clock news, the sound muted. She shrugged off the T-shirt. I dropped my towel. We stumbled into bed, kissing again, hands probing each other. She was not afraid to be aggressive, pulling this way and pushing that. When we were finished, she dozed with her head on my shoulder until the end of Letterman. Then she snaked a hand underneath the sheets and said let's do that again.

At the end of round two, I was glad the neighbors hadn't called the police. I was glad I could still move. The covers lay at the foot of the bed in a tangle, not unlike the two of us, naked and intertwined at the other end.

"What's that?" Tess placed a finger on the puckered white spot the size of a nickel just above my hip.

"I got shot by some bad guys a couple of years ago."

"And this one?" She pointed to a jagged scar on my left calf.

I didn't say anything.

"Did somebody shoot you there, too?" She licked the healed wound on my leg.

"No." I reached for the TV remote and turned up the sound.

CHAPTER TWENTY-FOUR

Billy Barringer saved my life for the first time when I was fifteen.

We were on the Brazos River in a flat-bottom johnboat, casting spinner bait for river bass, drinking Buckhorn beer for lunch, and telling lies about how far we'd gotten with the eighth-grade slut, Evangeline Pearson.

It was August in Texas. During that time of year, the heat became an entity in its own right, a physical force outsiders didn't understand and natives ran out of adjectives to describe. The air grew heavy, swollen with moisture, indolent. The blue sky faded to pewter. The sun seemed larger than normal. People moved slower. Life revolved around swimming holes and air-conditioning, anything to stay cool.

Our boat was tied to a tree jutting over the tepid water from the red sand bank. Both shorelines were an almost impenetrable mass of post oaks, cottonwoods, and dense shrubs thick with spikes and thorns. The air smelled like fish and lake water; the only sounds were an occasional cattle egret trilling overhead or a turtle plopping into the water from the bank.

Billy made me laugh with a new description for Evangeline's breasts. Then he reminded me that he had swiped a *Playboy* from his dad and we could look at it when we got back.

I downed the rest of my beer and dove into the brackish water to cool off. As soon as my head broke the surface I felt a rope or vine against my ankle. The river was thick with trotlines used to catch the big channel catfish, unmanned fishing setups strung across the water and supported by makeshift buoys.

I turned and saw a bobbing plastic milk container a dozen yards away. The cord shifted suddenly, signaling that a catfish was caught on one of its hooks.

I tried to move my leg, but the cord wrapped around my ankle.

"Billy."

"Yeah?"

"There's a trotline." I grabbed the side of the boat.

"Where?"

I didn't reply, instead listening to the sound of an outboard motor sputtering somewhere upriver. The cord dug into my flesh and became tighter. The owner of the trotline was retrieving his catch for the day.

"Shit." I gripped the side of the boat harder. The little craft dipped toward me. The line pulled more. One hand slipped from the metal of the boat.

"Hang on, Hank." My friend dropped his beer.

"*Billy.*" My other hand lost its grasp on the boat. My head went under the water. The cord tightened around my leg. A hook pierced my flesh, the pain intense and far away at the same time. I banged against an underground stump, and my lungs filled with water.

The next thing I remembered was clinging to a cottonwood tree on the bank about forty feet downriver from the boat. Billy was next to me, holding a lock-back knife and a length of trotline.

I vomited river water and beer. My leg throbbed. I saw a red sheen to the water a few feet away. I said, "Thanks, amigo."

"Don't worry about it," Billy said. "You'd do the same for me."

CHAPTER TWENTY-FIVE

We woke at dawn. Tess reached for me and we made love again, softly and slowly this time. We fell back asleep.

When I woke the second time, the house smelled like bacon and coffee. I grabbed last night's towel from the floor, wrapped it around my waist, and padded to the bathroom. I took another shower, running the water lukewarm to get myself awake.

When I stepped out, Tess was in the hallway again, wearing my T-shirt and holding a cup of coffee in one hand. Her hair was mussed, one lock dangling in front of her eyes, making her look sexy and vulnerable at the same time.

"Made myself at home." She handed me the mug. "I found the washing machine, did my clothes from yesterday."

"Fine by me." I took a sip of coffee as she stepped around me and into the bathroom. Thirty minutes later we sat down and ate: bacon, scrambled eggs with chives, hot biscuits.

"Didn't know there were chives anywhere in this kitchen." I speared the last mouthful of eggs.

"They were on the bottom shelf of your pantry, next to a pair of panty hose and a box of shotgun shells."

"Oh." I racked my brain trying to remember why I had left a box of ammunition in the food closet.

"Today . . . ?" Her voice trailed off.

"It's Sunday," I said. "Lucas Linville will be at church. I'm betting in Pleasant Grove."

Tess opened her mouth as if to say something and then shook her head. She slapped some butter on a biscuit and took a bite.

"Rundell hangs at a bar on Industrial which won't be open." I carried my plate to the sink. "I want to talk to Vernon Black again, find out if he's had any more contact with . . ."

"My father . . ." Tess stood up.

"Yeah?"

"What if he's done something wrong?"

I frowned. It hadn't occurred to me that there my be another bent character in this little drama. Was I breaking the first law of the business: letting my feelings for her color my judgement?

"What if he's getting what he deserves?" she said.

"What do you mean?" I placed one arm over her shoulder.

"Nobody's perfect, are they?" She pinched the bridge of her nose between her thumb and forefinger.

"No, you're right." I wanted to hug her but sensed that this wasn't the proper time for that. "There's a shortage of perfection in this world."

"He's still my father, Hank." Tears welled up in her eyes.

My truck wasn't at the office as promised. I called Nolan's home and cell and left messages both places. I tried Olson's cell but it was turned off. I tried to reach Delmar on the three numbers I had for him but to no avail.

"Looks like we'll be taking the Bentley again today." I backed the big car out of the driveway of my office and headed toward the freeway.

We drove in silence through East Dallas, deserted on a Sunday morning, past the empty bars and full churches. The sun was still low in the sky and the temperature was a relatively comfortable eighty-six degrees, according to the thermometer on the dash. I got on Interstate 30 and headed east until the Buckner Boulevard exit, where I turned south toward the area euphemistically known as Pleasant Grove.

The neighborhood was located in the extreme southeast quadrant of the city of Dallas and was neither pleasant nor a grove, though there had reportedly been a stand of cottonwoods 150 years ago that had provided the name.

The trees and any charm the area might have had were long since gone.

Pleasant Grove at the dawn of the twenty-first century was thirty-five-year-old grandmothers living in trailer parks and red-tagged shotgun houses. Pleasant Grove was Laundromats and pawnshops, abandoned Dairy Queens and tiny grocery stores run by Iranians that advertised their acceptance of food stamps and WIC cards. Pleasant Grove was Jerry Springer country.

I headed south on Buckner, past the orphanage and Section-8 apartments. At Lake June Road I turned right and came to the Church of the Harvest a few blocks later.

The church sat at the end of a gravel driveway beneath two old cedar trees. The structure was white clapboard, paint peeling here and there, one side of the porch sagging. About ten cars were parked haphazardly underneath the shade of the big cedars.

I parked next to a beat-up Pontiac Grand Prix. We got out. I smelled the turpentine odor of pitch from the trees and the leaking oil and bad exhaust of automobiles driven too long past their day of reckoning with the salvage yard. The sounds of singing came from several open windows.

Tess stood beside me, raised her eyebrows in a question.

I walked up the rickety wooden steps leading to the entrance and pushed open the front door. I stepped inside and stopped. Tess bumped into me and looked around my shoulder. She gasped.

Lucas Linville sat in a wheelchair next to the pulpit. The right side of his face looked normal; the other was like soft plastic left near the fire too long, gooey and slack. His cheek sagged, and drool trickled from the corner of his mouth. His left hand lay in his lap, curled into a claw.

His good arm stretched outward at a forty-five-degree angle. The rattlesnake he held just behind its head writhed and wrapped its body around Linville's forearm. It seemed to move in rhythm with the singing of the worshippers. The angry shake of its rattle was plainly audible over the noise in the small auditorium.

A young man, maybe thirty years old, stood on the other side of the lectern. He wore a burgundy three-piece suit. He held his hands up, palms toward the pitched ceiling. His eyes were closed, and tears ran down his cheeks.

The audience was small, about two dozen people. Most were white and elderly. They too held their arms outstretched. They sang without musical accompaniment.

"They're Pentecostals," Tess said.

"What?"

"They believe handling poisonous snakes shows their faith."

I turned and looked at her without saying anything.

"There's a church like this," she said, "not far from where I grew up."

I turned back to the pulpit. Lucas Linville's good eye was staring at me. Half his face twisted into a grimace or a smile; it was hard to tell. He dropped the snake into a wooden box and swung a hinged door over the top.

An old man with a thick shock of white hair stood. He wore a threadbare suit that hung on his bony frame. He raised one hand toward the ceiling and began talking to the sky, words that had no meaning, a lyrical stream of vowels and consonants, gibberish but for the soothing tone in which he uttered them. Across the aisle, a woman in her midthirties rose and did the same, the words different but the feeling and tone similar.

After a few moments, the preacher in the burgundy suit raised his arms and the two parishioners sat down. The old man looked drained, breathing ragged, his face damp and pale. The preacher said a prayer, followed with a reminder about the evening service and a benediction.

We moved to one side as the congregation left. After a few minutes no one was in the sanctuary but us, Linville, and Burgundy Suit.

Linville's good eye followed me as I walked to the front of the church. The snakes hissed and rattled in the wooden crate resting beside his wheelchair.

"You must be the one they call Lee Oswald," Burgundy Suit said.

"Who are you?" I asked.

"I am Pastor Bob." The man grabbed the wide lapels of the wine-colored suit and puffed his chest out. His voice had the mellifluous cadence of a televangelist.

"Hi, Pastor Bob." I smiled. "You ever hear the joke about Oral Roberts?"

The man looked perplexed but didn't say anything.

"How did you know my name?" I said.

"Arthur called, seeking after Pastor Linville." Bob rocked on his feet, thumbs still tucked behind his lapels. "What can I do for you?"

I stepped up onto the platform and pointed to the half-paralyzed man in the wheelchair. "How bad is he?"

"He's had a stroke."

I knelt beside the chair, on the side opposite the box with the pissed-off rattlesnake. "Can you hear me, Linville?"

The old man nodded once.

"You lied to me."

No response. Pastor Bob said, "He can't talk."

"But he can play with rattlesnakes?" Tess spoke for the first time.

"People are dying." I continued to speak to Linville. "That file. I need to know what was in it."

The old man gritted his teeth. His good eye seemed to look into my soul, trying to communicate something.

"You could have told me at the beginning, when you hired me, what was going on." I stood up. "It would have saved a lot of problems."

Pastor Bob placed one hand on my arm. "He can't help you. Even before his stroke, you couldn't have gotten what you seek."

"Why?" Tess said.

"Let's take a walk." The younger man motioned us toward the door where we had entered only a few minutes before. We followed him outside. The temperature had risen. A hot breeze skipped across my face; I smelled sewage from a long way off.

"Pastor Linville has been like a father to me." Bob pulled a yellow silk handkerchief out of his coat pocket and mopped his face.

"People are dying because of something he had," I said, "and I need to know what."

"In the end times, the forces of evil shall multiply." He stuck the yellow cloth back in his breast pocket. "I watch as the harlots and fornicators roam these streets. They grow stronger while the faithful become weaker."

"Save it for the flock."

"Is that your car?" Bob pointed to the Bentley. "I've always admired the fine styling of classic British automobiles."

"We're getting nowhere fast," Tess said.

"I truly am sorry he can't help you." Pastor Bob actually sounded sincere. "Since his son disappeared, only the angels have been able to speak to him."

CHAPTER TWENTY-SIX

I pulled out of the driveway leading from the Church of the Harvest and headed west on Lake June Road with no particular destination in mind. Tess was silent beside me. In a logical fashion, I lined up the activities and participants in my mind.

I had tried to unravel the ties among Linville, the stolen file, and Rundell. For the moment, a dead end had presented itself.

There were two areas of inquiry left: the Barringer connection to Tess's family, and the Barringer connection to Rundell. Both required a trip out of Dallas, back into areas of Texas and of my life that I would have preferred not to visit again.

I made a decision, pointed the car north, and headed toward Parkland Hospital and a certain fifth-floor room where a retired wise guy spent a fair amount of time these days.

Victor Lemieux and I were *muy simpático* after helping each other out of a sticky situation one sultry evening in a French Quarter alley. Depending on whom you talked to, at the time Victor was either the number-two or -three guy in the family that controlled most of the illegal activities in south Louisiana.

A few years later an unsanctioned assassination attempt by a rogue Jamaican drug dealer left Victor in poor health and in a melancholy state of mind unsuited for his chosen line of work. So he moved to Dallas to be near his only daughter and her children. We reconnected and helped each other out here and there. Life was good for Victor Lemieux until forty years of Marlboro Reds turned the soft tissue in his lungs to the consistency and color of shoe leather.

Emphysema, the doctors said. Oxygen masks, steroid shots, breathing machines—none of which added up to a particularly pleasant way to live.

I explained all this to Tess as we drove to the county medical facility, a mammoth building located a few minutes north of downtown in the middle of a row of other hospitals. I parked the Bentley in a pay lot across Harry Hines Boulevard from the main entrance.

Tess and I got out and threaded our way through the other cars to the street. At the curb, we stopped by the crosswalk, where we waited for the light to change. Two Hispanic streetwalkers stood next to us. One of them had her arm bandaged in what looked like a dirty T-shirt. She used her good hand to hold a cell phone to her ear.

The light changed. We crossed the street, entered the hospital, and got on the elevator. On the fifth floor, I asked a skinny red-haired guy standing behind the nurse's station where Victor Lemieux was.

He looked at me blankly for a moment before pointing to the room directly across from where we stood. The door was open. I told Tess to wait outside.

My friend had aged considerably in the two months since I had seen him. His features were shrunken, the alabaster flesh withered and waxy. An oxygen tube looped under his nose, the regulator bubbling on the back wall. The room smelled like hospital disinfectant and decay.

He opened his eyes. "This is the shits, ain't it, Hank?"

"How're you doing, Victor?" I shook his gnarled hand.

He closed his eyes and took several deep breaths, chest rising with a visible effort. Then, "Whatchoo need, boy? You didn't come all this way to see an old man wheeze."

I sat down in the high-back chair by his bed. "Tell me what's going on." I pointed a finger toward the window. "Out there."

He frowned.

"The street reads like somebody new is taking over."

"Dallas is open." He shifted in his bed and sighed as if the new position felt better. "That's why I could retire here."

"Hookers are getting the squeeze. Other stuff, too." I leaned back in the chair and looked around the tiny hospital room. A spray of flowers sat by the window. Several crude crayon drawings dotted the far wall. At the bottom of each, the caption read, "We love you, Grandpa. Get well soon."

"Ah, that's nothing." He waved his hand as if to dismiss a fly. "Small-time bullshit."

"Maybe not." I related the two incidents that had happened to Olson.

We were both quiet for a few moments. The oxygen dispenser hissed and bubbled. Victor wheezed. "Take a lot of juice to get to that crazy sonuvabitch, Olson. There's some important people in Houston that like him."

I didn't say anything, filing away that previously unknown tidbit about my friend.

"What else is—" Victor stopped talking as a dry cough ripped from his lungs. After a few minutes he regained control of his breathing. "Anything more?"

"You know Vernon Black, the state senator?"

"Rich old boy from East Texas," he said.

"Right." I related the bizarre blackmail story, leaving out the name Jesus Rundell for now.

"What are you not telling me?" he said.

"Remember the Barringers?" The question was a formality. Asking Victor if he recollected the Barringers was like asking the retired president of General Motors if he knew anything about Buicks.

"Uh-huh."

"People keep mentioning them."

"They run a great operation." He smiled and stared at a spot on the ceiling. "Gambling and gash, they owned it in that part of the world."

"Uhh . . . right." I reminded myself that even though we were friends, we came from different sides of the fence. "What if they are trying to move into Dallas?"

"They wouldn't," he said. "They know where they belong."

"Maybe not with Billy dead."

"It wouldn't be allowed."

Neither of us wanted to mention the circumstances of Billy's fall from power. Victor disagreed with my actions but respected my choice. I sometimes wondered if the fact that I was still alive was due to his intervention.

The door opened and a woman in baby blue scrubs came in, carrying a tray of food. She placed it on the rolling table by Victor's bed. He pulled off the plate warmer and stared at his lunch.

"Look at this shit." He stuck a fork into a piece of what looked like meat. "Used to be, every Sunday I'd eat at Galatoire's."

"Maybe we can hop a Southwest flight one of these days, grab some lunch in the Quarter and get back by dark." I stood up.

"Sit down." He poured salad dressing on a bowl of wilted iceberg lettuce. "I ain't finished talking to you."

I sat.

"This thing I was involved in," he said, "it breeds a certain type of man. But sometimes you get a bad apple, even by our standards. You hear what I'm saying?"

I didn't understand but nodded anyway.

"His name is Jesus Rundell." Victor turned and stared out the window. "But I bet you figured that out already."

I didn't say anything. A certain protocol existed for the communication between two friends operating in different positions on the turnpike of the outlaw life. Names were rarely mentioned in an enclosed area. Listening devices could be anywhere, even in the hospital room of a breathless and dying retired chieftain.

"It's not good to upset the order of things," Victor said. "Stability is the key to business."

"What are you telling me?" I stood again.

"I've said too much already." Victor poked at his food with the fork. "Leave an old man in peace, whaddya say?"

CHAPTER TWENTY-SEVEN

Tess was in the waiting area by the elevators, standing next to two men. One was in his late forties, the other appeared just out of college. She looked at me, her face blank.

The men wore dark gray suits and narrow striped ties. They turned my way when I approached. I could tell by their movements that they were toned underneath the conservative business attire.

The older of the two had short sandy blond hair, like a military cut that had started to grow out. He held a black wallet in front of my face and let it drop open, exposing the shield and ID of the Federal Bureau of Investigation.

"Special Agent Lance Hitchcock." He held the card in front of my face for a long five seconds. "We'd like to talk to you and your friend for a moment, if we could."

"About what?" I pushed the DOWN button.

"Let's not get into that here."

The door dinged open. I stepped inside, motioning for Tess to follow. Hitchcock and his partner stepped inside the narrow compartment after us.

"What if we don't want to?" I crossed my arms.

The older agent shrugged.

"You need to do better than that," I said.

"I've been chasing wise guys for going on twenty years." Hitchcock leaned against the wall. "I can spot a person in the life from across the room."

"What's your point?"

"You're not one. Which means you might just be legit," he said. "And if that's the case, then why wouldn't you want to have a friendly visit with me?"

"Maybe because I've got a lot to do today?"

"A few minutes is all I ask." The federal agent smiled and turned to his partner. "Lenny, do it."

The other man pulled a small but complicated-looking apparatus out of his pocket, like a PDA/cell phone amped up on growth hormones. He held the thing in front of his face and tapped a few keys. The machine beeped a couple of times.

The elevator stopped on the ground floor. The doors opened.

"There's a diner across the street," I said. "My friend and I are gonna get a cup of coffee, maybe have some lunch."

Hitchcock nodded once. His partner put away the PDA. The four of us walked out of Parkland Hospital and into the midday Sunday heat, past the patients in robes and wheelchairs sitting quietly in the shade, smoking. Another pair of hookers stood at the crosswalk, heading away from the hospital this time.

We crossed when the light changed. A diner named Burl's Home Cooking was on the corner. The place was worn Formica and patched Naugahyde, filled with people in hospital scrubs, work clothes, and the occasional business suit.

I asked Burl, a skinny guy with shifty eyes at the front counter, for a booth in the back. He led us that way. Tess slid in first. I sat next to her, the Feds across from us. Everybody ordered coffee from a waitress in her teens with a safety pin through one nostril and dyed black hair styled into a Mohawk. She wore a cross around her neck and tattoos on her arms that said, "Jesus Saves." Kids today.

Special Agent Lance Hitchcock pulled out his own PDA/cell phone geek gadget and punched a couple of buttons. "Victor Lemieux is a capo in the Marcello crime family," he said. "Why were you talking to him?"

"Does the FBI really use the term 'capo'?" I said.

The waitress brought our coffee. Nobody spoke as she set the mugs down.

"Mr. Lemieux is not a nice person." Hitchcock picked up a container from the middle of the table and dribbled sugar into his cup.

"Victor is a retired businessman from New Orleans." I poured cream into my mug.

Lenny, the younger agent, laughed and tapped some more on his PDA. After a few seconds he looked up. "Your name is Lee H. Oswald." He pushed another series of buttons and recited my date of birth and the address on my driver's license.

I wondered how he got that information. I hadn't told them my name. I waited for the punch line, the inevitable joke about assassinations and dead Kennedys. When none was forthcoming, I said, "Go on. Get it out of your system."

"Huh?" The younger agent frowned.

"You know, the Kennedy thing."

"What are you talking about?"

"How old are you?" I said.

"What's that supposed to mean?" He dropped his PDA on the table and glowered at me.

"Easy, Lenny." Special Agent Hitchcock placed a hand on his partner's arm. "Oswald is obviously used to getting jokes about his name."

"I don't get it." Lenny turned to his coworker. "What do you mean?"

Hitchcock looked like he was going to say something but shut his mouth instead.

"Guess they're not teaching much history at Quantico these days."

I stirred my coffee. "Pretty cool how you came up with my name so fast. Does that thing have a camera in it?"

"The homeland security boys aren't the only ones that get the cool toys." Hitchcock waved his PDA at me, his voice displaying just the faintest trace of jealousy at the mention of the antiterrorist group. "Facial recognition software. Directly linked to a half dozen databases."

"It's good to see my tax money at work," I said.

"Let's talk about why you were visiting a known mobster." Hitchcock took a sip of coffee. "That guy's suspected of ordering the deaths of at least twenty people."

"Victor's in his seventies with one foot in the grave and the other standing in a puddle of grease at the front door to hell." I took a drink. "What do you guys care?"

"Something's up here in Dallas," he said. "And we think Mr. Lemieux might know what."

I didn't reply. Tess asked the passing waitress for a bottle of mineral water. Mohawk laughed and told her she'd bring a pitcher of tap.

Hitchcock took a long drink and put his mug down. "You're not a wise guy but you're not a CPA either. You know something's going on, too."

I remembered the name of the Vietnamese hood from the restaurant the other day, the one who ran the Asian modeling studios on the west side of town and was sporting a fresh bruise on his cheek. "You know a guy named Tran Huang, runs Oriental girls out of some cribs over by Denton Drive?"

Hitchcock nodded. "He got whacked last night. Somebody put a twenty-two in his belly button."

Tess gasped. I felt cold inside.

"Took him an hour and a half to bleed out, they figured." Hitchcock spoke while tapping on his PDA device. "Says here you served in Kuwait."

"Yeah." I took a sip of coffee and tried to control my breathing.

"Remember that old Schwarzenegger movie, with the invisible

monster from outer space?" The older agent sat back in his booth and placed his hands behind his head.

I nodded. "*Predator,* right?"

"Yeah, that's it." He leaned forward. "Remember how you couldn't actually see the alien, but you could see the space where it was, the air kinda moved?"

I nodded again.

"It was invisible but you could sense its presence."

I didn't say anything.

"The same thing's going on here." Hitchcock lowered his voice, cupped his hands around the mug of coffee. "We can't see anything, but we know it's there."

I thought about Jesus Rundell, debating whether to relay that information to the sandy-haired federal agent.

Hitchcock looked around the diner before continuing. "Every few years some of the higher-ups in organized crime get together. Like a summit meeting or something."

"A retreat?" I said. "Goal setting for the coming year?"

"Right." He leaned forward. "And this time around, they're coming to Dallas."

"Because this is neutral territory."

"Bingo." Hitchcock smiled.

"But this invisible player is a new wrinkle?" Tess asked.

"Yeah," the FBI agent said. "And what if this new guy tries something way out there, like taking out everybody at the meet?"

"So much for neutrality," I said.

"Uh-huh. Which means Dallas is a plum that gets picked. By somebody."

The waitress came back with the coffeepot. We all declined refills and pitched some money on the table. I asked Hitchcock where the meeting was supposed to take place, and when.

"We don't know. In the next two or three days. The get-together is usually at a strip club. Most of them are owned by some connected entity."

I slid out of the booth and got up. Everybody else did, too. We left the café without talking. Lenny walked away and pulled out his hand-held device. Probably downloading porn off the Internet. Tess went in the other direction, toward a convenience store next door.

I turned to Hitchcock. "Why did you tell us all that?"

"I recognized your name," he said. "You're the guy that busted Billy Barringer."

I sighed. Sometimes it's better to be associated with a presidential assassin. "You think his family could be involved?"

"Maybe. There's a new generation coming online." His expression was quizzical, bordering faintly on incredulous.

"What?"

"Nothing."

"Why are you staring at me?" I grabbed my fly, made sure it was zipped.

"That was pretty amazing what you did, turning him in like that." He nodded slowly, almost reverently. "I mean, the guy had just saved your life."

CHAPTER TWENTY-EIGHT

A city bus drove by, diesel smoke streaming into the hot and muggy air along Harry Hines Boulevard.

"This is a shot in the dark," I said.

"What?" Hitchcock arched one eyebrow.

"The twenty-two in the gut was a Billy Barringer trademark."

"I know what you're thinking." The FBI agent shook his head. "Not a chance. Billy Barringer is dead."

"You sure?"

"Without a doubt," he said. "We even had them send the coroner's file to Quantico to verify the ID process."

"You do that often?"

"When it's a world-class piece of slime like Billy Barringer, we do. The dental match was one hundred percent."

"Then somebody is trying to make it seem like he's still around."

"Wise guys are not known for their originality." He shrugged.

A private jet screamed overhead, headed for Love Field or maybe Addison Airport, farther north.

"You want to try a name on that fancy little doodad of yours?" I said.

"Go." Hitchcock pulled out his handheld computer.

"Jesus Rundell."

He tapped for a few moments, then looked up. "Guy's an enforcer for a family in Houston, the Frantinis. Pretty clean as lowlifes go. About a thousand arrests but only two convictions, assault and man one. Did eighteen months in Florida twenty years ago."

"He's in town, making waves."

Hitchcock shook his head. "He's a nobody."

"What if he wants to be a somebody?"

"Guy's pushing fifty, too late to be a player. Besides, he's got no family juice; the Frantinis were never exactly major players. And their kind is a dying breed in organized crime."

I raised my eyebrows.

"Italian Americans don't count anymore. The new OC is Russian, Asian, Mexican, especially in this part of the world." He punched some more buttons on the handheld computer, squinted at the screen. "Besides, the profile on this guy is all wrong. He doesn't have the cojones to make a move to management."

"You might still keep an eye out for him."

"Profiles are usually right." Hitchcock placed his PDA in the breast pocket of his suit coat.

"Like the D.C. sniper?" I walked away.

Tess was sitting on the curb in front of the 7-Eleven. She held her cell phone in both hands, seemingly oblivious to the homeless guy leaning against the corner of the building, jabbering to himself, and the crew of landscapers guzzling soft drinks and eating hotdogs by the front door.

I sat down beside her. Together we watched the two FBI men cross the street and disappear into the throngs of people in front of the hospital.

Tess said, "We're not really closer to knowing what's going on, are we?"

I shook my head.

"We need to go to East Texas." She stood and faced me.

I nodded and pulled myself up off the curb.

"I thought I'd left all that behind," she said.

"Me, too." I didn't understand what she meant but didn't particularly feel like asking.

"Shit." She headed toward the street and the parking lot where we'd left the car. I followed her, and in a few minutes we were in the Bentley, headed toward the center of town. I called Nolan, looking for my truck. No response.

I tried Delmar next, and this time he answered. He was in Olson's room, at the hospital. My friend had suffered a concussion. They were evaluating a very small hematoma underneath the back right quadrant of his skull. Delmar said I could keep the Bentley, as far as he was concerned. And to quit coming around and getting Olson in trouble.

I hung up and headed to my house. Once there, I packed a couple of things in a duffel bag and arranged for my neighbor to look after the dog. We got back in the car.

Tess said, "I need some clothes, too."

"The Galleria's not too far away." I headed toward Central Expressway, which would take us north to stores or south to our destination. The Galleria was an upscale, multilevel mall on LBJ Freeway. It had a lot of options, Gap, Nordstroms, Saks Fifth Avenue.

She pointed to the Target coming up on our left. "That will do."

"The Galleria has a Victoria's Secret." I pulled into the lot and parked.

"I've decided not to wear underwear for a while." She grinned and kissed me on the lips once before bounding out of the car.

I watched her saunter toward the entrance and wondered what it would have been like if we'd met under different circumstances, if I would still feel the same way about her. I smiled and wondered how I actually did feel about her. Before I could think much more about Tess McPherson, my cell phone rang.

"Hello."

"I saw you called," Nolan said.

The smile slid off my face. "Where's my truck?"

"You slept with her, didn't you?" My partner's tone was accusatory even over the static-filled airwaves.

"What's it to you?"

"I worry about the choices you make with women sometimes."

The sheer number of possible responses to this statement overwhelmed me. I didn't reply.

Nolan continued. "I've done a little research."

"And that was okay with Larry?" I tried to sound as sarcastic as possible.

"He was a cop, too, Hank. He understands."

"Whatever."

The open line crackled and hissed for a few moments, neither of us making a sound.

Nolan said, "Lucas Linville is not an ordained minister. At least not a Baptist one."

"How do you know?"

"Larry's first cousin's wife's best friend is here. She works for the Southern Baptist Convention."

"The guy's lied all along, what's one more mean?" I watched a Nissan Maxima pull into the space in front of me, its grille only a few inches from the front of the Bentley.

Sergeant Franklin Jessup and I looked up at each other at the same time. He was behind the wheel of the rice-burner, an attractive woman about his age next to him. She twisted the rearview mirror her way and began to apply lipstick.

"Hank?" Nolan said. "You still there?"

"Gotta go." I ended the call.

Other than a twitch in one eye, Jessup's face was totally blank. The woman put her lipstick away. She said something. He shook his head. She raised her eyebrows, spoke a few more words, and got out of the Maxima. Jessup never quit looking at me. I cut my eyes and saw that the woman was almost to the front door of the store.

Jessup and I got out of our respective automobiles at the same time. He stood by the driver's door of his; I did the same. The parking lot was busy, Sunday-afternoon shoppers scurrying across the hot asphalt. I smelled popcorn from a machine by the front of the store. A low-riding Chevy with neon lights along the front fender drove by, a wall of Mexican rap pouring from its open windows.

When the noise subsided, Jessup pointed to the Bentley. "Fancy car."

"Uhh . . . yeah." The gears clicked in my head and I realized I was standing next to a $250,000 automobile.

"Going private must pay pretty well these days." He patted the top of his Maxima. "Only twenty-seven more payments and this baby is all mine."

"The car belongs to a friend."

"Must be a good friend."

"What do you want, Jessup?"

"Nothing. Just took my wife to church." He pointed in the direction of where the woman riding with him had entered the store. "Didn't think I was gonna get to. Work's been pretty busy lately."

"Oh?" I tried to keep my tone neutral.

"Buncha shit going on," he said. "Something major went down behind a gun store on Ross Avenue." He smiled. "You wouldn't know anything about that, would you?"

"Ask your buddy Rundell."

Jessup snorted.

"Guy is a nutcase," I said. "Needs his hard drive reformatted."

The detective walked to the passenger side of the Bentley. He peered inside and whistled. "Nice interior. Got a navigation system and everything." He looked in the backseat. "You got a bag in here. Not planning on leaving the county, are you?"

"What's it to you?"

"We still like you for the dead guy in the boardinghouse."

"Then why don't you arrest me?"

"Because we both know you didn't kill him."

I sighed and shook my head. "Then what's your point?"

"The stiff's uncle is connected to a couple of city councilmen. The pressure is on to make an arrest."

"Maybe you should do like O. J. and look for the real killers."

Tess walked to the passenger side of the Bentley, a plastic shopping bag in one hand. She nodded at Jessup and then at me, a question in her eyes. Jessup moved away from the door and let her get in the car. I opened the driver's side.

"Hey, Oswald," Jessup said.

"Yeah?" I looked at him across the top of the car.

"Watch yourself, okay?"

CHAPTER TWENTY-NINE

My mother lived with her third husband, a retired dentist named Buford, in a ranch-style house on the north side of White Rock Lake.

They had a good life together, I supposed. Buford smoked a meerschaum pipe while he built scale dioramas of famous World War II battles and bitched about the ethnicity of his neighbors. Mom drank a lot of pink Zinfandel, smoked those skinny cigarettes favored by topless dancers and senior-citizen bingo addicts, and thought about new ways that her children had disappointed her.

I figured I would be safe for a quick visit before leaving town. I wanted to ask her just one question. About the Barringers.

I turned onto her street. The houses were all the same: low-slung, one-story brick structures looking like two-level homes someone had squashed.

Mom's house was the only one with a mimosa in the front yard. I parked the Bentley underneath the pink blossoms of the tree and got out. Tess did likewise. A minivan pulled into the driveway next door and what appeared to be three generations of a Korean family disgorged themselves.

We walked up the concrete sidewalk to the minuscule front porch favored by builders of that era. The grass was green like a golf course and smelled of pesticides, a remnant of Buford's other hobby, carpet bombing all suburban flora and fauna with an array of chemicals.

I rang the bell. Through the frosted glass that served as the top half of the front door, I could see a female-shaped figure approach.

The door opened. My mother stood in the entryway. She wore a loose-fitting flowered housedress and a ball cap with a couple hundred rhinestones glued to the surface. In one hand she held a clear plastic tumbler full of pink liquid with a cigarette between her index and middle fingers.

She smiled. "Hank."

"Heya, Ma."

She looked at Tess and frowned. "And who is this?"

I introduced the two women. Tess stuck out her hand.

My mother ignored her proffered shake and repeated Tess's name, a look on her face that was meant to be a smile but the curled lip and arched eyebrow conveyed anything but pleasure.

After a few awkward moments, Tess lowered her hand.

"Can we come in for a minute?" I said.

Mom moved out of the way and motioned us into the interior of her home. The entryway was tiled but every other room was covered with a brown sculpted carpet. To the left was a living room about the size of a broom closet. The beige sofa was covered in a protective plastic cover. The carpet was freshly vacuumed, the tracks in the pile plainly visible.

"Let's go to the den." Mom walked to the back. Tess and I followed.

The family room dominated the house, a vaulted-ceiling chamber with about a thirty-foot leather sectional sofa facing a console TV. An episode of *Bonanza* was on at the moment, the sound muted. In one corner of the room, under a cloud of pipe smoke, sat a card table covered in pieces of colored plastic, papier-mâché landscape props, and tiny paint bottles.

Buford looked up from his work—an olive drab half-track troop carrier in one hand, a paintbrush in the other—and nodded a hello.

Smoke billowed from the bowl of his pipe. He looked as if he were going to say something but then returned to his toils. Judging by the color scheme of the half-finished battle scene on the worktable, I guessed he was doing a series on Rommel's North African campaign.

"You've got a nice home," Tess said.

Mom ignored her and sat in a La-Z-Boy recliner. She stubbed out her cigarette in an overflowing ashtray. "Your sister needs money again." My younger sibling lived in a mobile home park in Hot Springs, Arkansas, with husband number four.

I sat on the sofa and fell back into it, the springs long since worn out. Tess sat beside me. The divan enveloped her, too.

I didn't say anything.

"The workers' comp thing for Max fell through." My mother pulled a cigarette from a sequined holder with a snap on the top and a pocket on the side for a lighter. Max was my sister's husband-of-the-moment.

"Mom, remember when we lived near Waco, before moving to Dallas?"

"I hated living there." She lit her cigarette. "No damn culture."

Mom went to the opera once. In 1967. She never got over it or the fact that my father had relegated us to live in an area without such social opportunities. Dad's idea of a good time was a bucket of wings, a twelve-pack, and a night at the tractor pull.

"You were friends with Billy Barringer's mother."

Tess looked at me with a raised eyebrow.

"Why on earth you took up with that hooligan, I'll never know." She blew a plume of smoke upward toward the wagon wheel chandelier.

"Vivian," I said. "That was her name."

Mom nodded.

"Where was she from?"

"What do you mean?" Mom took a long drink from her glass.

"Where was she born?" I tried not to sound exasperated. "What town did she come from?"

My mother squinted at Tess. "Are you and my son dating?"

"No." Tess shook her head. "He's helping me with a problem."

"Vivian Barringer," I said. "Where did she come from?"

No reply.

"Her maiden name was Carmichael, same as Billy's middle name. Vivian Carmichael from . . . ?" I raised an eyebrow.

Mom pointed to her husband. "Buford's son just got a job at the Pontiac dealership."

Buford left the room, pipe in hand.

I swore under my breath and extricated myself from the quicksand designed to look like a sofa. I offered a hand to Tess, who got up also. "You need anything around the house, Ma? Any help?"

My mother stood. "You're never going to meet a nice girl, living like you do. Chasing thugs, going to God knows what kinds of places."

"See you around." I headed toward the front of the house.

Tess followed me, my mother bringing up the rear. I opened the front door and stepped outside. Buford stood by the flower bed, a spray bottle of weed killer in one hand, pipe clenched between his teeth. I was halfway down the sidewalk when she called out to me.

"Hank. Wait."

I turned around. Tess went on to the car.

"Don't go back there," my mother said.

"I have to."

"Please." There were tears in her eyes.

"Where was Vivian Barringer from?"

My mother looked at me for a long time. The children from next door came outside and began playing in the front yard. Buford went back inside. Finally she told me the name of the town. I kissed her on the cheek and left.

CHAPTER THIRTY

Interstate 35 starts at the south end of the state, in Laredo, and winds its way northward, ending up in Minnesota. In the process it splits Texas in two, in more ways than one. To the west the soil was thin and rocky, well suited to raising cattle on large, open tracts. The dirt in the eastern section was rich and dark, a deep loam perfect for growing things like plantation crops. Mesquite and cactus to the west; magnolias and pines to the east.

Cows to one side, cotton to the other. John Wayne versus Scarlett O'Hara.

The dotted white lines blurred underneath us as we barreled down the highway, making good time. Half an hour into the drive, Tess asked me about our last stop.

"Why do you care about where Billy Barringer's mother came from?"

"It's the only piece of information I didn't have."

"And it's important how?"

I was silent for a few miles and then said, "I don't know."

An hour later, we made our way through the northern part of Waco, the city on the Brazos, home to Baylor University, the Branch Davidians, eight or nine thousand Baptist churches, and more bookies and dice games than the Jersey Shore, if you knew where to look.

We stopped and ate at a place called George's, thick slabs of chicken-fried steak swimming in cream gravy, fresh-cut french fries, and iceberg lettuce salad. We washed it all down with Miller Lite served in goblets the size of softballs.

We got on the road again as the early evening sun stretched westward. We left the interstate and headed east on a state highway. The land on the outskirts of the city had changed significantly since my last trip, pastures giving way to new subdivisions. The growth wasn't as dramatic as in parts of Dallas, where rain forest–sized tracts of black dirt were being transformed into miles and miles of tract housing, but it was still noticeable.

Our destination was an old cotton town on the Brazos River called Seldon. Tess's family lived in the northern portion of the county, near where the new interstate was going through. Twenty years ago, the Barringers owned a roadhouse a few miles south of town. Though their base of operations was a couple of counties east, Seldon seemed like a good place to start.

The shadows lengthened as we made our way eastward. After a while we came to the city limit sign for Seldon. Population: 4,000 and change. City water: drinkable.

The number of people was hard to verify, as the streets were deserted with only an occasional truck lumbering by. Most of the houses were in some state of disrepair, unpainted, yards overgrown. Plywood covered the windows of several places, as if they were waiting for an inland hurricane. These homes had bright orange No Trespassing signs tacked on the outside walls. Each place had six or eight cars parked in the front yard.

Tess pointed to the second one. "Know what that is?"

"Meth lab." I nodded. It was hard not to know about the hillbilly heroin and the swath of destruction it was cutting through the Texas countryside.

"Yep." She nodded. "My high school boyfriend grew up in that house."

"Does he still live there?"

"Last I heard."

Since Seldon was the county seat, the downtown was dominated by a three-story limestone courthouse. The storefronts that ringed the square originally formed the commercial district for the area. Now most were empty, with a few antique stores and lawyers' offices the only businesses in the town center.

The interstate cutoff was a few miles past downtown. This was where the economic destiny of rural Texas lay at the dawn of the twenty-first century: a mom-and-pop video place; an unbranded motor hotel, probably owned by someone named Patel; and an all-in-one store selling liquor, beer and wine, groceries, and hardware items. The booze business was brisk. A steady stream of people emerged from the store, cases of beer tucked under one arm, a bag of ice in the other hand.

We passed the cluster of stores and the highway cutoff and soon were on a two-lane farm-to-market road, little more than a narrow valley between walls of trees and vines on either side. Every mile or so, a clearing would appear, an empty pasture or a mobile home visible in the diminishing light.

Both of us remained silent as the vegetation blurred by in a solid mass of dark green.

The road curved eastward, and we crossed the Brazos River. After a few more miles on the farm-to-market road, Tess directed me to turn right on a narrow gravel-and-dirt track.

The trees formed a canopy overhead. I flipped on the lights and slowed as the road meandered, following no discernible course. Tess rolled down her window, and I could smell the river and the dust from the narrow track we followed.

The thick mass of vegetation abruptly ended as the road shifted left into what appeared to be a driveway. The gravel surface led to a cattle guard serving as a break between two rows of white fencing.

The Bentley rattled over the livestock barrier. I stopped when we were across. A small pasture lay in front of us, maybe four or five acres dotted here and there by cottonwood trees ringing stock tanks. A couple of quarter horses grazed contentedly.

A two-story home sat a few hundred yards away. The structure was red brick with white trim and bracketed by two old magnolia trees on either side. The driveway snaked to the right of the house.

"This is where I grew up," Tess said.

I nodded and looked at the black, extended-cab pickup sitting in the driveway by the garage.

"That's Dewey's truck." Tess's voice was curious.

"Who is he?" I took my foot off the brake and let the big auto have its head and idle toward the house.

"A guy my sister knew in high school." Tess shifted in her seat, appearing anxious now. "He always gave me the creeps. I wonder why he's here."

"Let's find out." I parked behind the pickup. The garage door was open. The space where two cars belonged was empty, two matching greasy spots on the concrete. Tess walked to the center and stood there, hands on her hips. She looked around for a moment and then opened the door at the back leading into the house. She walked in; I followed closely. I had my hand on the Browning but didn't draw.

We were in the kitchen: green Formica countertops; appliances that weren't new but weren't old, either; a row of cereal boxes on one side of the sink, several vitamin bottles on the other side, next to a small black-and-white television. The lights were on and the air conditioner blowing.

"Hello?" Tess walked toward the dining room.

I opened the Frigidaire. A refrigerator is a lot like a medicine cabinet: Both reveal a great deal about their owners, their strengths and weaknesses, sins and indulgences, hopes and dreams, even.

The McPherson refrigerator contained a case or so of Bud Light, a half-empty bottle of ketchup, a packet of Velveeta cheese, five cans of

Skoal, and an open container of baking soda. In the vegetable crisper was a head of lettuce about a week past being edible.

Tess came back into the kitchen. "No one's here."

"Mom and Dad drink a lot of Bud, do they?" I stood aside and let her peer into the refrigerator.

"My dad doesn't drink very much. When he does, it's usually red wine. He's allergic to beer." She picked up the can of chewing tobacco. "What the hell?"

"Is that your mom's?"

"That's not funny, Hank."

I closed the door and went into the dining room and then on through the downstairs of the house. The place was nicely if not extravagantly furnished. No plasma TVs or expensive-looking antiques.

I was in the front of the house, at the head of the stairs debating whether to go up, when I heard the whine of a motor. It sounded like a dirt bike.

Tess appeared in the foyer. We looked at each other. The sound got louder, just outside the front entrance. Then it stopped.

I walked to the door, opened it, and met Dewey.

CHAPTER THIRTY-ONE

He was standing by the dirt bike, a can of chewing tobacco in one hand: early twenties, close-cropped hair on the tops and sides, long in the back. News traveled slow to some parts of the world that the mullet was passé. The eyes were a little too far apart. He wore the uniform of a young male from rural Texas: lace-up Roper boots; skintight, faded Wranglers jeans; a plaid shirt with the sleeves ripped off, accentuating the muscles of his arms and shoulders.

"Who are you?" he said.

I didn't reply.

Tess came up and stood beside me. "Dewey."

"Heya, Tess." Dewey pointed at me with the can of Skoal. "Who's the old dude?"

I sucked in my gut a little but didn't say anything. Old, indeed. Forty wasn't for a few more years.

"Why are you here?" Tess crossed her arms under her breasts. "And where are my parents?"

"They're out of town." He put two fingers' worth of shredded tobacco in his mouth. "Asked me to look after the place."

"They didn't tell me they were leaving."

"Shit, Tess." He laughed.

Nobody spoke for a moment. Dewey reached into a saddlebag on the side of the motorbike and pulled out a Bud Light. He opened it and took a long drink.

"The Barringers still own that place south of town?" I said. "Near the county line."

"Why don't y'all go on back to the city." Dewey spat on the concrete driveway.

"Cowboys and Forty-Niners play next week. I want to place a bet."

Dewey shrugged. "I'll take your action."

I shook my head. "You don't have the math skills to be a bookie."

"What the—" He frowned and his eyes clouded. "You saying I'm stupid?"

"The Barringers." I kept my voice low but took a step forward. "Do they still own that bar?"

"Tess, who is this sumbitch?"

Tess shook her head and went back inside.

"It's a yes-or-no question," I said.

The young man frowned and nodded warily.

"Thanks." The front door was closed, and Tess was nowhere to be seen. I turned back to the young man standing beside the dirt bike. "Where are her parents?"

"I dunno. Vacation, like I told you."

"When are they coming back?"

"I'm supposed to watch the place." He puffed up his chest.

"We've already covered that."

"Y'all need to get some gone." Dewey drained his beer and tossed the bottle on the front lawn. He reached in the saddlebag and got another one.

"This is Tess's house. She can stay if she wants."

"Mister, you ain't getting the situation, are you?"

The front door opened and Tess walked out. "Their room is a wreck. Stuff 's gone. Like they're not coming back."

The sun had set now. A mercury light on the side of the house flickered and then turned on, the buzz of electricity loud in the still of the early evening.

I spoke to Tess. "Let's go."

She walked over to where Dewey stood. She put her face about six inches from his. "I want to know where my parents are."

Dewey took a step backward, until he hit the dirt bike. "Get out of here, Tess. You was supposed to stay in Dallas, anyway."

"You piece of trash." Her face flushed, cheeks going almost purple with rage.

"Get in the car." I grabbed her arm and pulled. She leaned against me, breathing hard, still staring at the young man.

Dewey looked at us standing together and raised one eyebrow. The scant movement spoke volumes about how he interpreted our body language.

Tess shook her head and walked to the passenger side of the Bentley. Dewey spat out the wad of tobacco. It hit the driveway with a wet-sounding plop.

"Got anything else you want to say?" I asked.

Dewey giggled, a greasy little laugh full of sexual innuendo.

I took a step forward. He swung the beer bottle at my head. His eyes had telegraphed the move a long time ago so I was more than ready. I grabbed his wrist, yanked it up into the small of his back. The bottle shattered on the pavement.

"You were gonna say something else, Dewey?" I spoke in a low voice next to his ear.

"Fuck off, old man."

I swept a foot into his shins and pushed his back. He went down hard on the concrete.

turned the headlights on high beam and barreled down the rocky driveway toward the highway. Once on the farm-to-market road, I pointed the car south and said, "You want to tell me what's going on?"

Tess leaned across the seat and stuck her tongue in my ear, one hand groping along my crotch.

I jerked the wheel reflexively. The right-side tires rattled on gravel.

"God, you're hot," she said. "The way you handled Dewey. I want you, right now."

"Maybe not while I'm driving, huh." I yanked the car back onto the road and pushed her away.

"I'm sorry, baby." She eased back across the console and rested her head on my shoulder, fingers tracing a slow pattern on my thigh. "I'm just so scared."

I nodded and patted the hand that was on my leg.

"My parents are gone." She sniffled once and inched her fingers upward slowly. "I feel like I'm all alone now."

"Any chance they might really be on vacation?" I concentrated on driving and tried to ignore the warm feel of her palm on my leg.

"You won't leave me, will you, Hank?"

"Uhh . . . no." Maneuvering down a narrow road combined with the pressure of her fingers on my groin made talking hard.

"Every time I care about somebody, they leave." She kissed my cheek, her hand pressing harder on my crotch.

"Tess . . ." My voice was hoarse now, the road blurry in front of me. "What about your parents? Would they have left without telling you?"

The groin groping stopped, as did the cheek kissing. Tess moved back to her side of the car. "Give it a rest, will ya, Hank?"

I blinked a couple of times and focused on the road and tried to figure out what had happened.

"I should have told you that I'm not that close to them," she said.

I didn't reply.

"I was the oldest. My mother and I didn't see eye-to-eye on much of anything."

We passed the interstate cutoff. There were more cars at the liquor store, a full-scale party happening in the parking lot.

"What about your dad?" I slowed to let a pickup truck full of people in the back exit onto the highway. "Would he have gone off without letting you know?"

"Just because you share the same genes doesn't mean you know somebody." Her voice was distant, almost plaintive. "Did you ever wonder what you might have been with different parents?"

Her question seemed rhetorical, so I made no attempt to answer.

Neither of us spoke as we made our way through Seldon. People were milling around the front yard of the meth house where Tess's high school boyfriend lived. On the southern edge of town, we passed a police cruiser parked by a convenience store. The car was at least ten years old and had a dented and rusted back bumper.

The meager lights of the town faded in the rearview mirror as the night pressed all around us, a wall of coal black trees on either side, a swath of stars overhead. The bar was about twenty minutes south, right before the next county.

The Bentley chewed up the miles and we made good time. I pulled into the gravel parking lot a few minutes before nine. The place had been called the Seldon County Social Club when I was a child. Since then it had undergone something of a face-lift and was now called the County Line Bar.

The building was made from cinder blocks with a tin roof and no windows. A blue neon sign over the door announced the name of the place. A similar strip of red tubing to one side said, OPEN. I parked between a Chevy Malibu and a Ford pickup. The parking lot was almost full, and the Bentley appeared to be the only foreign car.

"Let's go." I got out of the car.

CHAPTER THIRTY-TWO

An outsider walking into a place called the County Line Club in backwater East Texas required a certain amount of swagger and self-confidence. That is, if he didn't want to get his ass whipped when he started asking hard questions.

I pushed open the metal door and let the smoke and noise wash over me. A stage was to the left; a five-piece band in baby blue tuxedos was playing seventies funk. To the right, at the front, was a bar. Farther on were pool tables.

The room was full. The crowd was half black, half white, one of the only places in this part of the world where skin color didn't matter.

A white bouncer-looking guy the size of a Buick sat at a table by the front door. He wore a starched denim shirt and pressed Wranglers over cowboy boots. He was staring at the door when we walked in, and his gaze followed us as we made our way toward the bar.

He stood up and intercepted me halfway there.

"Can I help you?"

"Not unless you can get me a drink." I had to shout to be heard above the noise of the band and the crowd.

"This is a private club."

"How much for a membership?"

He stared at me for a moment, obviously wondering who I was and where I would fit into the pecking order. Tess looped her arm through mine and said, "What's it take to get a beer around here?"

The bouncer chewed his lip for a moment more. "You can use my membership tonight."

I nodded a thanks and threaded my way to the bar, Tess holding my hand behind me. People were lined up, covering every inch of the bar, even the waitress's station. The ages varied, from barely legal to collecting social security. Most people seemed to know one another, and I caught more than a couple of curious glances.

After waiting for a few minutes, a fiftyish man with dyed black hair styled in an Elvis pompadour stepped away from the bar carrying two longnecks in each hand, a cigarette dangling between his lips.

I slid into the vacant spot and waited for the bartender to approach. Tess squeezed in beside me.

"Drink a beer, then wait for me in the car." I handed her the keys to the Bentley. "If I'm not there in twenty minutes, head toward Waco or Austin."

"What are you doing?"

"Mixing things up a little."

"I'm not gonna leave you here."

"Twenty minutes." I squeezed her hand. "I mean it."

The bartender approached. I ordered two Coors Lights. He pulled a pair of bottles from a cooler under the bar, popped the tops in a practiced motion, and placed them in front of me. I handed him a twenty, and one of the beers to Tess. She took the drink and stared at me for a few moments before melting into the crowd.

The bartender brought my change back. I stuffed it all in the tip jar and tilted my head his way.

I leaned across the bar. "Need to talk to Mr. Barringer."

"What?" He frowned, looking as if he hadn't heard correctly.

"The old man," I said. "Clayton Barringer."

The bartender shrugged. "Dunno who you're talking about."

I flipped one of my business cards on the bar and walked away. There was an empty stool against the far wall, by the pool tables. I sat down and looked at my watch. Tess was nowhere to be seen.

Twenty seconds later the bouncer approached me. He pointed to a door leading to the rear of the bar. "In the back. You first."

"No." I remained seated.

"You asked for something." He shrugged. "It's this way or not at all."

"Sorry." I took a drink of beer. "I'm not looking for a knife in the back tonight."

He frowned and peered at me as if I were a three-headed alien or someone from Europe, a creature completely outside his experience.

"Whoever wants to talk to me can come out here," I said.

"It doesn't work that way."

"It does this time."

He hesitated for a moment, eyes squinting. "Wait here."

I took another swig of beer as he disappeared into the back. Some might have seen giving my name out in a Barringer-controlled operation as tantamount to a death wish. Though they saw me as responsible for Billy's death, I knew from past experience they might also have viewed my sudden arrival in their part of the world as an opportunity for a little information gathering. Or so I hoped.

Three minutes later the rear door opened and Mr. Bouncer emerged with a smaller man wearing khakis and a western-style white dress shirt, his skin creased from the sun and a lifetime of hard choices. He was in his midforties, and had the look of one in charge of things.

The band took a break and a jukebox kicked in, playing a vintage Waylon Jennings tune, "Lonesome, Ornery and Mean." The smaller man walked to where I sat, nursing a beer.

"I'm the manager," he said.

"How's that working out for you?" I put the bottle on a built-in ledge running along the wall.

"What do you want?" He held my business card between his thumb and forefinger, as if it were infected.

"You know."

"I want to hear it from you."

"Clayton Barringer," I said. "He'll be interested in talking to me."

"Are you the same Oswald that—"

"Yeah."

The man shook his head. "They never told me you were stupid."

"That's funny." I stood up. "They never told me anything about you."

The manager looked like he had a good comeback worked out but couldn't quite remember how it went. He opened his mouth and pointed a finger at me.

The bouncer said, "You got any idea how many people in this part of the world want a piece of you?"

"Tell Moose we're operating a little above his level now." I pointed to the bouncer but spoke to the manager. "Where can I find the old man?"

"I'm gonna tell you a place to go," he said. "Mr. Barringer will be nearby."

"In case you were wondering," I said, "several really unpleasant people know where I am and are expecting me to check in on a regular basis. Bad things will happen if I don't."

The manager stared at me blankly and then gave me directions to a house in the next county.

I silently repeated the information several times so it would store in short-term memory until I could get to the car and write it down. I would have made a bad spy, all that memorize-the-secret-password-and-then-eat-this-communiqué BS.

The bouncer said, "Time for you to leave."

I sat back down, picked up my beer, and made a mental note to call Olson and Delmar and ask them to nose around a little if I didn't surface in the next day or two. Whenever I made similar requests, Olson always seemed a tad disappointed when I was okay and denied him the opportunity to go on a rampage.

I took three swallows of beer, pausing ten seconds between each. After the third, the bottle was empty. I put it back on the ledge and stood again.

"Okay, Moose. Now I'm leaving."

The jukebox changed songs. "Purple Rain" by Prince blared through the overhead speakers. Moose followed me to the front door. "Be careful out there." He laughed.

I was pretty sure he wasn't really concerned for my welfare. I was also more than a little concerned about what waited for me outside. Sometimes the grapevine can spread a message faster than the Internet.

I pushed open the front door and stepped out into the humid night air. The parking lot was illuminated by two weak lights at either corner of the property.

A man stood in the middle of the parking lot, his shadow canting toward me. He took a long drag from a cigarette. The way he held the cancer stick and let the smoke dribble from his nose reminded me of a guy I knew years ago, a casual acquaintance who ran with Billy.

I took a few steps and saw the man's profile, recognized him as the same guy. I couldn't remember his name. I did remember that nobody liked to be alone with him for any extended period.

He took one last puff from the cigarette and dropped it onto the gravel parking lot, grinding it out with the toe of his boot. "Been a long time, Hank."

"Yeah. It has." I tried again to recall his name. The Bentley wasn't visible from where I stood.

"What brings you to town?"

"You already know or you wouldn't be standing here in the dark, waiting for me."

"Things are changing."

"That so?" I eased my hand under my shirt toward the Hi Power.

"Population's grown. Lots more people now," he said. "It's all a numbers game."

"The old man used to say that, didn't he?"

"Yeah." He pulled another cigarette out and stuck it in his mouth. "It's good for business, more people."

"So what's your point?" I saw the Bentley now, Tess behind the wheel, maneuvering the big auto through the parking lot toward the front door near where I stood.

"We don't want nothing to mess up business." The Bentley pulled up behind him but he didn't turn around. "You get what I'm saying?"

"I'm just looking for some answers." I headed toward the passenger side of the car.

"You don't even know the right questions to ask," he said.

I climbed inside the car.

CHAPTER THIRTY-THREE

Tess drove back to town. I wrote down the information given to me by the manager and told her what had happened. By the time I had finished, we were driving through Seldon, vacant and forlorn-looking on a Sunday night at ten o'clock.

I suggested going to Tess's house and spending the night.

"No." She shook her head.

"Why not?"

"It's not my home anymore."

"Is this about that guy being there?"

She shook her head, turned down a side street, and cut through a tiny neighborhood of shotgun houses. A few minutes later, we pulled up to the motel at the interstate cutoff. The throngs of people in the parking lot in front of the liquor store had disappeared. Empty ice bags and beer cans littered the ground.

Tess stopped in front of the office of the motel. "Let's stay here."

"Only if they have a massage bed." I stepped out of the Bentley. The minuscule lobby stunk of curry and cleaning bleach. The Indian man behind the counter took my $29.95 and, at my request, gave me a key to a room on the second floor, near the back and away from the highway.

Tess parked the car by an overflowing Dumpster. We got our stuff and lumbered up the stairs to the honeymoon suite, 350 square feet of Triple-A-approved luxury. Threadbare carpet, stained bedspread, and a gurgling toilet; the room had it all. Even HBO on the television bolted to the dresser.

We were both exhausted. We fell into bed and tried to go to sleep.

The problem was that our room was between a guy who sounded like he was going through heroin detox, and a woman wearing a Dairy Queen uniform and living with three kids in a tiny, two-bed unit.

I knew all of this because Mr. Detox threw his TV through the window at around eleven, screaming about the ants on his body. While the one police officer on duty in Seldon chased him around the parking lot, the waitress ambled outside, told her children to shut the hell up, and then asked if I wanted to party.

Tess came out at that point. She yawned and squinted at the girl, a bemused look on her face. The waitress looked at her, then at me. She stuck her finger in one ear and scratched and said, "Well, shit." She disappeared back in her room. A few minutes later, the cop managed to subdue the whacko in the parking lot. Tess and I crawled into bed again.

I was awake now, more than a little wired after the evening's excitement. I reached across the lumpy mattress. Tess rolled over, kissed me on the cheek. "Let's pretend we don't know each other."

"Huh?"

"My husband thinks I've gone to see my sister." She snaked one hand down the front of my boxer shorts.

"U-uh, okay."

"Please. Let's just do it." She placed her index finger on my lips. "No names, okay?"

I nodded and we had sex by the light of the flickering neon outside the window.

The next morning we woke at about seven as the Monday-morning traffic rushed by on the highway outside the window. We showered and ate breakfast at the "café" part of the convenience store across the parking lot, a series of wooden booths overlooking the gas pumps. The food was hot and the coffee strong. We finished, got our stuff from the room, and went to the car.

I opened the trunk and rooted around.

"What are you looking for?" Tess asked.

"Not sure." Delmar always had interesting things stashed here and there. The last time I borrowed his car, I had a flat and found a grenade launcher and a five-foot-long elephant tusk in the trunk.

"Want me to help?"

"No." I found a tool kit next to a can of fix-a-tire stuff and a roll of duct tape. Next to that were two boxes of ammunition for some obscure Eastern bloc military rifle. A shoe box in the back had a dozen or so switchblades. They were Microtechs, expensive little buggers that retailed for about four hundred a pop. I stuck one in my waistband. Delmar wouldn't miss it.

Underneath the jumper cables on the other side of the trunk I found a padded briefcase made out of black nylon. I opened it and pulled out a Dell laptop.

"What are you gonna do with that?" Tess said.

I turned on the machine without replying. After it ran through its interminable boot-up procedure, a tiny blue light winked on the front. A small screen popped up and said, "No wireless networks in range." A click on the battery icon showed a full charge.

"Let's go." I shut the trunk and hopped behind the wheel. Tess slid in the passenger seat, and I pulled out of the driveway.

She gave me directions. A few minutes later, I pulled under the shade of a sweeping elm tree in front of a faded redbrick building. The structure was old, mortar missing between some of the bricks. A stone inset sat over the front door, identifying the library as a gift of the Carnegie Foundation.

"They were supposed to get a grant and build a new one," Tess said. "Don't know what ever happened."

I opened the laptop without replying and held my breath. The hard drive whirred. A screen popped up: "Wireless networks available."

Tess leaned over and looked at the screen. "Checking your e-mail?"

"No." I surfed my way to Google and typed in the address given to me by the manager the night before. I hit the FIND button and waited.

Nothing.

"Crap," I said.

"What?"

"It was a long shot." I threw the piece of paper with the address on the console. "Wanted to see if I could get a phone number to the place."

Tess picked up the paper. "Try River Bend Road."

"Huh?"

"This says County Road 191." She tapped the slip of paper. "They also call it River Bend."

"Okay." I typed in the same address with the new street name. Nothing happened. The wireless connection was lost.

"Damn," Tess said.

I took a deep breath and hit REFRESH. The wireless screen appeared, showing a faint signal. I pushed the search button again. Five seconds later I was at a Web page for Burt's River Bend Kennels. At the bottom was a phone number.

"You ever heard of this place?" I pointed to the screen.

"Uh-uh."

"What about Burt . . ." I squinted at the screen. "Gomez?"

"Never heard of him."

"Let's go say hello." I shut down the laptop and we pulled away from the Seldon library.

Tess navigated. We headed east by southeast on a two-lane road badly in need of patching. The countryside changed as we drove. The impenetrable mass of oaks gradually gave way to pines. There were no more new subdivisions, just miles and miles of trees with the occasional double-wide nestled deep in the shadows.

We drove through several tiny towns, if that was the right word. Each was nothing more than a small collection of frayed and decrepit buildings clustered at a deserted intersection. These communities were so small, they didn't rate population signs, only small white-on-green markers denoting the name.

I stopped at a service station to fill up the gas-swilling Bentley. The pumps were the old style, digits twirling mechanically behind the glass. An old man in overalls and a greasy Houston Astros cap came outside and asked if I wanted my windows cleaned. I shook my head, topped off the tank, and paid him.

Twenty minutes later we drove past a one-story brick home that appeared to be relatively new, that is, built in the last forty or fifty years. There was a picket fence in need of a coat of paint running along the front of the property. The gate was padlocked.

Behind the house I could see a long building with chain-link fencing serving as the outside walls: the kennel.

I pulled the Bentley into a driveway about a quarter of a mile down the road and parked behind an oleander bush, leaving the car unable to be seen from the street. There was no house here, just a vacant rectangle about the size of a mobile home where the vegetation didn't grow.

Tess said, "What are you gonna do?"

"You stay with the car." I handed her the keys. "Give me one full hour this time."

"And then what?"

"Get the hell out of here." I grabbed the roll of duct tape. It was about nine-thirty now, pushing eighty degrees. The sun cut through the pines to the southeast, narrow beams of light reflecting on the dust in the air.

The kennel was a few hundred yards to the west. I pushed my way through the brush and headed that way.

CHAPTER THIRTY-FOUR

The trees and shrubs were thick but not impassable. I avoided the densest part and struggled to keep my sense of direction. Fifteen minutes later, I climbed over a barbwire fence without snagging anything important and continued.

Another few dozen yards brought me to the edge of a cleared area. The house was maybe thirty yards away. A couple of dogs barked in the distance.

I pulled out my cell phone and dialed the number.

A man's voice answered. "Burt's Kennels."

"Is this the dog place?" I held the mouthpiece as far away from my face as possible.

"Say again." The connection crackled and hissed.

"You got some dogs loose, running around on River Bend Road."

"Shit." More voices sounded in the background. "Where'd you say?"

"Right in front of your kennel."

I heard the man speak to someone other than me: "I gotta go. I'm responsible for them dogs." Though I couldn't make out what the other person was saying, it was obvious he didn't want the man on the phone to leave.

"You better hurry," I said. "Lotsa traffic out here."

"Who is this?"

"Oh, crap. One just got hit by a pickup." I ended the call and dashed to the corner of the house. From there I crawled toward the entrance, staying beneath the windows.

There was no porch, just a couple of steps leading up to a front door. I stood to one side and waited.

After about ten seconds, I heard the door open. A middle-aged man stepped out and squinted. He looked toward the road and then back at the kennel. I tackled him. We hit the ground on the other side of the front door.

The move knocked the wind out of him. He wheezed and tried to stand up. I stuffed a rag in his mouth and bound his wrists with a piece of duct tape.

"Screaming would be a bad tactical move on your part right now." I pulled the makeshift gag from his mouth. "How many are inside?"

"W-w-what about the dogs?" His breathing was labored.

"They're okay."

"But—"

"How many?" I put one hand on his sweaty throat and squeezed.

"T-two."

"Are you sure that's all?" I squeezed a little harder.

"Honest to God. Only two."

I stuck the gag back in his mouth. I made sure he could breathe and dragged him to the side of the house, staying below the windows. The dogs went batty, barking and howling.

In the middle of the side yard was a brick barbecue pit, rising about four feet above ground level. I wrestled him behind the cooker, out of sight from the house, and taped his ankles. Around a minute had gone by.

I sprinted around to the back door and waited. Thirty seconds passed, then a minute. The dogs had just begun to quiet down when I heard the front door slam shut. That meant either one or none was now in the house. I liked those odds better than two.

The back door was unlocked. I opened it as quietly as possible and stepped into a dirty kitchen. The coffeepot was on, full ashtrays everywhere. A two-year-old *Sports Illustrated* swimsuit calender hung on one wall, next to an electric clock over the door leading to the dining room.

I strained to distinguish the noises filtering through the dirty kitchen: dogs barking outside, coffeepot gurgling inside.

And a muffled cough from the front of the house.

I pressed against the far wall by the door. Heard floorboards creak. Smelled sweat and tobacco. A man stepped into the kitchen. He was about my size, in good shape, vaguely Hispanic.

People on the frontlines of the hard life often develop an extra sense of danger, a knack that tells them to look behind them even though no sound was made. This guy had the gift. He turned toward where I stood, one hand reaching for his hip.

He was exceptionally fast but I had the advantage of surprise. He was still in motion when I moved.

An open palm slap to the right ear with everything I had, simultaneous with my left knee to his groin. He fell over on one side and huddled in a ball, moaning. I tied his hands and feet. He offered no resistance.

"Where's Clayton Barringer?" I kept my voice low.

"Uuhhh." He shook his head, trying to make the ringing in his ear go away.

I asked him again. More groaning. I put a strip of duct tape over his mouth.

The front door opened and then shut.

"Ricky?" The man's voice was muffled.

I pulled the semiconscious man away from the door of the kitchen.

"Ricky. Where are you at?"

I heard footsteps.

"Shit. You got the runs again?" The man's voice got louder.

I drew the Browning, eased a round into the chamber as quietly as possible, and moved toward the refrigerator, away from the entrance.

The second man stepped over the threshold. He held a short-barreled shotgun in one hand, casually, as someone would carry it in a nonthreatening situation.

"Drop it." I moved away from the fridge and pointed the Browning at his face.

He gulped and clutched the gun to his hip, not bringing it to bear on me, but not letting it go, either.

I shot the kitchen clock over his head. Bits of broken plastic flew everywhere. The big hand landed on the back of his head, sticking straight up like a cowlick. He dropped the gun and raised his hands, cowering underneath the hole in the Sheetrock where the clock used to be.

"On your knees," I said. "Hands on top of your head."

"You are screwing up big-time." The man eased to the floor. "You let me and Ricky go, and there won't be no trouble."

I stepped behind him, put a foot in the middle of his back, and pushed. "Hands behind you."

"It's your funeral." The man crossed his wrists against the small of his back as if he might have done it a time or two before.

I lashed his hands together and rolled him onto his back. He sneered at me. His partner groaned and tried to turn over but gave up after a few seconds.

"You really do have a death wish, don'tcha?"

"Where's Clayton Barringer?"

"It don't work this way." The man was regaining his confidence, moment by moment. "You let me go and I'll take you to him."

"I bet you will." I opened the cabinet under the kitchen sink. "But I want to see him on my terms. You understand how it is."

"Then you're shit out of luck."

I made no reply. There was an assortment of fun things under the counter: matches. rubber gloves, baking soda, plain white vinegar used for cleaning, a small bottle of bleach. I placed all of the above on the counter in plain view of the man.

I said, "What's your name?"

He looked at the array of products but didn't reply.

"C'mon. You're not going to get in trouble for telling me your name."

"Freddy," he said. "Hey. What are you doing with all that stuff?"

I ignored him and opened the closet in the far corner of the kitchen. The cooker where I had hidden the first man had looked recently used. On the floor of the closet, I found a nearly full can of lighter fluid. I added it to the other stuff on the counter.

"Freddy, did you study much chemistry in high school?"

"W-what are you talking about?"

"You mix up certain household chemicals the right way . . . bad things happen." I dumped a couple of tablespoons of vinegar into the fingers of a rubber glove.

"Hey, wait a minute." Freddy began to sweat. "What are you doing?"

I filled the thumb of the rubber glove with baking soda, careful to keep it from mixing with the vinegar. I turned my back and grabbed the bleach and lighter fluid and acted as if I were adding each.

Cautiously, keeping the two substances from contacting, I pressed the end of the glove together and lit a match, holding the flame to the rubber until it melted into itself, forming an airtight seal.

"Hope I added enough sulfur hydronium oxide." I turned back around.

"W-w-what?" Freddy was shaking now.

"The stuff that makes it go boom."

"That thing is a bomb?"

"Yep." I shook the sealed glove a couple of times and dropped it a few feet from his face.

"*No.*" Freddy gyrated and bounced as much as his bonds would let him.

I walked outside and waited. Chemistry had not been one of my better subjects, and I had no idea how to make a bomb out of household chemicals or what sulfur hydronium oxide even was. Olson could take the stuff found under the sink and make weapons-grade plutonium, not me.

All I remembered was how to make carbon dioxide by mixing vinegar with baking soda. A liquid combined with a solid and formed a gas. A rapidly expanding gas, trapped in a sealed container, would cause a detonation of sorts: not very loud, not even remotely harmful, just very scary if you didn't know what was happening.

A few moments later the rubber glove exploded, a muffled bang like an overinflated big balloon.

I went back inside. Freddy had managed to roll to the kitchen door but couldn't get through before the glove gave way. The room smelled like vinegar.

"Crap," I said. "Didn't use enough reactant."

"Please." Freddy was hyperventilating. Sweat drenched his clothes. "W-w-what do you want?"

I ignored him and got another glove.

"If it's money . . ."

I turned around. "Tell me where Clayton Barringer is."

"They'll kill me."

I waved the glove. "The next one gets taped to your crotch."

He stared at the yellow rubber in my hand and trembled. "You take River Bend Road east. There's a town that ain't there anymore, called Morton. Just past where the state highway crosses is a feed store. Most days the old man works out of the back of there."

I dropped the glove on the counter and went outside. I grabbed the first man and brought him into the house. I placed everybody in a different room and made sure their ankles and wrists were fastened securely.

I ripped the telephone off the wall, confiscated all their cells and car keys, and left.

CHAPTER THIRTY-FIVE

I went back the same way, over the barbwire fence and through the brush. It was hot now, no wind whatsoever in the thick mass of vegetation. About halfway through, I stopped and threw the goons' car keys in one direction and their cell phones—minus batteries—in another.

I had fifteen minutes left before the hour was up and Tess was supposed to leave. I crashed through the brush with five minutes to spare.

Tess and a man about her age stood behind the Bentley, talking.

Tess said, "This is Cedric."

Cedric had on a pair of khaki cargo shorts, hiking boots, and a Che Guevara T-shirt. A muslin carryall was slung over one shoulder. He had scraggly red hair and a beard and ears too big for his head.

"Hi, Cedric." I grabbed a bottle of water from the rear of the car and took a long drink. "Would love to chitchat but we've got to run."

"Cedric and I were friends in high school," Tess said.

"That's nice." I stared at the young man. "Did you dress like that back then?"

"Do you know how many gallons of fuel this thing burns for every mile?" Cedric tapped the bumper of the Bentley with an aluminum walking stick.

"He was telling me about the new highway that's coming through," Tess said. "It's going to cut through one of the last places in East Texas where the red-cockaded woodpecker inhabit."

"Really." I tried to sound like I cared. "The red cock pecker?"

"Cock-*aded*." Cedric emphasized the last syllable.

"Ohhh. That pecker."

"And then there's the pollution," he said.

"So what are you doing here at the moment?" I drained the last of the water.

"Counting grackles." Cedric looked smug.

"You're kidding, right?" I frowned. Grackles were the cockroaches of birds. Drop a nuke and there would be grackles, roaches, and tax collectors left when the dust cleared.

"No, I am not kidding." He crossed his arms. "It's a project for my master's."

I turned to Tess. "We need to go."

"Bye, Cedric." She smiled and waved.

"Wait," he said. "When will I see you again?"

I could feel his hormones raging from ten feet away.

"I don't live here anymore." Tess's tone was gentle.

I got in the car. Tess opened the passenger door and slid in next to me. I said, "Unrequited love?"

"You don't have a clue, Hank." She buckled her seatbelt. "Where are we going now?"

"A town called Morton."

"I've never heard of it."

"Me, neither." I cranked the steering wheel and pointed the nose of the Bentley toward the highway. "That's the point."

The town of Morton, Texas, was nothing, a null set, the essence of emptiness: three or four houses that looked abandoned, a brick building that might have been a general store a century or so ago. Now it was a skeleton, the roof gone, windows missing.

I drove slowly, looking for signs of life. No cars or even stray dogs disturbed the narrow road. A few hundred yards past the general store was a wood-framed building. It had been white a long time ago. Now the paint was a memory, a few thin strips clinging to the gray wood. A barely legible sign overhead said it was the Morton Feed Store. There was a FOR LEASE notice in one window.

A late-model navy blue Chevrolet pickup was parked on the gravel and dead grass that served as a parking lot. A few hundred yards later, I pulled to the shoulder and turned around.

I drove back the way we'd come and stopped across the road from the store.

Tess opened her door.

"Stay here." I got out and jacked a round into the chamber of the Browning. "Clayton Barringer's mean enough to make a psychopath cross the street."

I jogged across the highway and stopped next to the pickup, parked under the shade of a pecan tree growing to one side of the building. The hood of the Chevy felt hot. I heard the engine ticking.

The front door was ajar. I closed my eyes for a few seconds, trying to get them ready for a low-light situation after the sun.

I opened my eyes, kicked the door, and dashed inside, sweeping the building with the muzzle of the Browning.

Clayton Barringer stood behind a counter in the center of the room, counting a stack of currency. He looked up for a moment before going back to the pile of money. I did a little calculating myself. He was probably in his midsixties now, still looking fit in a white button-down shirt and a straw cowboy hat.

The room smelled like fertilizer and weed spray and was empty except for the counter and a couple of chairs lying here and there. The floor was dusty.

Clayton finished counting and stuck the money in a canvas bag. "You can put the gun away. I've been expecting you."

I didn't reply.

"You been running around half the state with that McPherson slut." He sighed. "You think I wasn't gonna get wind of it?"

I was glad Tess had, for once, followed my instructions and hadn't come inside.

"You always were a persistent bugger, even as a kid."

"How's business?"

"Better than ever." He patted the bag and smiled.

"Tell me about Jesus Rundell."

"Times are changing." Clayton came out from behind the counter and sat down in a wooden chair. I could see a .45 automatic in a slide holster on his right hip.

"Why didn't you have me killed?" I kept the Browning pointed his way. "After Billy."

"One thing at a time." He pulled a pack of Winstons from his breast pocket and stuck one in his mouth. "You know how much this state is growing?"

I nodded.

"Mexicans pouring over the border." He lit the cigarette with a battered Zippo lighter I remembered from twenty years ago. "They made Interstate 35 a NAFTA highway. More traffic, more people."

"There doesn't seem to be much going on around here."

"Dallas is growing east. Tyler and Longview are getting bigger, too. It's just a matter of time before it gets here."

"One big city."

Clayton Barringer nodded. "And that's good for business."

"Thanks for the lesson in demographics," I said, "but where does Rundell fit in with all this?"

Clayton walked to the window on the far wall. The glass was dirty, streaked with decades' worth of dust and grime, diffusing the light from outside. He stared out the window for a long time without answering, smoking quietly.

Finally, he dropped the cigarette on the floor and ground it out with the heel of his boot. He turned around and said, "Rundell offered me something I couldn't turn down."

"What?"

"You could have worked for me. You and Billy would have made a great team."

"That's not my way." I shook my head. "I break enough laws trying to stay honest."

Clayton stared at me without speaking. His expression was a cross between paternalistic and condescending.

"I'm sorry about Billy." I sat down on one of the chairs scattered about the room, the Browning dangling by my side.

"No worries, son. You played the cards the way you saw fit."

I felt twelve years old again. A wave of emotion rippled across my chest.

"My operation grew west." Clayton walked back to the counter. "Rundell and his people wanted to move into Dallas. I had places close by. It seemed a natural fit."

"Dallas is an open city."

"Things change."

Tires crunched on gravel outside. A car door slammed. I stood and gripped the Browning tighter.

"You don't need that," Clayton said.

There was something about the way he spoke the words and held his mouth that was unsettling. My stomach fluttered. My mouth tasted metallic. My skin felt clammy.

I went to the front door. Opened it. Saw Tess locked in a passionate embrace with a dark-haired man. He had one hand on her neck, the other at her waist.

They broke apart. Tess stepped aside and looked at me, a blank expression on her face. The man she had been kissing looked at me, too. His goatee and hair were inky black, an obvious dye job.

He smiled. "Hey, Hank. How's it going?"

I tried to speak but nothing came out.

What do you say to a ghost?

CHAPTER THIRTY-SIX

Billy Barringer smiled again and stuck his hands in the pockets of his jeans.

Tess leaned against the Bentley.

I felt dizzy.

"It's okay," Billy said. "I'm not gonna hurt you."

"What the hell?" I finally found my voice.

"Rundell got me out."

"Alive?"

Tess rolled her eyes and snorted.

"Yep."

Clayton Barringer stepped outside. He stuck a cigarette in his mouth and tossed the pack to Tess. She pulled one out and placed it between her lips.

I tried to process all that was happening but couldn't. I looked at Tess. "What about your parents?"

"Shit, Billy." Tess lit her cigarette and blew a cloud of smoke up toward the hot sky. "You didn't tell me he was so damn stupid."

"What about 'em?" Billy said.

"Somebody's putting the squeeze on Vernon Black."

Billy laughed. "It don't take much to get a city boy like him scared."

Tess shook her head and looked at me as if I were flunking out of the special ed class for private investigators.

"Tess here always has been the wild child." Billy ran his fingers through the woman's hair. "Mama and Daddy couldn't understand how their oldest turned out the way she did. Isn't that right, darlin'?"

Darlin' pushed Billy's hand away and continued to smoke.

"Rundell gets you out." I frowned and thought it all the way through. "And in exchange, the Barringers help him move into North Texas?"

"More or less," Billy said.

"So why am I here?" I looked at Tess.

"Because you owe me."

"Hank acts like a tough guy," Tess said, "but he doesn't have what it takes."

"What's she talking about?" I looked at my friend.

"You're gonna get that damn file back." Billy smiled. "And kill Jesus Rundell."

The farmer in the faded overalls fed quarters into the slot on the pool table. The balls dropped into the gutter on the side with a clatter.

I watched him rack the balls on the worn felt. We were in a roadside barbecue joint a few miles from the feed store. The place was called the Beef Barn and served beer and setups for hard liquor as well as smoked meat and bad-smelling potato salad. The building had low ceilings and wood-paneled walls decorated with beer signs and nothing else.

The bar last night had been the Ritz compared with this dive.

A steady stream of people disappearing into a back room told me something else was going on beside food and beverage service.

Billy and I were sitting at a table by the front door. The room was smoky and dark and heavily air-conditioned. Tess was at the bar, talking to a guy in a sleeveless Harley shirt and leather chaps.

Billy took a drink of iced tea. "It's good to see you, Hank."

"You, too." I was still trying to get a grip on the fact that he was alive.

"Thanks for coming here."

I shrugged.

"It means a lot."

"Billy, I'm not killing anybody for you."

"Life is good for me right now." He leaned back in the chair and put his hands behind his head. He had on his most charming smile, the kind he used when we were kids and in trouble. "I sure don't want it to end."

"Then why take out Rundell?"

"Hank, you need to understand." My friend leaned forward. His blue eyes gleamed in the dim light of the bar. "I'm not in the business anymore."

I raised one eyebrow.

"You think I can live like this if I was?"

"He got you out, thinking you were gonna help him?"

"Right." Billy smiled.

"And now you're not. And he's pissed off."

"Right again."

"A couple of days from now, there's supposed to be a big meeting in Dallas." I related the information given to me by the FBI agent.

Billy nodded. "I heard."

"The Feds are worried somebody might try something stupid. Like a hit on the whole lot of them."

"If he takes out a bunch of players, that's bad for everybody. They'll come this way . . ." Billy raised his hands.

"And mess up your life." I finished the thought for him.

"Yeah." He spoke softly.

I heard laughter from the bar and turned that way. Tess and the guy in the Harley outfit were yucking it up over another round of beers. Billy chuckled and shook his head. He said, "You tapped into that yet?"

I didn't reply.

"She's a pistol." Billy rubbed his goatee with one hand.

Tess laughed again and pointed to the two of us sitting at the table.

The man in the Harley shirt frowned and gave us a tough-guy look.

"Must not be from around here," Billy said.

Harley Guy downed a shot of something amber-colored followed by a long pull of beer. He spoke to Tess, who didn't respond. He said another few words and grabbed her arm.

She twisted free and moved a few feet down the bar.

He looked back at us. I kept my expression blank. Out of the corner of my eye, I could see Billy doing the same.

Harley Guy stood up.

I eased my chair back a few inches. Billy was closest, facing away from the table. He didn't move.

The man approached. He was average-sized, but his biceps were thick and ropy like a gym rat's. He stopped a few feet away, hands on his hips.

"What can I do for you?" Billy spoke to him in a low voice, his eyes barely visible beneath the slits in his lids.

I pushed my chair back a little more but stayed seated.

Harley Guy stuck his chest out. "You got a problem with me?"

Billy didn't say anything. I saw him wiggle the fingers of each hand. Not a sign of pleasant things to come, as I recalled.

The man standing in front of the table cocked his head to one side and squinted, as if he were really giving us the once-over before he commenced to kicking butt. I wondered how Billy would let this play, being out of the life and all.

"Is that your old lady?" Harley Guy jerked his finger toward where Tess sat at the bar.

"A word of advice." Billy's voice was low but forceful. "You are in the wrong place to start anything."

"This joint used to be owned by that family from a couple of counties over, didn't it?" The man made a big show of looking around the place. "I hear they ain't such a big deal anymore."

Two more guys in similar garb were on the far side of the room, drifting our way like sharks slicing through the water.

Harley Guy stepped a foot closer, swaying a little. The booze had made his eyes filmy.

"Bitch offers it up, then shoots me down. Says she's with you now."

Billy shrugged.

"Hey." The man kicked Billy's foot. "Stand up when I'm talking to you."

Billy flicked his wrist and the contents of his plastic tumbler hit the man in the face. Harley Guy sputtered, wiped sweetened iced tea out of his eyes. Billy moved so fast it was hard to tell what was happening, the action nothing but a blur of hands and feet. The man was on the floor bleeding and moaning a few milliseconds later.

I looked to the left as his two friends approached. One swung the heavy end of a pool cue at my head. I timed the movement, letting the stick hit the meaty part of my left forearm and grabbing it with my fingers.

The man pulled back as I pushed, an unexpected move on my part. With the momentum going my way, I directed the tapered end of the cue toward his face, connecting with a solid crunch to the nose.

The third person in the mini–motorcycle gang was a wannabe tough guy. He stood with his hands up like a boxer ready for the bell. Billy grabbed his right fist before he could react and twisted. The man screamed and fell over, moving in the direction of his breaking arm.

Two large men appeared from the back. They looked at Billy. He waved them away. The rest of the lunchtime crowd stared for a few moments and then went back to their pool, beer, and barbecue.

Tess wandered up, a beer in hand, cigarette dangling from her lips. "Fucker's got an attitude, doesn't he?"

I stared at her but didn't say anything.

"What?" She frowned at me. "I got something between my teeth?"

Billy grabbed the first biker by the back of his neck and pulled him up. The man's eyes were unfocused. He shoved him toward a bouncer. "Take out the trash, will ya?"

The man shuffled the biker away.

"What about helping me?" Billy turned my way. "With Rundell."

"I'm not a hit man."

"You always did like to dangle your foot on the other side of the line." Billy smiled. "You're lucky you get to pick and choose."

Tess drained her beer, stubbed out the cigarette.

"Didn't know you smoked," I said.

"There's a lot you don't know about me." She walked back to the bar.

Billy put one hand on my shoulder. "Let's go outside for a minute, okay?"

I followed him out into the early afternoon sun. The light reflected off the white gravel of the parking lot. He walked down the side of the building to the back. Nobody was there. A Camaro sat under the shade of a post oak tree.

"How about you and me take a ride?" Billy opened the driver's door.

I didn't move.

"Shit, Hank. You'd be dead by now, if that was the way it was gonna be."

I got in the passenger seat. The interior had that peculiar musty smell of an old car. The dash was cracked. The seatbelts didn't work. Billy cranked the ignition, put the car in drive, and drove past the vehicles in the parking lot. He turned left on the highway and kept the speed at a sedate fifty miles per hour.

Neither of us spoke.

Ten minutes later he turned down a narrow dirt road. Cane pole grew thick on either side. We passed a shack on the left, a tiny wooden home where chickens scratched in the dirt and the front yard was ringed by plastic jugs full of colored liquid.

Billy saw me looking at the containers. "Keep the evil spirits away."

I nodded but didn't say anything.

"Funny what people will do if they believe in something."

I nodded. "Yeah. It is."

A few minutes later he maneuvered the Buick through a break in the bamboo and down an even narrower path. I could hear the river. He stopped in a cleared spot on top of the bank. We both got out. The water was below us, a twenty-foot drop down a red dirt slope.

"You know where we are, Hank?"

"Near where we went fishing and I got caught in the trotline."

Billy nodded and smiled.

"Why'd you bring me out here?"

He moved to the rear of the Buick and opened the trunk. I looked inside and saw biker guy number one, hands and feet tied, a piece of duct tape across his mouth. His eyes were wide and unblinking and he was drenched in sweat.

"What the hell?" I looked at Billy.

My friend grabbed the bound man by his belt and dragged him out of the trunk, letting him drop to the dirt with a plop.

"Guy disrespected me."

"I thought you were out of the life."

"I am." Billy dragged him to the edge of the bank.

Everything seemed to be happening in slow motion. The air was hot and still like a greenhouse. Billy's smile seemed crooked, his eyes loopy. The tied-up man tried to wiggle his way to freedom until he turned over and saw how close he was to the edge of the bank.

"Billy. Whatever you're gonna do, don't."

"Quit acting like you've never done the deed." He pulled a Ruger .22 semiautomatic pistol from his waistband.

"Oh, crap." I took a step forward.

Billy yanked the biker's shirt up and stuck the muzzle in his belly button. The man grunted and his eyes went wider than I thought possible. Billy jerked the gun away and fired into the ground a few centimeters away from the guy's stomach.

The biker's flesh mottled with powder burns, a dark gray, speckled stain.

Billy turned around and faced me. "Back in the day, I'da gone ahead and popped this motherfucker one in the gut."

I didn't say anything.

"But I'm clean now."

The biker looked at me, his eyes pleading.

"What do you want?" I tried to control my breathing.

"Jesus Rundell." Billy turned to the river, gun dangling by his side.

The biker grunted.

Billy leaned over the man. "Don't come back to this part of the world, you hear me?"

The man nodded.

Billy pulled a lock-back knife out of his pocket and cut the cords on the biker's wrists. He gave him a little shove and watched as he rolled down the red dirt bank into the Brazos River.

"You owe me." He turned around. The muzzle of the gun moved up a few degrees, not aimed at me, but not pointing straight down anymore either.

I stared at the pistol in his hand.

"If you can get me close to him, I'll pull the trigger."

"Billy . . ." I couldn't find the right words.

"Don't make me do something I don't want to, okay?" The muzzle of the gun rose another couple of inches.

I ignored the weapon and walked to the edge of the bank. The far side was about three or four hundred yards away. A little upstream a row of milk jugs bobbed in the current, another trotline aiming for some of the big river catfish. A pair of cattle egrets flew overhead, gliding in the thermal caused by the warm water. I thought about choices already made and the utterly futile notion of free will.

I turned to my friend. "How do you want to play this?"

CHAPTER THIRTY-SEVEN

We were on Interstate 35 headed north. Tess was asleep in the backseat of the Bentley. Billy sat in the front, next to me. Just north of Waco I said, "What's in the file?"

Billy closed his eyes and ran his hand over the leather-trimmed dash but didn't say anything. The terrain on either side of the highway was flat and open, dotted every few miles with farmhouses surrounded by plowed fields.

After a few miles he said, "Wonder what it would be like to get off on one of these roads and head west."

"You've never been the running kind."

"I've never been to California, either." He opened his eyes and stared straight ahead. "I'd like to see the Pacific Ocean, maybe take a tour of where the stars live."

"Want me to drop you at the airport when we get to Dallas?"

He shook his head. "There was this guy in the cell next to me. The cat thought Willie Nelson was Jesus returned to earth. Used to sing "Whiskey River" over and over again like it was a hymn or something."

"What's that got to do with anything?" I entered the passing lane to go around an eighteen-wheeler.

"Nothing much. He welshed on a bet and got shived one day." Billy shook his head. "It's a whole 'nuther world on the inside."

"I can imagine."

"No, you really can't." Billy's voice was low.

I didn't reply, and we were silent for a number of miles, a current of awkwardness filtering through the car. A few miles north of Hillsboro I swung into the passing lane again to get around another lumbering truck. I pressed the gas on the Bentley and felt the transmission shift into overdrive as the motor purred beneath the hood. The speedometer was nudging eighty when I topped a small rise. I pulled back into the right-hand lane and saw a black speck on the side of the road, maybe a thousand yards away.

More highway peeled by. The black-and-white markings on the vehicle were visible now, as was the distinctive silhouette of the light bar on top: a Texas Department of Public Safety cruiser.

"Dammit." I tapped the brakes and brought the car down to a legal sixty-five.

Billy pulled the Ruger out of his waistband and slipped it under the seat.

A couple of hundred yards in front of us the cruiser began to move along the shoulder of the highway. As we went by the blue and red strobes turned on. The siren sounded.

Tess stuck her head up from the backseat. "What's going on?"

"Hank was speeding," Billy said. "Everything's gonna be all right."

"Uh-huh. Except for the fact that you're a wanted felon."

"Not to worry. I'm a ghost." He looked in the rearview mirror. "Give the nice officer a little skin, okay, honey?" His voice was tight.

"What the hell do you think I am?" Tess said. "A piece of meat?"

"No, you're a woman for the new millennium, in touch with herself and her goals and desires." Billy turned and faced the backseat. A thin layer of sweat beaded on his forehead. "Your one flaw, however, is that you like to screw guys like me, which means you are, in fact, a piece of fucking meat. *So show the officer some fucking skin so that maybe we can get the fuck out of here without me getting busted.*"

"Thought you were a ghost." I eased the Bentley over to the shoulder.

"Rundell's loose and gunning for me," he said. "There's no telling what my status is at the moment."

When the speedometer read twenty, I pressed on the brakes and brought us to a stop. Through the rearview mirror I could see two things: Tess knotting the bottom of her shirt to show off a very trim and tanned midriff, and a DPS patrol car about a foot behind the Bentley.

I rolled down the window, shifted the transmission into park, and placed my hands on the top of the steering wheel. Billy wiped the sweat off his brow and folded his hands in his lap.

The officer stopped at the rear window, where Tess sat displaying some skin and trying not to be a piece of meat. He was about thirty, with a fair complexion and freckles that would someday turn into pre-cancerous lesions. He wore the standard uniform, olive khaki pants and shirt, and a gray felt Stetson hat.

"How are you doing today?" His voice was friendly even though he kept his right hand on the butt of his service pistol.

"Doing fine, Officer." I kept my fingers glued to the steering wheel.

"Sir, I clocked you going seventy-eight in a sixty-five zone."

I nodded.

"Could I see your license and insurance?"

"Sure thing." I held up my right hand. "I'm gonna reach into my back pocket and get my wallet, okay?"

"Yes, sir." The highway patrolman nodded. "Please go ahead."

I eased my hand to my hip pocket and realized we had a small problem. This wasn't my car. I didn't know where the insurance papers were. If I started opening compartments and consoles, there was no telling what would pop out. Like Delmar's .44 Magnum, or the ball of plastic explosive; maybe the odd hand grenade or two.

I pulled out my Texas driver's license and the handgun carry permit, which was required by law to be shown to an officer if he or she requested identification. "Here's my stuff. I am permitted for concealed carry, too."

"Are you carrying a weapon on you at the moment, sir?" He took the two ID cards.

"Yes." I put my hands back on the steering wheel. "I have a pistol underneath my shirt on my right side."

The cop looked at my licenses for a moment and then stared at me. I felt a trickle of sweat dribble down the small of my back. He leaned against the top of the car and peered inside. "And who are you?"

"Hey, how ya doing there, Officer." Billy smiled the smile that had let him skate through a lifetime of trouble. "My name is Billy Reynolds."

"Are you a private investigator, too?"

"No, sir." Billy laughed. "I am in the food supply business. You got a restaurant, I got your menu items, lemme tell you what. You name it: lobster tails, prime filets, salmon, whatever you need." He reached over and handed the man an embossed business card.

The cop looked in the backseat. "And who are you?"

Tess said her name. Then, "These are my boyfriends. Can't decide which one I'm gonna marry, though. If you were me, which one would you pick?"

"Huh?" The highway patrolman blinked.

"Guess I should go with the biggest dick. Don't you think?"

"Uhh . . . I . . . uuhh." The officer looked at me and then back at Tess.

"I just want someone to treat me right," she said, fanning herself with one hand, her accent sounding like a southern belle. "Is that so much to ask?" In my peripheral vision I saw Billy's smile stretch tight and a fresh film of perspiration coat his face.

The cop looked at me again, his eyes confused. He shook his head a couple of times. "Oh, yeah. I need the insurance card."

"The insurance?"

"Yep." He nodded. "Proof of liability coverage."

I tried to sound sincere and nonthreatening. "I'm borrowing this car. And I'm not real sure where my friend keeps his card."

The cop frowned. He cut his eyes to Tess for one more quick look. He didn't appear confused anymore. He looked professional—and suspicious. He said, "I'm gonna go to my car now. I'll be back." He walked away.

When the officer opened the door of the squad car, Billy turned toward the back and slipped his arm between the two front seats. He grabbed Tess's hand and twisted.

"Shit, Billy, that hurts."

"You stupid fucking slut." His voice was low but charged with anger. "It's like you want us to get caught."

"*Billy.*" Tess's voice was ragged, tears visible in her eyes. "Please. That h-h-hurts."

"Let her go, Billy." I could see the cop talking on his radio and staring at the back of our car. I didn't dare turn around to help her.

"Lessons need to be learned, Hank." He moved his arm another few inches, and Tess screamed.

"That cop hears her yelling and we're all going for a ride." I was sweating now in spite of the air-conditioning.

Billy gave her one last squeeze and snaked his arm back into the front seat. I looked in the rearview mirror and saw the highway patrolman walking our way. I wiped sweat off my face. Billy reached under his seat and pulled out the Ruger. He put the weapon in his lap and covered it with a section of newspaper that had been lying on the floorboard.

"What the hell are you doing?" I said.

"Just being careful."

I started to reply but the cop was at the window.

He said, "This car is registered to the Elm Street Benevolent Society."

"It's my friend's. His name is Delmar."

"Delmar?"

"Yeah."

"Well, it's clean . . . not reported stolen or anything."

"Like I said, I'm just borrowing it."

"Is everything all right?" The cop squinted at me. "You look like you're gonna get sick."

Billy rustled the newspaper slightly.

"I'm fine," I said. "Haven't had a ticket in a while."

"Ma'am?" He looked in the back. "Are you okay?"

"I-I-I'm fine, too." Tess's voice was hoarse with emotion.

"We're all fine," Billy said. "Hey, you know what, why don't I send you some steaks? I got a case of New York strips you can cut with a spoon."

"No, thanks." The officer handed me a clipboard. "I'm citing you for failure to provide insurance and speeding. Sign on the line at the bottom, please."

I did as instructed and handed the papers back to him. He looked in the back one more time and then told us to have a good day before walking back to the squad car.

Billy let out his breath and slumped forward. I put the car in gear and pulled onto the highway.

Billy eased his seat back and closed his eyes. "Tess, you ever pull that shit again, I will fuck you up sixty different ways to Sunday."

CHAPTER THIRTY-EIGHT

During the rest of the trip home I drove the speed limit and tried not to think about the second time Billy Barringer had saved my life, only to have me repay the favor by turning him over to the police.

The frame-up fell on a mentally handicapped guy named Teddy from Nacogdoches, a small town deep in the pines of Southeast Texas.

The story at the time was that the Barringers had paid Teddy's mother ten grand, with the promise of ten more if her son got the death penalty. Mama, a third-generation welfare recipient and no Mensa candidate herself, didn't really care one way or the other about any of her five kids, especially when that kind of loot was being waved around. Money was tight and selling the family retard made as much sense as turning out one of the thirteen-year-olds to hustle the long-haul drivers at the truck stop behind the family double-wide.

So an emissary of the Barringers paid the cash and drove Teddy to the resort town of Port Aransas, a skinny barrier island at the mouth of the Corpus Christi Bay. Once there, he met Billy Barringer in the parking lot of the Dunes Liquor Store and transferred Teddy to his new guardian.

This was midmorning of June fifth of the prior year, a little over twenty-four hours before a crooked police officer from Beaumont,

Texas, sat down to lunch with his family and had his brains splattered all over the onion rings and his twin daughters' new swim cover-ups, which, unfortunately, the nine-year-old girls were wearing at the time.

After Billy picked up Teddy from the parking lot of the liquor store, he took him to eat at Pizza Hut and then to the beach to watch the college girls loll around on the sand, all oily and tan.

Billy sat on a dune underneath an umbrella with Teddy and explained what he needed to do the following day. It was really very simple. Just sit here on the beach and look at girls. Billy showed him the shirt he was going to wear. Teddy nodded occasionally and scratched his beard, grunting an affirmative when it seemed necessary.

After sitting by the ocean for a while, they went to a rented house two blocks from the beach, where Billy ran over it again and made sure that his young friend understood completely what was expected of him. To seal the deal, Billy brought in a Mexican prostitute to service Teddy, guaranteeing lots more lovin' if he did as promised the next day.

I didn't know any of this when I drove my rental car into the sandy parking lot of the Beachcomber Bar and Grill late in the morning of June sixth.

Like so many things in life that were complicated, that day started out deceptively simple. A very wealthy man from Amarillo wanted me to give a package of money to a cop from Beaumont so that a piece of fake evidence would disappear.

I didn't know that the bearded man in the Metallica T-shirt sitting by the jukebox was a freelance shooter out of Laredo who worked for cheap due to his unreliability and substance abuse issues.

I didn't know he had just ingested two grams of cocaine to get amped up for the hit, in direct violation of the instructions given to him by my childhood friend Billy Barringer.

I didn't know he was hearing voices in his head that told him to go ahead and pop the mark a full twenty minutes before schedule.

Instead, I sat at the bar a few feet from the cop and his family and watched a freighter slice through the glassy waters of the Gulf of Mexico. The windows were open and a warm breeze blew through the place, mixing with the pleasant smell of hamburgers cooking on a grill and beer being poured from the taps.

I sipped from a glass of iced tea and waited for the cop from Beaumont to finish eating lunch with his family. The brown paper bag stuffed with one-hundred-dollar bills was wedged between my legs.

A dark-haired girl in a bikini so small it was probably illegal in certain states wandered in from the beach-side door and ordered a Corona. She rolled the icy bottle across her brow and then took a long drink, spilling a thin stream out of the corner of her mouth.

I was watching the beer trickle over her chin and down her tanned chest and failed to see the man in the Metallica shirt stand up.

I turned away from the girl when she caught me staring. Saw Metallica Man three feet behind the cop from Beaumont, his eyes jiggling as if they were plugged into an electric socket.

A small-caliber revolver appeared in his hand. The muzzle blossomed with flame, and a flawed man died in front of his family for reasons I never quite understood, the moment forever seared into the crevices of their souls as forces far outside the bell curve of human decency ripped their lives to shreds.

The girl in the bikini shouted and dropped her beer.

The wife of the cop brushed a piece of her husband's skull from her hair and began to twitch uncontrollably, as if her nerves had been short-circuited. Her mouth opened but no sound came out.

I jumped up and grabbed for the weapon on my hip. It wasn't there; I'd flown into the Corpus Christi airport only an hour before and had no opportunity to find a local piece.

Metallica Man stood stiff-legged by the booth, the gun still pointing at the dead police officer. He yelled something unintelligible as Billy Barringer rushed into the room.

Billy looked at him for a half second and then at the cop, slumped facedown in his half-eaten cheeseburger.

Metallica Man scratched his beard and said, "Oh, shit."

Billy said, "Have you fucking lost your mind?"

Metallica Man's cheeks puffed up, as if he were blowing on a trombone. He fired again, the bullet striking the dead cop in the back. He turned and pointed the gun at me. He cocked the hammer. I became very still, weighing my options: an open room, no cover, the threat only a few feet away. I willed myself to be as small a target as possible.

The girl in the bikini and the wife of the victim screamed. Billy lunged and tackled the shooter. The murder weapon skittered across the hardwood floor. I scooped it up.

Billy seemed to see me for the first time. He didn't waste time on the niceties. "Bring the gun." He shoved the killer through a side door and down a narrow set of stairs.

I followed instinctively, murder weapon in one hand, bag of money in the other.

The restaurant sat perched on a grass-covered dune. Forty yards from the stairs Billy stopped underneath a pair of palm trees. A line of saw palmettos blocked our view of the beach.

"What the hell was that about?" He threw the shooter against the trunk of one of the trees.

I dropped to my knees and sucked in a deep breath of salty air. The gun in my hand was a blued Smith & Wesson, already damp from the humidity. I tossed it on the ground.

Billy picked it up and slapped the shooter across the face with the barrel. "You fucking idiot."

"We need to take him back. There's a dead cop in there." I pointed toward the beachfront restaurant.

Billy looked at me for a long few moments, a half smile on his face. "How long's it been, three, four years now?"

"He blew the guy's brains out in front of his little girls." I nodded at the shooter, who was holding one hand against his nose, trying to staunch the flow of blood.

"It wasn't supposed to happen that way." Billy backhanded the shooter with the revolver again. "Shit. We just wanted a different MO, not traceable to the family."

"What the hell are you talking about?"

"How's life been treating you, Hank?" Billy hit the killer again, across the mouth this time. A couple of teeth landed in the sand. "You doing okay as a PI?"

"Leave something for the police to throw in jail, will ya." I took a step forward, trying to stop my friend from pistol-whipping the man in the Metallica shirt to death. The reality of what had just occurred was slowly dawning on me.

"God, you are so not getting it, Hank." Billy pressed the muzzle of the Smith & Wesson against the temple of the shooter and pulled the trigger. The discharge sounded like a pop gun, the sand and sky soaking up the noise like an immense silencer. The shooter fell over on one side.

"Billy." I jumped to my feet.

My friend stuck the revolver underneath his shirt and trotted toward the beach. I stared at the corpse and then ran after him.

I caught up with him at a spot a few feet from the surf, underneath a faded yellow umbrella. He was standing next to a bearded man in a Metallica T-shirt. The guy was much younger than the now-dead shooter from the restaurant, but his coloring and build were similar. He showed no concern for the blued Smith & Wesson resting in his lap, his concentration fixed on a pair of young women sitting a few yards away.

"You gonna be cool, Hank?" Billy pulled a Mr. Pibb from a small ice chest resting on the sand. "I saved your life back there, you know."

"The Barringers took out the cop." I spoke the words more to myself than to Billy.

"We needed a public display." He pulled open the tab on the soft drink. "Didn't quite happen the way it was supposed to, but it'll still work out."

I looked at the sack full of money in my hand.

"Won't it, Hank?" Billy Barringer smiled the smile perfected after years of avoiding the consequences of his actions.

"You usually take someone out with a twenty-two, don't you?" I looked away from the surf and saw a Port Aransas PD squad car squeal to a stop in front of the Beachcomber Bar and Grill. "One bullet in the belly button."

Billy shrugged, the grin never leaving his face. Two more police cars arrived at the restaurant, lights flashing. One of the cars pulled away and headed down the beach.

"What about the other one?" I jerked my head toward the dune where the body of the shooter lay.

"In a couple of hours somebody will get him," Billy said. "The police are gonna be busy with the crime scene and then with my friend here." He pointed the can of Mr. Pibb at the younger man holding the Smith & Wesson.

"A Ruger semiautomatic twenty-two." I nodded slowly. "That's the gun used, according to the papers."

The squad car was getting closer.

"You used to gunsmith those Rugers yourself, back in high school. Always did like them to have a hair trigger."

"What of it?"

"Nothing. Just recollecting." I heard a helicopter overhead. An ambulance stopped at the restaurant.

"One thing, though." I crossed my arms and frowned. "A revolver, like that Smith, has a gap between the chamber and the barrel. When you fire, some of the blast escapes from between that gap."

Billy frowned as the squad car stopped a few feet away.

"Leaves a residue they can test for."

"You ain't gonna turn me in, are you, Hank?" Billy's face went pale. "That guy was bad like you wouldn't believe."

The first Port Aransas police officer approached, gun drawn. He was plainly focused on the man in the Metallica shirt.

"How come, Billy?" I shook my head slowly.

"A man's got to do what a man's got to do."

I wanted to say something more but couldn't, the beach now filled with police pointing weapons at the man sitting on the sand with the Smith & Wesson in his lap.

CHAPTER THIRTY-NINE

We passed the Dallas city limit sign about the time rush hour hit. Most of the traffic was going the opposite way, out of the town center, heading to the sprawling suburbs ringing the city. The skyline loomed ahead, a jagged protrusion from the black prairie.

"Let's go to your house," Billy said.

"It's in a crappy neighborhood," Tess said.

"Good." Billy smiled. "You think Rundell knows where it is?"

"Doubt it." I jammed on the brakes as a sea of red lights materialized in front of me. We were on Woodall Rogers Freeway, on the north side of downtown. I was heading in that general direction while trying to come up with a better plan, like maybe dropping both of them off at the Nut Hut.

"Nothing like the big city to turn a country boy's head." Billy peered out the window at the concrete-and-glass labyrinth of the central business district.

I took the Pearl Street exit and headed north, past the Federal Reserve Building and the Crescent Court Hotel.

"Hot damn." Billy peered out the front window as the Parisian-inspired Crescent whizzed by. "This *is* the fancy part of town."

I cut through Routh Street, heading toward Central Expressway. That was a mistake.

"Hey." Billy grabbed my arm. "What's that place?"

"It's a bar." The Gingerman was in an old house, near the Quadrangle and a side street full of art galleries. The place had four or five million lagers and ales on tap and outdoor seating in a beer garden.

Billy suggested getting a drink. I suggested not. Tess told me I was a wuss. I stood my ground until Billy started twitching and running his hands over the barrel of the Ruger. I parked and the three of us walked inside. The room was all dark wood, even the tables and chairs. A bar ran the length of the place on the right, the wall dotted with hundreds of taps for various brews. A jukebox was opposite the bar, next to a dartboard. The Monday-evening happy hour crowd was small but lively, most of them twenty-something men in business attire.

Billy and Tess went to the bar together. I stood a few feet behind them. A long discussion ensued between Billy and the bartender, a skinny woman with enormous breasts barely contained in a denim halter top.

Billy wanted something different, beerwise. The bartender jiggled her way to a stack of menus near the wait station. She opened one. Together she and Billy pored over the choices, arguing the merits of a Chimay wheat versus a more traditional lager from a new Pacific Northwest microbrewery.

Tess looked at me and rolled her eyes. Billy asked for a sample and the big-bosomed bartender obliged, filling three tiny plastic cups with different brews. Billy tasted each one as if he were the sommelier at Spago. He made a big production of smelling and then swishing the beer in his mouth.

"Ahhh." He smacked the last cup down. "That's the one. We want three pints."

The beer was from a microbrewery in Arizona called the Goat Scrotum Ale Company of Tucson. The bartender set down three glasses.

I took a sip of mine and placed it back on the bar. The muddy liquid tasted like peat moss and compost.

"Oh, yeah, that's good stuff." Billy took a long pull and surveyed the room. For just a moment he lost the hard-nose look. In the low light he appeared younger and almost innocent. After a few moments I realized what was happening.

Billy Barringer wasn't scanning the room looking for trouble. He was looking around to see if he fit in. Billy was in the big city, and just a mite insecure.

I took a few more sips of the nasty beer and then ordered a Shiner Bock. Billy and Tess approached a couple at the dartboard.

The man's tie was loosened, his cuffs rolled up. The woman wore a tailored linen skirt and a sleeveless blouse. Both had e-mail/cell devices attached to their waistbands. They were young and attractive, professionals who worked in one of the nearby office towers. Billy said hello, asked if they wanted to play a game of darts. They said hello back and invited them to join.

Everybody introduced themselves except for me. I milled around a few feet back and watched as Billy Barringer, a murderer and extortionist and the onetime leader of a vast network of pimps, bookies, prostitutes, and thieves, hung on their every word.

After a while, Tess and the woman sat down while Billy and the man played some more. I leaned against a post near the dartboard and listened to my friend talk to the other man.

Billy asked him what he did for a living. He asked what part of town he lived in, where he was from, what movies he'd seen lately, where were the cool places to eat and drink.

After each response Billy nodded sagely, as if that were the expected answer, as if they were two people of similar background and education sharing a few beers after work. At that moment I felt something for Billy Barringer that I never thought possible.

I felt sorry for him.

Why did we wonder what our future would hold when the path pointed only one way? Did Billy Barringer have a choice, or just the illusion of one? Do any of us?

They played another two games. Tess and the girl giggled and smoked. Billy and the man laughed and drank tar-colored beer. I nursed another Shiner Bock. After an hour, the man and woman said their good-byes, paid their tab, and left. Billy and I joined Tess at the table where she'd been sitting with the young woman.

"Have fun with that city boy?" Tess drained her beer. "I thought you were gonna let him fuck you up the ass."

The temperature at the table dropped a dozen degrees. Billy's eyes went narrow. His fingers flexed, and his breathing was shallow.

"Shut up, Tess." I leaned between them, eager to diffuse the situation. "Billy had a few beers with the guy. No big deal."

Tess laughed but didn't say anything.

Billy licked his lips, flexed his fingers again.

"Let's get out of here, okay." I kept my tone upbeat.

Tess got up and wandered to the front door. I started to follow her until Billy put a hand on my forearm.

He said, "Don't ever pity me, okay, Hank?"

CHAPTER FORTY

By the time we left the Gingerman it was almost nine o'clock. The sky was moonless, stars partially obscured by what looked like thunder-clouds. A Hummer stretch limousine made its way down the street. I waited and then pulled away from the curb and pointed the Bentley north on McKinney Avenue. We passed the Hard Rock Café and a half dozen trendy restaurants and nightclubs.

"Let's go to your house and figure it out," Tess said.

I nodded to her in the rearview mirror and headed east, across Central Expressway. The refurbished cottages of the M-street section of Dallas, so named because all the avenues started with that letter, gave way to the rougher-edged area near my place of residence. A few minutes later we turned on Sycamore. I was going to pull in the driveway until I saw my Tahoe there. Nolan, my erstwhile partner, must have seen fit to return it after her reunion with Larry. The spots on the street were limited, so I parked the Bentley a couple of houses down, and we all got out.

"How come you don't live in a better neighborhood?" Billy spoke for the first time in a quarter of an hour.

I ignored him and headed toward my home, making my way in the darkness down the drive to the rear entrance. I unlocked the back door, stepped inside, and stopped.

The alarm wasn't beeping. It chirped once, indicating the door had opened. I drew my Browning and jacked a round in the chamber.

"What?" Billy stepped inside the kitchen, the Ruger in his hand.

"The alarm's off." I strained to hear.

Faint footsteps from the hall. I pointed the Browning at the doorway leading to the rest of the house. Billy eased to the left, his gun trained in the same direction as mine. I heard the refrigerator compressor kick on, then a woman's voice.

"Hank?"

"Nolan?" I lowered the Browning.

"What the hell are you doing here?" My partner appeared in the doorway, a Glock semiautomatic pistol in her hand, muzzle pointing at a forty-five-degree angle to the floor.

"It's my house, remember?" I drew a deep breath and placed the Hi Power on the countertop.

"Who the hell is that?" Nolan tilted her head toward Billy.

"Who the hell are you?" Billy kept the Ruger pointed at her.

Tess walked into the kitchen and took a look around. "This is a cluster fuck."

Nolan frowned at me. "Where have you been?"

"Somebody tell me who this is." Billy was sweating now.

"Put the gun down." I placed a hand on his arm. "That's my partner."

"Partner?" Billy lowered his weapon a fraction.

"Yeah."

I looked at Nolan. "This is Billy Barringer."

Before she could respond, I heard a popping sound and the lights went out.

CHAPTER FORTY-ONE

I felt on the counter for the Browning, willing my night vision to improve. Nobody said anything.

My fingers brushed the grip of the pistol right about the time I heard movement outside the kitchen window. I ran toward the front of the house and collided with Nolan, her head ramming my cheekbone. We went down in a jumble of arms and legs.

Shots fired, and I knew it was Billy's Ruger. The sound of the tiny .22 was like a champagne cork popping. Each round was a spark in what was otherwise darkness but showed me nothing other than Billy's outstretched hand.

Nolan extricated herself from where we lay in a tangle on the floor. There was just enough ambient light from outside for me to sense her moving to the dining room.

I did the same as a quick burst of fully automatic fire swept the kitchen. I heard my new refrigerator gurgle as a round hit.

In the dining room, I felt my way toward a cardboard box in the corner. Among other things, the container had a new pair of night-vision goggles that Olson had given me. I found the box and rummaged through it as quietly as possible.

"What the hell is going on?" Nolan brushed against me, her voice a whisper.

"No clue."

"Billy is alive?"

"Not now, okay?" I found the goggles and put them over my eyes, my finger fumbling for the ON switch. I clicked it up, down, side to side, and every way in between. Nothing happened. Then I remembered taking out the batteries to use in the TV remote.

"Shit." I ripped the goggles off.

"What?"

"Nothing."

Another string of gunfire ripped through the silence.

"What about trying the front?" Nolan said.

I started to say something but was interrupted by a *whoomp* from the back of the house.

"Don't shoot, it's me." Billy's voice was a whisper. A barely visible figure scuttled into the room on his hands and knees. "What was that?"

"Hell if I know." I stood up.

The room grew brighter. And hotter.

"Holy shit." Nolan got to her feet also.

Billy hopped up as the first of the flames became visible. They were coming from the part of the house where my bedroom was.

"The front door." He motioned toward the street side of the house. "We've got to get out."

I shook my head. "No. They'll be waiting."

"Then what do we do?" Nolan said.

"Follow me." I ran toward the fire. Once in the hallway, I looked left. The flames had engulfed half of the house already. To the right was a small door leading to the basement.

"Uhh, Hank." Billy's voice was high-pitched now. "It's pretty damn hot right here."

"Hang on." I opened the door and plunged down the narrow stairs, hands out on either side to feel my way along the brick walls.

I reached the bottom without tripping. The darkness was total now. I bumped my way past exercise equipment and a workbench. In the far corner was shelving where I knew I could find a flashlight.

My hand explored the area and touched an aluminum tube. I turned it on and a thin shaft of light illuminated my cluttered basement. A gun safe was in one corner, next to a heating and air-conditioning unit.

Billy and Nolan tripped down the stairs, stumbling toward the light.

On the far wall another short row of stairs led outside. At the top was a set of doors at an angle to the house. Ten seconds later the three of us were standing in the side yard next to my neighbor's place, on the opposite side from Mr. Martinez. The wooden privacy fence was all but a ghost and we slipped into the next backyard.

I turned and looked at what was left of my home, a bonfire of my worldly possessions.

Nolan touched my arm. "Hank, I am so sorry."

I didn't say anything.

"I don't know where Tess is." Billy leaned against a fence post and watched the flames burn.

"Who did this?" Anger surged through my body. "Who were you shooting at?"

"Rundell's people," Billy said. "He's found out where you live."

We snuck through two more backyards and finally emerged where the Bentley was parked. A siren howled nearby but it was hard to tell if it was headed our way or just part of the general mélange of crime in my little section of Dallas.

I took a step toward the car but Nolan grabbed my arm. She pointed to a figure sitting on the parkway.

The three of us aimed our weapons. I turned on the flashlight with my free hand. Tess sat on the grass, leaning against the side of the Bentley.

Billy got there first and knelt beside her.

She held her arm close to her body, as if it were injured. There was a patch of blood on her forehead, and her clothes were covered in soot and dirt.

I knelt beside Billy. "What happened?"

"There was an explosion." She was stuttering and shaking.

I placed a hand on her shoulder. "Did you see anybody?"

"The fire was so fast." She looked at me and then at Billy.

"It's okay." He stroked her hair.

"How many were there?" I said.

"Don't know."

"How many did you see?" I was eager to get as much information as fast as possible. She looked as if she could go into shock at any moment.

"Get off her ass, Hank." Billy shoved my arm. I lost my balance and fell over.

I jumped up, one hand out, the other close to my torso for a quick punch. Billy lunged, going for a bear hug. We rolled together and fell into the gutter next to the Bentley. Billy landed on top, knocking the breath out of my lungs. I braced for a blow and brought my hand up for a strike of my own when he was suddenly gone.

I sat up. Nolan had Billy flat on his back, with the Glock pointed about a foot from his forehead.

"Maybe you two could settle who's got the bigger dick later." She looked at me for a millisecond before returning her attention to Billy. "Because we got a shitload of problems at the moment."

Billy and I looked at each other.

"Let's get out of here." I stood up and got in the car, everybody else doing the same.

I headed away from the flames. Nolan rode in the front seat, Billy and Tess in the back. They might as well have not been there. He held her close and whispered things in a soothing tone.

"Sorry to have scared you like that," Nolan said.

"Where's Larry?"

"We broke up."

"That didn't take long." My shirt was stained with something greasy from rolling around in the gutter. I tried to wipe it off but only got more of the substance on my hands.

"Go ahead." She crossed her arms. "Get it out of your system. Say I told you so."

"I told you so."

"He said all the right things." She shook her head. "Then he went and got drunk and punched out the manager at Sizzler and we got kicked out and then he starts in on me like it's my fault and—"

"I still don't get why you were at my house." I turned onto Gaston and headed toward downtown.

"Larry went a little crazy. Started stalking me."

"So he's out there, too?"

"Doubt it. I'm pretty sure he ran into a parked car and got thrown in jail again."

I kept driving through the dark streets of Dallas.

CHAPTER FORTY-TWO

The powers that be in this city have always had a schizophrenic, love-hate relationship with adult entertainment venues, specifically topless bars.

On one hand, the city fancied itself a convention town and went after the big-money trade group meetings with a vengeance. An important element of the hospitality business that nobody really talked about was the desire of convention-goers to partake in some of life's spicier offerings, activities not always available back home in one of those Midwestern states that begin with a vowel.

On the other hand, the moralistic streak that permeated so much of the southern United States ran deep in the fiber of the city.

The result was a hodgepodge of laws designed to appease the puritans while still allowing the middle-aged tool-and-die salesman from Des Moines the chance to watch a twenty-year-old mother of three shake her silicone breasts to the thumping rhythm of a 1980s hair band.

Connie the Crack Whore had told me that Rundell hung out at a strip club on Industrial Boulevard, on the west side of town. I decided to clean up a little and make that my next destination.

I mentally debated the options for a few seconds and then headed to Delmar and Olson's house.

"Where are you going?" Nolan said.

I told her.

"With them?" She tilted her head to the backseat.

"Uh-huh."

"Is that smart?"

"I'm out of ideas."

She didn't reply.

When I was a block away I dialed Olson's cell phone.

Delmar answered. "Yeah."

"It's Hank."

"What the hell do you want?"

"Where's Olson?"

"Where's my car?"

"I'm bringing it back."

He hung up without replying.

Billy stuck his head in front. "Who're you talking to, Hank?"

"I'm gonna take you someplace safe." I turned onto Delmar and Olson's street. "And get us cleaned up a little."

Billy pulled out the Ruger and dangled it between the two seats. "You wouldn't be trying to trick-fuck me, would ya?"

Nolan sucked in a loud mouthful of air.

"Don't you think we're a little beyond that now?" I parked in the driveway, underneath the magnolia tree. By the time I stepped out of the Bentley, Delmar was on the front porch.

"Who the hell is in my car?"

"Hey, Delmar." I walked across the yard.

"Don't you even care about Olson?" He stepped off the porch.

"How is he?"

"Quit acting like you give a shit." His voice was shrill, tinged with a measure of fear that I had never heard before.

"Things are in play at the moment." I looked at the Bentley and then back at Delmar.

"It always is with you."

"I need a place to stash some people."

"What do you think this is?" He put his face inches from mine. "Motel 6?"

"They burned my house down."

"I ought to . . ." He frowned. "What?"

"Rundell's people did it."

He looked at Nolan, Tess, and Billy standing by his car.

"We're out of places to go," I said.

"All right." His shoulders slumped. "They can come in." He turned and walked up the steps leading to the front door.

I motioned to my three traveling companions and went inside.

They'd redecorated again, a minimalist theme this time: chrome-and-glass furniture, white walls, black accessories. An M-16 with two clips taped together back to back was leaning in the corner.

Olson stood by the stairs. He had a bandage on his head and a mildly confused look on his face. "Heya, Hank."

I looked at my friend but didn't say anything.

"The docs think he'll be all right." Delmar watched as Tess, Nolan, and Billy spilled into the room. "It was rough there for a day or so when the swelling wouldn't go down."

I looked at Delmar. "I need two things."

"What?" He crossed his arms.

"A clean shirt and no questions."

Nolan took charge. She asked for a first aid kit, told Billy to wait in the living room in one of the fancy chrome-and-leather chairs. Delmar left to get the medical supplies while Olson squinted at the man with the dyed black hair sitting in his front room.

I hesitated for a second and then introduced them. Olson frowned but didn't say anything.

Delmar returned at that particular moment. "Who the hell did you say that was?"

Nolan took the first aid kit and reminded him he was gonna get me a clean shirt. Then she grabbed Tess by the arm and took her to the bathroom in the back to clean the cut on her head.

Delmar went upstairs and came back in a few minutes with a plain spread-collar white oxford-cloth shirt. I took off my denim one and put on the fresh garment.

It didn't look right untucked, so I removed the inside-the-waistband holster with the Hi Power.

Olson watched me place the gun on a glass-topped table in the entry-way. He nodded a couple of times as if he remembered something and then began to rummage around in the hall closet. A few moments later he handed me a Sig .380 that fit perfectly in the hip pocket of my jeans.

He seemed quite pleased to have accomplished this simple task. I hoped that nothing permanent had been jarred loose in his oversized cranium.

Delmar and Billy were looking at each other warily when I walked into the living room. I told Billy it was time to go.

"Is this who I think it is?" Delmar said.

"Yeah."

"But he's supposed to be dead."

"As far as you know, I still am." Billy stood up.

"Or what?" Delmar turned and faced the undead one.

Billy flexed his fingers.

"You responsible for this?" Delmar pointed to Olson, now leaning against the banister.

"You blame the clouds when it rains?" Billy smiled the bad smile.

I stepped between the two of them. "Let's go."

Billy followed me outside. We got in the Bentley. Delmar stood on the porch and watched us drive off.

CHAPTER FORTY-THREE

Sugar Babies prided itself on being an upscale establishment for the value-minded consumer, a hybrid, of sorts, occupying the territory between the low-end dives and the thirty-dollar-per-table-dance places where the women all looked like turbo-breasted supermodels.

Ten-dollar cover charge, decor only slightly less garish than an off-strip casino waiting for the wrecking ball, dancers without too many tattoos and most of their teeth.

I valeted the Bentley and gave the guy a twenty to park it by the front. A girl in black fishnet hose, butt-cheek-high hot pants, and a velvet halter top sat behind a counter just inside the front door. She took our cover charge and stamped our hands.

The music was loud, a thumping bass line belonging to a band whose name I couldn't quite bring to mind but remembered seeing a couple of years earlier on *Behind the Music,* talking about the night it all went to shit when the lead singer ingested twenty grams of Peruvian flake with Miss July 1987.

We ventured inside. A large main stage was on one mirror-lined wall, a level below the rest of the place. The main stage had a circle of chairs around it with a ring of tables after that. This lower section was occupied by what looked like two busloads of Japanese tourists.

A red-haired young woman in pigtails, knee-high white stockings, and a hot pink bikini was dry-humping the brass pole in the middle of the stage. Every few seconds she would lie flat on her back and spread her legs for the cheering crowd.

I counted five more smaller stages dotting the room. Each one had a dancer clad only in a G-string, shaking all her jiggly parts to the beat of the music.

The place was full, not an empty seat visible from where I stood, and people milling about in the aisles. Every dozen feet or so was a tuxedo-clad manager.

"You've got a plan, right?" Billy leaned close to be heard over the music.

"Not even a bad one." Which was the truth. Things were moving too fast. No time to plan.

A girl wearing the same fishnet hose and halter top getup as the cashier approached us. She carried a small cocktail tray in one hand. A bandolier of shot glasses bisected her chest, a fifth of tequila resting on her hip like a pistol.

"You guys want a table?" She looked about nineteen, pretty with a button nose and flawless skin. She smiled and her face came alive, green eyes sparkling in the strobe lights of the bar.

I smiled back. "Sure."

"This way." She threaded her way through the crowd to the back of the room.

I followed her to a two-topper near the DJ booth and one of the smaller stages. I wondered how a girl like her had come to be in a place like this.

I said, "How did a girl like you come to be in a place like this?"

"Save it for a dancer, okay?" She smiled again but it didn't light up her face this time. She put two cocktail napkins on the table. "What do you want to drink?"

"Shiner." I motioned to where I thought Billy was. "And he'll have a . . ."

Billy was gone.

The waitress jerked her thumb backward. "He's that way."

I looked where she indicated. Billy was standing next to one of the other stages. A blonde was kneeling down, knees and thighs bracketing his shoulders, his head between her cantaloupe-sized breasts.

"Crap."

"Whaddya expect," the waitress said. "It's a titty bar."

I left the table and walked up to Billy. "What the hell are you doing?"

He didn't reply. I guessed it was because his ears were blocked by the dancer's breasts. Maybe it was the music, though.

"Billy." I tugged on his arm. "Not now."

"Mmmpht." His voice was muffled by silicone and flesh.

I yanked and he broke the connection with the dancer. "We've got stuff to do."

"Goddamn, I haven't seen tits like that since . . . shit, I dunno when." Billy tossed a five-dollar bill at the girl as I pulled him back to the table.

The music changed. Now playing was the Dixie Chicks' ode to trailer park trash everywhere: "Good-bye Earl." The dancer on the main stage had stripped off her bikini and wore only a miniscule thong, the white hose, and seven-inch platforms.

I dragged Billy back toward our spot. The waitress was placing a bucket of champagne on the table while a Rubenesque woman with a tattoo of Kid Rock on her shoulder performed a lap dance for a young man in a wife-beater undershirt and baby blue nylon warm-up pants.

The waitress handed me a beer. "That'll be seven dollars."

"Who's that?" I gave her a ten-spot.

"You want a tequila shot?" She stuffed the bill into the nether regions of her cleavage without offering change.

"I'm looking for somebody." I ignored her offer. "A new guy. Been in and out of here a lot lately."

"A guy. In here. That narrows it down."

"He shaves his head and dresses like a high-class pimp."

Her eyes got wide for a millisecond before returning to normal. "Sorry. I don't know who you're talking about."

"Pass the word to the manager." I handed her a twenty.

She ignored the bill and left, looking over her shoulder as she made her way down the crowded aisle.

I turned back to our table. Billy had sat down in the only available seat and was gaping at the woman grinding her crotch into the man in the other chair.

The man looked over. "Ain't this the shits?"

I took a long swallow of beer.

The song ended and the dancer stopped dancing. She grabbed the bottle of champagne, poured two glasses, and handed one to her friend.

"Hey." He drank half of it in one gulp and stuck out his hand to me. "I'm Iggy."

"Hi, Iggy." I ignored his offer of a shake. "Why are you sitting here?"

The man laughed. He smacked the table, which made the fake diamond dial on his oversized watch spin.

His eyes never seemed to blink.

"Dude, needed a place for a table dance." He patted the woman's bare ass. "This here is Nicky."

"Hi, Nicky." I stared at the woman's breasts. They were so big they needed their own zip code.

The woman leaned over and kissed me on the lips, one hand giving my inner thigh a good squeeze.

Another song cranked up: Bon Jovi, "You Give Love a Bad Name."

Billy said, "Heya, Nicky? How about a dance?"

"Sure thing." The woman killed the rest of her champagne and slid over to Billy, managing to drag her thigh against my crotch in the process.

"Oh, yeahhh . . ." Billy leaned back and spread his legs.

I rubbed my eyes and tried to remember when I had last eaten anything of substance. This was not going as planned. But things with Billy rarely did.

"You need a pick-me-up?" Iggy handed me a tiny square of folded paper. "This shit will do you right."

"Iggy." I dropped the paper in the bucket of ice containing the champagne bottle. "Why don't you go away?"

The younger man laughed again. When he stopped, his eyes seemed wider and more bloodshot. He grabbed me by the arm. "Hey, it's all cool and shit."

I wrenched free.

He stood up and leaned over. He smelled sweaty, with a metallic stench coming off his breath. "Don't cause a scene. You're in enough shit already."

"What the hell are you talking about?"

"The man needs to talk to you." Iggy developed a tic on the left side of his face.

"You need to lay off the drugs. Your heart's gonna explode."

"You think they didn't tell us to watch out for you?" Iggy smiled. His teeth were gray, the color of mold.

"Do you come with subtitles?" I let my hand slip from the table, getting it a little closer to the pistol in my back pocket. "Because I'm not following what's going on."

"That thing you stole, whatever the hell it was." His eyes jiggled in their sockets. "It's, like, real important that they, like, get it back, you know, dude?"

Nicky had her mouth on Billy's crotch. His eyes had rolled upward until only the whites were visible.

"Iggy, this is the major leagues. Do yourself a favor and go away before you get hurt."

The song ended, and Billy handed Nicky some money.

"Hey, I am just the messenger."

Billy stood up and looked at the brunette dancing on the stage behind Iggy.

I said, "How about you pass a message back to whoever sent you over here?"

"It don't work that way." A small pistol appeared in Iggy's hand. It was pointed at my stomach and impossible to see in the dark club unless you were standing a foot or less away. "The man needs whatever it is, in the worst way."

"Tell him I've got it. But not with me."

Billy squinted at a platinum blonde on the stage behind Iggy. He staggered that way.

"We're gonna take a walk." Iggy's lips were flecked with spit, his hair greasy with perspiration. His gun hand shook. "Your buddy can stay here and get his unit rubbed on."

"No."

"I will so pop one in your kneecap." He pressed the muzzle against the bend in my leg but didn't sound very convincing.

Suddenly the pressure against my flesh was gone. Iggy's mouth twisted in pain. His fingers holding the gun were bent back at the wrong angle. Billy had hold of the pistol, one finger behind the trigger so it couldn't fire.

"Dude." Iggy's voice was tight with pain. "This is so wrong."

"You think?" Billy twisted a little more, and Iggy's index finger snapped.

The man howled but I couldn't hear him. The next song had started with an extra-loud screech of feedback. God bless Ted Nugent.

Billy threw Iggy against the DJ booth. He hit with his head and fell into a twitching bundle on the floor.

"They know we're here," I said.

"I guess this means I'm not gonna get another table dance."

Two big guys in ill-fitting tuxedos appeared by the table.

"Uh-oh." I whacked the first one on the side of the head with the half-full bottle of champagne before he could do anything. Billy shoved a chair into the other one's diaphragm. They landed on top of each other.

We headed toward the front door, not running but not dillydallying either.

A group of camera-toting Japanese men in the aisle slowed us down. They were scurrying after a six-footer with Marilyn Monroe hair and implants so big they cast a shadow in the low light of the bar.

We were in the middle of Japanese men when the third tuxedo showed up, blocking our way to the front. He had a headset on, covering one ear, a mike by his mouth.

He saw us and stopped, blocking the aisle.

The blonde stopped, too, which caused all the Japanese men to run into her and her enormous breasts.

Tuxedo yelled something into his boom mike.

The dancer swatted the Nipponese tourists. "You little yellow fuckers quit following me. I told you already: No cameras allowed in Sugar Babies."

An older Japanese man in a red sleeveless golf sweater stood at the edge of the group, a Nikon in his hand.

Billy tapped him on the shoulder. "You want me takee picture?" He pantomined using a camera.

The man said something in his native tongue and bowed. He handed a very complicated-looking digital camera to Billy.

"Hey." Tuxedo elbowed his way past the blonde and reached for Billy between two Japanese men.

A Ted Nugent set was under way. "Free-for-All" gave way to "Cat Scratch Fever."

"Miss Chesty?" Billy yelled at the Monroe-esque dancer. "You wanna stand over there with Mr. Toyota?"

More Japanese tourists had materialized, crowding the aisle, forcing themselves between Tuxedo and Billy. They jabbered back and forth as their friend moved toward the dancer. The music got louder.

"No fucking pictures!" The blonde tried to get away but the crowd forced her next to the man who had given his camera to Billy.

"Drop the camera and place your hands on your head." Tuxedo's fingers were within inches of Billy.

"Everybody smile." Billy put the Nikon to his face.

"I told you to assume the position." Tuxedo grabbed Billy's shoulder.

Billy turned and hit him in the face with the camera.

Feedback from the music wailed across the room. The yellow-and-blue strobe light kicked on as did the fog machine, filling the air with a surreal-colored haze that seemed to fit perfectly with the screeching guitar.

Mr. Tuxedo covered his nose with one hand while fumbling with his boom mike with the other. The blood that dripped between his fingers appeared green in the weird lighting.

Billy tossed the camera to the Japanese man.

I looked around for more bouncers but it was hard to see who was who with the strobes, fake tits, fog, and all the tourists crowding us.

Billy pushed his way through the crowd. Mr. Tuxedo still stood in the aisle, green-black blood staining his white shirt. Billy punched him in the stomach, and he fell to the floor.

"Hey, what the hell do you think you're doing?" The dancer grabbed Billy by the hair and pulled at the same time that I managed to break through the bottleneck of tourists and run into both of them.

The three of us dropped to the floor, next to Mr. Tuxedo. A couple of Japanese fell on top of us, along with a petite brunette dressed in a barely there French maid's outfit who appeared from out of nowhere.

Someone bit my forearm. A nipple poked me in the eye. Cameras flashed. Japanese men jabbered at one another in Japanese. My face was pressed into the dirty carpet of the bar.

I tried to get up until a foot hit my solar plexus and everything shut down.

CHAPTER FORTY-FOUR

Noise all around. Angry voices. Yelling. The chatter of the Japanese tourists grew faint.

Rough hands held my arms and dragged me somewhere. My stomach felt like I'd swallowed a box of glass shards. My head hurt and I wasn't sure why. I didn't remember getting hit there.

Another song was playing: "Highway to Hell" by AC/DC.

I opened my eyes. The hands holding me gave a shove, and I hit the door at the rear of the club with the side of my face. The door opened inward and I fell onto a tile floor.

The harsh fluorescent lights killed my vision. The music was muffled now, a dull throbbing that matched the pain in my gut and head. More hands grabbed me, pulling me upright and hustling me down a corridor.

My vision had just about returned to normal when I was thrown into another, darker area. I blinked a couple of times and saw the room was an office. Two men in tuxes stood on either side of me. I smelled Old Spice aftershave.

One-way glass formed the far wall, looking out over the VIP area. Next to that was a bank of closed-circuit television monitors showing various sections of the club. On the wall opposite the video devices was a stack of liquor cartons arranged haphazardly around a metal desk.

Jesus Rundell sat behind the desk. He had a cigar in one hand and a red-haired dancer in his lap. The girl was sobbing quietly, one hand over her eyes, the other covering her chest.

"Shit, girl, quit acting like that hurt." Rundell blew a smoke ring across the desk. "You know you like it."

The dancer shuddered, her shoulders shivering as the sobbing grew louder.

"Get this out of here, will ya?" Rundell pushed the dancer off his lap. She fell on the floor and rolled into a ball. A bouncer grabbed her arm and pulled her toward the door.

"You've sure been messing with my business." Jesus Rundell looked at me and rubbed one hand on his thigh lightly. "And your boy Olson made a serious mistake when he stuck me with that knife."

I started to say something, but one of the tuxes punched me in the stomach and I hit the floor hard, landing next to an empty pack of cigarettes and a black bra.

"Enough of that shit, already." Billy was in the room.

I got to my hands and knees and tried not to vomit.

"I thought you were going to stay out of Dallas," Rundell said.

"I thought you weren't gonna fuck things up." Billy knelt beside me and grabbed my arm. "Try standing up, Hank. Nobody's gonna hit you again."

I stood. My legs were wobbly.

"Where's the file?" Rundell relit his cigar.

"Maybe it burned up in my house." I took several deep breaths.

"Uh-uh." He shook his head. "You're not stupid enough to keep it there. That was just a welcome home message."

"You almost fried me, too, dumbass," Billy said. "Thought you were supposed to keep it safe."

"And I thought we'd reached an understanding about showing me the proper respect." Rundell's skin seemed to get tight on his cheeks. His eyes narrowed to slits.

"That's when you don't screw things up."

The bouncers shifted slightly beside me. Rundell stared at my friend, his anger a physical presence in the room.

Billy kept talking. "We had a deal."

"And your buddy's messed it up." Rundell pointed to me with his cigar.

"What the hell are you two talking about?" I massaged my stomach.

"Hank has the file," Billy said.

"Where is it?" Rundell stood up.

Billy looked at me.

I looked back. Tried to figure out all the permutations and angles. Couldn't make sense of anything. I said, "It's at my office."

"Hank's been keeping it safe." Billy smiled. "Now we're gonna go get it."

Rundell stuck the cigar in his mouth and grabbed a pinstripe sports coat off the back of his chair. The strobe lights in the club flashed on. A pair of dancers were in the VIP section, writhing on the same stage, back to back.

"And then what?" Rundell's head was wreathed in smoke.

Billy laughed and smiled the smile. "A deal's a deal."

The tuxedo-clad goons behind me relaxed.

"Damn straight." Rundell limped from behind the desk and stuck out his hand. He and Billy shook. "Let's go."

I drove. Billy was next to me, Jesus Rundell in the back.

"Nice fucking ride." He banged on the side panel of the back door.

"It's a Bentley," I said.

"That so?"

"They're made in England." I glanced in the rearview mirror.

Our passenger was chewing on his dead cigar. "That's in Europe, you know."

Billy made a noise, a have-you-lost-your-fucking-mind kind of sound.

"You ever been to Europe?" I peeked in the mirror again as I turned south on Harry Hines Boulevard and went past a Mexican biker bar on one side of the street and a country club on the other.

"Imagine yourself at the edge of a cliff, Lee Oswald, overlooking a deep canyon." Rundell's voice was so low I had to strain to hear it. "What possible benefit is there to poking at me?"

"No offense." I smiled at the mirror. "Just making conversation."

"Shut the hell up, Hank." Billy's voice was tight. "Just drive the car."

Rundell leaned back and chewed on the stogie. After a few miles, he pulled a disposable lighter out of his pocket.

"Sorry," I said. "Delmar doesn't want anybody smoking in his car."

Billy blew out a mouthful of air.

"Don't you even wonder why you can't see the bottom of the canyon floor?" Jesus Rundell lit the cigar and a cloud of smoke drifted into the front seat.

The rest of the trip was uneventful.

I pulled into the driveway of my office ten minutes later. I was no closer to having a plan or the elusive file than when we'd left the bar. Billy wasn't too helpful, either, especially since we couldn't talk without the baldheaded whack job hearing us.

I put the transmission into park and wondered what to do next. The answer wasn't long in coming.

A bullet ripped into the front windshield.

I ducked.

Billy opened the door and rolled out.

Rundell yelled and swore.

Another shot rang out. A cloud of safety glass filled the front of the Bentley. Delmar was going to have my ass over this.

I killed the ignition, opened the door, and dropped to the ground. The bullets came from in front of the car; I headed to the back.

"What the hell is going on?" Billy was kneeling by the rear bumper.

"You're bleeding." I pointed to a red line on the side of his neck.

"Shit." Billy grabbed the wound.

Another shot, this time striking metal. We both lowered our heads reflexively.

I reached for my Browning and remembered it was back at Delmar and Olson's house. The pistol Olson had provided had been taken from me by one of the bouncers back at the bar.

"Where the hell is Rundell?" Billy pulled out the Ruger.

Before I could reply, I heard the rear door of the Bentley open followed by a banshee cry.

"I think we found him." I peeked around the rear of the car.

Jesus Rundell stood by the side of the Bentley, screaming at the top of his lungs. He stopped for a moment, pulled a pistol out from under his coat, and fired toward the front of the car: four, five, six shots, as fast as he could pull the trigger.

I couldn't see what he was shooting at, nor could he, if I was to guess. The bulb that lit the driveway had been burned out for months.

What I was pretty sure he was hitting was the side of the wood-framed house that served as our office. Judging by the angle at which he stood, I guessed most of his rounds were hitting the back of the structure, about where my personal space was.

The unknown shooter returned fire, three quick shots. Rundell yelled and grabbed the side of his head. The rear window of the Bentley shattered.

"Who the hell is out there?" Billy snuck a quick peek from his side of the car.

"I dunno. But if they keep shooting, you may not have to worry about Jesus anymore."

"Shit." Billy stood up. "Rundell, get the hell under cover, will ya?"

I looked at my friend. "I thought you wanted him dead?"

Rundell stumbled to the back of the car. Even in the low light, I could see blood dripping down the side of his neck and onto the shoulder of his sport coat. Our unknown assailant had shot off Jesus Rundell's earlobe.

"*Who the fuck is shooting at us?*" He banged the trunk of the Bentley with one hand.

"Shut the hell up!" Billy grabbed the man's arm and pulled at the same time as another volley rang out.

Rundell yelped. I actually saw the bullet rip through the fabric of his coat, high on his shoulder. He fell to his knees and leaned against the bumper of the car.

"W-w-where are the pictures?" He grasped the front of my shirt.

"Pictures?" I stared at the wounded man.

Billy pushed me aside and grabbed Rundell by the collar. "The meet. When is it?"

Rundell frowned. "Huh?"

"The sit-down." Billy pulled at the wounded man until their faces were only inches apart.

"Told you already." Rundell shook his head. "There won't be any problem."

"When and where?" Billy said.

"Day after tomorrow. Sugar Babies." Rundell's breathing was labored, his face even paler than before, the shock setting in. "What about the file?"

"Forget the file." Billy shook his head. "Is everything set up?"

"Quit worrying." Rundell rolled his eyes. "I told you everything would be cool."

"T-thanks." Billy let out a sigh as his shoulders sagged.

"We had a deal, remember?" Rundell smiled for the first time. "Everybody's gonna be okay—"

Billy fired once from the hip, striking Jesus Rundell in the forehead.

His head snapped back, a tiny spray of blood barely visible in the low light.

"What the hell?" I fell backward, landing on my ass.

"Let's go." Billy scrambled toward the street, keeping low.

Another shot hit the Bentley.

I followed him into the night.

CHAPTER FORTY-FIVE

Streetlights were a hit-or-miss thing in this section of East Dallas. City Hall, a fiscally mismanaged scandal-making machine, could barely come up with enough money to put gas in the police cars, never mind making sure all the outdoor lighting was functional.

So we ran in the dark. Billy was ahead of me. The pain in my stomach slowed me down. He paused after three blocks. When I caught up with him, he was leaning against a stop sign, breathing heavily.

This particular section of town was on the edge of a neighborhood controlled by the Mara Salvatrucha, also known as the MS-13, a particularly violent gang formed by refugees fleeing the civil violence in El Salvador. The MS-13 wouldn't much like a couple of white homeboys walking on their sidewalk.

"We have . . . got to . . . get out of here." Each wheezing breath I took was agony on my bruised diaphragm.

"Who was trying to kill us?" Billy pointed the Ruger at my nose.

"What the hell are you doing?"

"You threw me to the wolves once. Why wouldn't you do it again?"

"Did it not register with you that they were shooting at me, too?"

The throaty rumble of a car with glass-pack mufflers sounded down the block. No sirens yet. A twenty-round firefight in gangbanger land was about as common as a car alarm going off. I wondered if anybody had even dialed 911.

"I'm not going back to prison." Billy's voice was shaky.

"This is gang turf." I turned toward the sound of the approaching automobile. "A couple of gringos on foot. Gonna be bad."

"Yo." A voice sounded from the darkness. The car, a twenty-year-old Chevy riding an inch from the pavement, pulled to the curb, the headlights illuminating two figures standing on the sidewalk.

I didn't say anything. Billy held the gun by his thigh, more or less out of sight.

"What's up, man?" The taller of the two spoke, his accent thick and exaggerated. The smaller one took a step forward. He was maybe twelve years old.

"We're passing through," I said. "I'm from a couple of streets over. No disrespect meant."

The older one nodded a couple of times as if he were pondering the situation. He looked at Billy. "And what's your problem?"

Billy didn't say anything. Instead he pointed the gun at the one closest to us. His hand shook.

"What the hell, bro?" The older one took a step back and raised his hands, not the actions of a hardened gangbanger.

"Billy." I kept my focus on the two in front of us. "Put. The gun. Down."

"Yeah . . . *Billy*." The older one backed away another foot or so. "No problems here, man. Just put the piece down."

"Okay, it's cool." Billy let out a long breath and relaxed his shoulders. That's when the Ruger went off, striking the youngster in the eye. The tiny .22 was like a loud pop gun.

The older one grabbed his mouth and fell to his knees. The car sped off down the street.

"I-I-I didn't mean to." Billy turned to me. "The trigger . . ."

I forgot to breathe, my skin cold. Everything seemed hazy, as if filtered through dirty glass.

"*Madre de Dios.*" The man beat his chest.

"It was an accident," Billy said. "I swear."

"You killed my little brother." He cradled the youngster's head in his lap and stared at us.

"Billy." I watched my friend point the Ruger at the man on the ground. "What the hell are you doing?"

"I'm not going back to prison, Hank." His voice was a whisper. "You have no idea what it's like."

"Put the gun down." I began to shake, my limbs trembling uncontrollably. "Don't make a bad situation worse."

The man holding his dead brother wailed.

I looked down the street. It was empty. "We need to get out of here."

Billy rocked on his feet a couple of times and lowered the gun.

I trotted back toward my office. When I got to the alley, I turned left and made my way down the narrow track. Billy followed a few feet behind.

I listened and watched for the police. I heard more dogs than I could count, three backyard domestic disputes (two in Spanish and one in a guttural language I couldn't identify), and a half dozen boom boxes playing Mexican radio.

I saw three squirrelly looking people smoking dope, two rats, and a dead dog. At the end of the alley I turned right and walked toward Rieger Street.

Billy said, "Where are we going?"

I didn't reply.

"You gonna turn me in again, Hank?" Billy's voice was shrill. "It was an accident."

I didn't say anything. I thought about the child lying on the sidewalk a few blocks over. I kept walking.

A hundred yards from my office I moved off the sidewalk and melted into the shadows of the neighboring buildings, hugging the shrubs. Billy was still behind me.

When I got to the place next door to my office, I stopped and waited, listening for any movement. After three or four minutes, it became obvious that the shooter was either waiting silently for us to return (not a likely scenario) or had left.

I dashed to the front door and saw that it had been forced open. The frame by the lock was in splinters. The inside was in near-total darkness.

Billy appeared beside me.

I ignored him and crept to my office. There was a cocked-and-locked Browning Hi Power in a small childproof box bolted underneath my desk. I grabbed the Browning and a SureFire flashlight and returned to the hallway as the night breeze flowed through the shot-out windows.

"Now what?" Billy's voice had a trembling quality to it.

"Stay here." I brushed past him and did a quick search of the interior. There weren't many places to hide. Once outside I pressed myself against the side of the building and did a quick circuit around the perimeter to make sure the shooter was really gone.

He wasn't.

CHAPTER FORTY-SIX

When I got to the backyard, by the alley where the bamboo grew thick, I smelled alcohol. Then I heard snoring.

I waited for a long 120 count but nothing else sounded except crickets and the faraway sounds of a city at night. I held the flashlight away from my body and the pistol at eye level and aimed at darkness. After another half minute I turned on the SureFire. The overgrown backyard lit up as if it were daylight, the powerful xenon bulb making everything a vibrant white.

Larry Chaloupka, Nolan's once again ex-fiancé, lay sprawled on the dirt, an almost empty bottle of Jack Daniel's in one hand, a Korean knockoff of a Glock nine-millimeter in the other.

His polyester short-sleeved dress shirt had come untucked, exposing a massive belly rising and falling in sync with the snores.

I slowly let out my breath and leaned against the side of the house. Unfortunately, there were only a few seconds to relax before I heard sirens close by and saw red and blue flashing lights. The gravel crunched in the driveway where the shot-up Bentley sat next to Jesus Rundell's corpse. Car doors slammed.

I killed the light and placed the Hi Power on a windowsill, after removing the live round from the chamber. A Dallas police officer broke through the shrubs and into the backyard.

He appeared to be concentrating on Larry's comatose form and didn't see me for a moment. When he finally did, he pointed his gun and light at my head. *"Freeze."*

I raised my hands.

More police entered the small area; lots of lights flashing, cops talking, radios radioing. An older officer, obviously in charge, sauntered in and took a quick look around before walking to where I stood. He was about fifty. The name tag on his chest said COOPER.

The younger cop who had entered first shoved me against the rough wooden wall of the office. A quick but thorough pat-down ensued. He removed my wallet and tossed it to his superior before pulling my hands behind me and snapping on the cuffs.

"You want to start at the beginning or where it gets fun?" Cooper said.

"Sergeant Jessup wouldn't be on nights, would he?" I smiled and tried to look as little like a murderer as possible.

"Who?"

"Frank Jessup. He works homicide."

"Son, let me give you some advice." Cooper smiled in an unfriendly way. "Don't start out dropping names of homicide guys. Makes me think you've got experience in that area."

A squawking radio saved me from having to answer right then. A garbled voice mentioned gang activity, a dead body, and the name of the street where Billy had just accidentally killed the youngster.

"Busy night here in the hood." Cooper fiddled with a control on his walkie-talkie.

"That so?" I kept my tone neutral.

He opened my wallet and chuckled. "Lee Oswald, huh?"

"I go by Hank."

"Sure you do." He squinted and rifled through cards and wallet junk. "And you would be a private investigator, right?"

"That's correct."

"Who's this?" Cooper pointed to Larry's snoring figure, over which a couple of officers were kneeling.

"That's Larry Chaloupka." I wondered when he was going to get to the dead body in the driveway. "My partner's ex-fiancé."

"This your office?" Cooper walked to the corner of the old house and scratched at what looked like a bullet hole.

"Yeah."

"Somebody shot it up pretty good." He turned to the rookie cop. "Anybody checked the interior?"

"Not yet." The officer shook his head. "The door looks jimmied."

"See what we've got going on inside."

My stomach constricted, vision tunneled.

Cooper walked a few steps and stopped in front of the window where I had placed my Browning. "Is this yours?"

I nodded as a line of perspiration dribbled down my temple.

Cooper smiled. "You hot?"

I didn't say anything.

"Let's stand out here where it's cooler, whaddya say?" He grabbed the Browning in one hand and my elbow in another and propelled me toward the driveway.

I resisted for a second.

"What?" The officer stopped. "You got a problem going out there?"

"U-u-uh, no." I was really sweating now. "It's just . . . all that shooting."

"It's secure now." Cooper tightened his grip on my arm and pushed until I was standing by the front of the ruined Bentley.

That was when I noticed there was no one standing behind the car, hovering over the body of Jesus Rundell. Two marked police units, lights still swirling, were blocking the driveway, only ten or twelve feet from where Billy had shot him. A small group of uniforms stood between the two squad cars, talking and doing cop stuff.

"Hey, somebody want to bag this for me?" Cooper held up the Browning.

An officer headed our way, walking right over the spot where Rundell's body was.

Or should have been.

Cooper handed him the gun and then turned to me. "Have you fired that weapon tonight?"

I stared at the officer as he walked back to his squad car with my Hi Power. I tried to understand what it meant that the body was no longer lying in the driveway behind the Bentley.

"Hey, Lee Harvey." Cooper snapped his fingers. "You still here?"

"Uh . . . yeah." I shook my head and blinked a couple of times. "I mean no. I haven't discharged a weapon."

He nodded slowly and left me standing there, joining the small knot of officers clustered between the two squad cars. After a couple of minutes, more uniforms joined them from behind the house. There was a lot of talking and gesturing and scribbling on clipboards.

Cooper frowned and spoke into his radio. He put the walkie-talkie back on his belt and pointed to my office, saying something to a couple of officers.

They walked toward the front door.

Cooper broke free of his little law enforcement confab and headed my way. When he got to where Rundell's body should have been, he stopped. He looked down, pulled out a flashlight, and turned it on.

I was standing in the ten feet between the Bentley and the outer wall of my office area. With the window broken, it was easy to hear the people moving in my room. I listened to them search the building where I had left Billy Barringer only a few minutes ago. I watched Cooper gesture to the ground where a psychotic hitman had fallen with a bullet in his head.

Broken glass tumbled in my gut. Sweat coated my face.

After a few moments, Cooper approached me. "Guess we better go inside and straighten this all out."

I let him pull me toward the front door.

CHAPTER FORTY-SEVEN

A squad car was parked in front of my office, more uniforms milling about. Crime scene tape delineated the property line. When I saw this, my last hope that Billy had somehow gotten out of the house vanished.

Cooper guided me through the front door. The air conditioner had been turned on. A blast of cool air enveloped me. I started shaking a little but not from the temperature change.

An officer walked into the reception area, an evidence bag in his hand. I couldn't tell what it contained. He and Cooper had a whispered conversation. Every few seconds they looked at me.

Cooper took the bag and approached me. "Where's your office?"

"In the back."

"Show me."

A few moments later, we were standing by my desk. The overhead light illuminated the damage: broken glass, far wall pockmarked from bullets. A stray round had hit the picture of my Ranger squad in Kuwait City. The bullet had punched through the image of Olson's chest.

"I wouldn't have bet on it, but you're clean. For now." Cooper unlocked my handcuffs. "You want to tell me what happened?"

"Pulled into the driveway and Larry shot out the window." I rubbed my wrists.

"Which direction were the shots coming from?"

"Here." I swiveled my head to indicate the office. "Outside, I mean."

"What time was this?"

I told him.

"Any idea why Mr. Chaloupka would be shooting at you?"

"He and my partner break up on a pretty regular basis. Plus he's drunk a lot of the time."

Cooper nodded and walked to the shot-out windows. He pulled aside the ruined curtains and looked outside. "We found a homicide victim a few blocks away, on the edge of a gang area."

I started sweating again.

"It wasn't a hit, though." He turned from the window. "Actually, it doesn't look as if he was a member, more likely a wannabe."

I tried to control my breathing.

"So you pull in and your partner's fiancé tries to take you out."

"Yeah."

"And then you returned fire?"

"No."

"Who shot back then?"

"I don't know."

"We found a pile of nine-millimeter cases. Looks like whoever was shooting was standing by the car at the time." Cooper strolled to the far wall and looked at the cracked picture. "Hard to understand why you wouldn't see who was shooting."

"Guy was behind me. Different guns spit out empties differently."

"Yeah." He nodded. "That's a good point."

A woman wailed in Spanish outside.

"We ID'd the kid." Cooper shook his head and sighed. "He was only ten."

I wasn't sweating anymore. My skin was cold and clammy. I could taste the muddy water of the Brazos River, feel the hook of the trotline dig into my flesh all these years later.

"One shot through the eye. Small-caliber, probably a twenty-two." He held up the plastic evidence bag. "From a gun like this, maybe."

I could see the outline of the Ruger .22 that Billy had been carrying.

"We found it on the floor in your office."

"You think the shooter broke in here, maybe?" I willed my voice to stay even.

"Don't know. I was hoping you could help."

"Beats me. All I know is what I've told you." I shrugged. The words that came from my mouth sounded far away.

Cooper nodded. "Let's go over that one more time, okay?"

By the time I had finished relating my made-up story for the third time, Sergeant Jessup arrived. It was now about three in the morning but his dress was impeccable, silk tie knotted just so, the cuff of his pants breaking perfectly over the toes of his polished loafers. He nodded at me and had a quick conversation with Cooper. The uniformed officer left with Billy's Ruger.

Jessup sat on the corner of my desk. "You want to tell me what really happened?"

"Just told it all to the other guy." I brushed glass off my sofa and sat down, suddenly very tired.

"You gonna stick with that?"

"Yeah." I leaned back and closed my eyes.

"Whose blood was behind the car?"

"Two federal guys were nosing around, asking about a big meeting supposed to happen here in Dallas." I reached in my wallet and pulled out the card the older FBI agent had given me.

"You're losing me," Jessup said.

"Tell them that nothing's gonna upset the balance of power." I stood up, handed him the card, and walked to the doorway.

"Where are you going?" Jessup pushed himself off my desktop.

The question took a while to worm its way through my frazzled synapses. "Got to get something to eat. Then sleep." I closed my eyes for a moment. "Then I need to take a quick trip to East Texas."

"There's blood on that Ruger, you know." He spoke softly.

I didn't say anything, just listened to the police and crime scene investigators and EMTs outside my office window. The woman's voice was wailing again.

"When they run a DNA test on it, what are they gonna find?"

"Beats me."

I wondered if ghosts could bleed.

There was a twenty-four-hour Taco Bell a few blocks away on Gaston. I had no car, so I walked. The streets were empty, the hour too late for even the hookers to be out. When I got to the restaurant I ordered one of everything and ate until nothing would go in anymore. Surprisingly, it made my bruised stomach feel better.

My cell rang as I was leaving. Nolan's number appeared on caller ID. I turned the phone off, stuck it in my pocket, and staggered back to my office. The crime scene tape was still staked around the property, but the police had left. The EMTs had taken Larry to the emergency room for acute alcohol poisoning. Delmar's shot-up Bentley hadn't moved. Judging by the bullet holes in the hood, it looked like it couldn't move.

Fatigue ravaged my body like a cancer, picking at every cell, draining any semblance of stamina.

But I had nowhere to rest. My home was gone, and I didn't want to face Delmar and tell him about his quarter-million-dollar vehicle.

The front door was wedged shut with a piece of cardboard. I opened it and made my way to my office. I stepped over the threshold and smelled sweat. No sound disturbed the room except for the low moan of a warm breeze coming through the busted window.

I saw a figure sitting on my sofa in the dark. When I got closer I wasn't surprised to find Billy Barringer drinking from a tall plastic water tumbler.

"You were in the attic, right?" I sat down next to him.

Billy didn't reply.

"You killed a child."

"Gets pretty damn hot up there." He drained the glass and put it on the floor. "You didn't turn me in."

"No."

"Why?"

There was no answer available that I could articulate. I had made a different choice, one I knew would haunt me long after this point in time passed from the fabric of my consciousness.

"I was in a hurry. Dropping the gun like that was pretty stupid," he said.

"It doesn't matter."

"I meant what I told you before."

"About what?"

"About being out of the life." He stood up.

I kicked off my shoes, wriggled my toes, felt my eyelids get droopy. "Rundell's body is gone."

"I put one in his head. It's over."

"I'm sure it is." I leaned over on the sofa.

"See you around, buddy." Billy Barringer walked out of the room.

CHAPTER FORTY-EIGHT

The voices in my head would not stop chattering. They were an incessant buzz, just below the volume needed for comprehension. I heard what sounded like my office mate, the lawyer with the Napoléon complex, whispering, his tone angry.

I felt heat, sensed light through my closed lids. I tried to remember where I was. I burped and tasted hot sauce.

"I think he's awake." My suite mate sounded louder now.

I opened my eyes and saw two people standing over me: Ferguson, the height-challenged lawyer whose office was in the next room, and our landlord, a foul-tempered Iranian man named Ebrahim.

Sunlight was streaming through the broken windows. Traffic noises came from outside. The events of the previous evening slowly came back to me.

My eyes felt gritty. I blinked and looked at the clock on the far wall. It was 9.30 A.M. I had been asleep on my sofa for a little over five hours.

"Goddmann, Oswald." Ebrahim's accent was thick. "Look at what you do. This this this . . ." The veins in his neck were throbbing.

"What are you talking about?" I sat up and rubbed my face. "It's just a little mess."

Ebrahim rattled off what sounded like a long invective in his native tongue. I got the feeling it involved me having carnal knowledge with a camel.

Ferguson made a tsking sound. "You've really outdone yourself this time."

"Shut up." I stood and both men took a step back.

"You. Get out now." Ebrahim pointed to the door. "No more Lee Oswald here."

"Hey, my rent's current." I walked to the closet in the corner and worked the combination on the small gun safe that was inside.

"No rent. No lease. No nothing for Oswald." Ebrahim was hopping up and down.

I opened the safe. The police had kept my Hi Power. I found another one and slipped it into an inside-the-waistband holster. I took off the shirt borrowed from Delmar and put on a spare denim one hanging in the closet.

"You not listening to me, Lee Oswald," Ebrahim said.

"Yes, I am. I'll move my stuff out of here in the next day or two." I twisted and something that might or might not have been important popped in my lower back. "If you touch anything before I get it out, I'll go jihad on your ass, you understand?"

He gulped and backed away from me.

I locked the safe and turned to Ferguson. "I need a ride."

"What am I, a taxi service now?"

"Yep." I grabbed his arm and pushed him out the door.

Fifteen minutes later, he dropped me off at Delmar and Olson's. I rang the bell.

"Hi." Nolan opened the door. "They had to take Olson back to the hospital."

I didn't say anything, just got the clammy-skin feeling again.

"Under his skull. The bleeding wouldn't stop."

"Where's my truck?"

"In the back." She jerked her thumb toward the rear.

"Keys." I held out my hand.

She fished them out of her pocket. "Don't you even care about your friend?"

"More than you can imagine." I took the keys and padded though the house, Nolan trailing after me. My Tahoe was parked under the old pecan tree that took up most of their backyard.

"What are you doing?" Nolan stepped in front of me.

"What do you care?"

"Shit, Hank." She shook her head, ran a hand through her hair. "I'm sorry I bailed on you."

"Talked to Larry lately?" I moved around her and walked outside.

"That's over for good." She followed me. "He's really unstable, thought there was something between you and me."

I got in the Tahoe.

"Where are you going?" Nolan opened the passenger door and stepped in.

"Nowhere with you."

"Uh-uh." She slid onto the seat and placed a hand on my arm. "You look like you haven't slept in a month."

"Where's Tess?"

"I don't know. She called a cab not long after you and Billy left."

I nodded and tried to understand what that meant.

"Hank, tell me what's going on."

"Your ex tried to kill me last night."

Nolan's face went white.

"He missed." I turned on the ignition. "Last time I heard he was still in the hospital."

She stared at me, eyes wide.

"Alcohol poisoning." I put the car in reverse and whipped around, heedless of Nolan's still-open door.

"You trying to kill me?" She grabbed the console with one hand and the door handle with other, pulling the latter shut before it slammed into the wooden privacy fence.

"You said you wanted to come."

"I asked where we were going."

"A little town called Spenser."

"Crap." Nolan put on her seatbelt. "Nothing good comes from that part of the world."

CHAPTER FORTY-NINE

Two hours later, we passed the city limit sign for Spenser. I tried to remember the last time I'd been there. It must have been twenty-five years ago or more. The circumstances of that trip eluded me at the moment.

Spenser hadn't changed much, unlike other places I'd been to recently. The square overlooked a small lake ringed with pine trees. All of the buildings in the center of town looked freshly painted. People were milling around on the sidewalks, going in and out of a place called the Blue Bonnet Café.

I stopped at a convenience store a block off the square, went inside, and asked the woman behind the counter for a phone directory. She handed me a thin book.

There was no listing for Barringer. I found it under her maiden name: V. Carmichael, 821 Rosemont Avenue. I tossed the book on the counter, headed back outside, and jumped in the truck.

"Where to?" Nolan asked.

I told her.

"Why do you think it's there?"

I didn't answer, just started driving. The good thing about small towns was that it's easy to find places since the options for looking are limited. A few minutes later, I turned onto Rosemont Avenue.

Vivian Carmichael's place was a one-story gingerbread house with a covered porch running across the front with two swings at either end. It was in the middle of the block, underneath a massive live oak tree so old it must have been a sapling during the Coolidge administration.

I parked across the street and hopped out. Nolan followed. The wooden porch creaked under my weight. I smelled fried chicken, heard a television blaring.

I rapped on the door frame. The TV muted. Dainty footsteps approached.

"Yes?" Vivian Barringer's soft face, framed by gray hair, appeared behind the screen door. She wore an apron over a faded housedress and held a spatula in one hand.

I smiled. "Heya, Mrs. B."

"Hank Oswald?" She squinted at me through the screen door. "Good Lord, I haven't seen you since I don't know when."

I knew but didn't want to say.

"How in the world are you?" She stepped outside and gave me a hug. She smelled like soap and fried chicken.

"Fine," I said.

"Well, come on in." Billy's mother held open the door and motioned us inside.

"This is Nolan." I gestured to my partner and entered the house. "We work together."

Vivian shook her hand. "Y'all come on back to the kitchen. I've got a fresh pot of coffee and some cobbler sitting out."

We followed her into a linoleum-floored room that looked out on a rambling backyard that seemed to go on forever. An old gas stove on one wall contained several simmering pots. I remembered now: Vivian Barringer loved to cook.

"Have some coffee." She poured us each a mug.

I took the cup and blew on the surface. It was about ninety degrees outside and not much cooler in the steamy kitchen.

Vivian fussed with some of the pots on the stove, her back to us.

Nolan looked at me. I shrugged. After a minute or so, Vivian turned back around. There were tears in her eyes.

"You gave him back to me, you know." Her voice cracked.

"Mrs. B." I put the coffee on the countertop. "I'm sorry."

"Don't be." She smiled and pointed the spatula at me like a sword. "You always were a good boy. Did the right thing."

I shook my head slowly but didn't say anything.

"He's returned now." She dabbed at her eyes with the end of her apron. "No more of that life his father would have for him."

"He told me he was going to stay straight."

"And he will, trust me." She worried the apron in her hands. "Once you take the journey, you come back changed."

I didn't understand. "Do you have something for me?"

"He lives not far from me now, did you know that?" She returned to the stovetop.

Nolan went to the kitchen window and looked outside.

"I had a hunch there might be something here for me." I moved to the side of the stove to catch her eye.

"Hank. You better check this out." Nolan's tone was insistent.

I looked outside. A narrow strip of Saint Augustine grass divided the yard, with vegetable gardens on either side, tomato and pepper plants on the right, melons and squash and corn on the left.

A Filipino man was in the middle, walking toward the house carrying a pail of vegetables. He had on a pair of baggy parachute pants like something M. C. Hammer might have worn back in the day, and a black wife-beater-style undershirt. The white music player was on his belt, the earpieces in place.

I went outside, Nolan right behind me. The screen door banged shut. The man looked up. His eyes went wide and he stopped walking.

"Hello, Arthur." I took a couple steps into the yard. "What a coincidence, seeing you here."

He threw the pail at my head. I ducked, and it hit Nolan on the shoulder. He ran away from the house, and I went after him. The thin strip of grass petered out and gave way to an overgrown series of flower beds, an uneven gravel path between them. Rosebushes grew unkempt everywhere, overhanging branches forming a barrier in the narrow passageway.

Arthur knew the territory better, but I was faster, heedless of the thorns tearing at my clothing and flesh.

I had just started to gain some ground when he passed a wooden worktable under a cedar tree. He grabbed a trowel as he went by, turned, and threw it at me with more force than I would have imagined.

The rusted tool went low and grazed the outer edge of my left knee. I lost my footing and hit the table, knocking it over on top of me.

"Quit jacking around, will ya?" Nolan hopped over me like a gazelle and pressed on through the overgrown garden.

I brushed potting soil out of my hair and stood up. Nolan shouted to me, her voice muffled by the garden. A man yelled.

"Where are you?" I limped toward the back of the lot until the gravel path forked.

No response.

"Nolan." I wiped sweat out of my eyes, dirt off my face.

"Over here."

"Here left, or here right?" I mentally flipped a coin and started down the right track.

"Hold o-o-on." She sounded exasperated. A few seconds later she appeared on the left path, pushing Arthur in front of her. One knee of his parachute pants was ripped and bloody.

"What happened?" I grabbed Arthur by his free arm. He looked at me, breathing heavily and sweating.

"He tripped over a wheelbarrow." Nolan mopped sweat off her forehead with one hand.

"Why were you running?" I squeezed the man's arm.

"Tired of getting punked by you." His look was icy.

"You want to tell us why you're here, in Vivian Barringer's backyard?"

He didn't answer.

"Arthur." I sighed. "Don't be the Filipino version of a dumbass. Tell us what's going on."

"Mrs. Barringer, she's been very good to me."

"You know why we're here, don't you?"

He didn't say anything.

"A man at Carlos's mother's apartment mentioned a *chino,* a Chinese," I said. "Made me think of you."

He nodded slowly.

"Where is it?"

His eyes cut left for an instant before returning to stare at the ground.

I turned and saw a narrow opening in an otherwise solid wall of honeysuckle vines.

Arthur chewed on his lower lip.

I shoved him toward Nolan and pulled the Browning from its holster before plunging through the opening. The honeysuckle formed a tunnel of sorts, about ten feet long. I exited to another, less overgrown backyard. The lawn was well watered but needed mowing. A wood-framed house with peeling paint was to the right, more or less even with Vivian Barringer's. I whistled once and Nolan and Arthur emerged a couple of seconds later.

"How many people are in there?" I kept the Browning by my side.

"No one that can hurt you."

"How many?"

"Only one." Sweat was running down Arthur's face now.

Nolan holstered her gun and blew a strand of hair out of her face. "God knows why, but I believe our friend."

I ignored both of them, walked to the house, and opened the back door. The place was not much different from Vivian's, with a linoleum-floored kitchen, old appliances, dated decor. I smelled moth-balls and dust as I went to the front of the home.

Lucas Linville was sitting in a wheelchair by the living room win-dows, staring at the hallway.

"Been. Expecting. You." He could talk now, though each word was an obvious effort.

"What's in the file?" I sat down on a chintz-covered armchair, sud-denly tired.

"Honesty." A thin line of spittle hung out of his mouth like a spider-web. "And ret . . . ret . . . r-r-retribution."

"Where is it?" I stood up so as not to let the fatigue overrun my body.

"Arthur hid it."

The Filipino man was standing in the hallway with my partner. He started to say something but Nolan made a noise and pointed to the win-dow. I looked outside and saw a yellow cab parked in front of the house.

The passenger door was open and Jesus Rundell exited, a bloody bandage on his head. He pulled a long-barreled shotgun out with him and pointed it at the window of the house.

Nolan said, "Oh, shit."

The gun fired and the window disappeared.

CHAPTER FIFTY

Time seemed to stand still. I saw a triangle of glass cartwheel toward my head but I was powerless to move. The shard hit my forehead above the right brow. My eyes snapped shut, and I fell to the floor.

I heard the shotgun fire again.

Nolan yelled.

Another boom from outside, closer this time.

Arthur screamed. I rolled away from the window, clawing at my waist for the Browning. Got the gun out. Rubbed blood out of my eyes with my left hand. With my right I rammed the rear sight on the Hi Power into my hip and pushed down, jacking a round into the chamber one-handed.

Opened my eyes. Everything was fuzzy and red. I brought the gun up. Pointed it toward where the front door should be. Was vaguely aware of a foot appearing out of nowhere, headed toward my hand. Gun disappeared. Fingers hurting now. Closed my eyes again.

When I opened them Jesus Rundell stood over me.

"You're supposed to be dead." I looked at his face. It was coated with dried blood. His eyes were askew, looking in different directions.

"T-t-told you I gotta hard skull." He put the shotgun to his shoulder and aimed at a spot two feet from my head. "Now tell me where the file is."

"I don't know."

Rundell made a sound like a frat boy after his twelfth tequila shot. He sat down and dropped the shotgun on the floor. His eyes glazed over as the skin on his face not covered in blood blanched.

"He gets that way every now and then." Tess McPherson stood in the doorway, a long-barreled revolver in one hand.

"I give up. Whose team are you on?"

"Not yours, chump."

"Then how did you know to come here?"

She laughed once. "You hang out with the Barringer boys long enough, you eventually learn where mama lives."

I looked to the other side of the room. Nolan was sitting on the floor, holding her bicep with one hand, blood trickling through her fingers. Her pistol was a few feet away. Arthur was curled in the fetal position, shivering with his hands over his ears. Except for a small cut on his cheek, Lucas Linville looked unharmed. He'd been in the corner, not directly in front of the glass.

"Why don't you tell me where this file thing is so we can get the hell out of here?" Tess pointed the revolver at my face to emphasize her point.

"Linville is the only one who knows and he can't talk."

"Or move, apparently." Tess walked over to the wheelchair. "So how did he hide it then?"

"I ... uh ... don't know." I glanced to my right and saw the Hi Power next to the chintz-covered chair.

"Let's find out, shall we?" Tess stuck the muzzle of the revolver on the old man's knee. "Okay, Uncle Lucas. Tell me where the file is."

Nobody said anything.

Tess looked around the room. "Anybody else want to take a guess before I blow this guy's leg off?"

"Wait." Arthur sat up. "I will tell you."

"Arrrgh." Everybody in the room turned and looked at Jesus Rundell as he returned to a near lucid state. Some color had returned to his face and his eyes were focusing again, still crossed but alert.

"Baby?" Tess stepped away from Linville. "Are you okay?"

Nolan and I looked at each other. *Baby?*

Rundell stood up, using the shotgun as a cane.

Tess grabbed his arm. "The gook was just about to tell me where it is."

Rundell blinked several times and looked at me before turning to Arthur. "Start talking."

Arthur licked his lips. "In the closet in the dining room. There's a wooden box on the shelf. It is there."

"Want me to get it?" Tess said.

Rundell grunted and wrenched his arm free of her grasp. He staggered into the next room. I saw him look to the left and then the right. Apparently, the closet was in that direction because he wobbled that way and was soon out of sight.

I heard a door open.

I heard Rundell grunt.

I heard wood scrape against wood, metal hinges squeak.

I heard the angry buzz of at least one pissed-off rattlesnake.

"What the hell is that?" Tess darted toward the dining room.

I stuck my foot out and tripped her. She fell onto a coffee table covered with broken glass.

"*Ayeeahh.*" Rundell's voice was beyond pain and fear, the tone primeval.

I scrambled to where the Hi Power lay, snatched it, and stood up. Nolan had grabbed her pistol and was pointing it at Tess. I headed to the dining room.

"*No.*" Arthur reached for my arm. "The snakes."

I stopped. Everyone was quiet, listening to the sound of rattling and Rundell's dying moans.

"You gotta be cool," Arthur said. "They're poisonous and shit."

"No fooling?" I tiptoed to the left side of the doorway leading to the dining room, opposite the closet. I leaned in and looked. It was hard to tell since they were all squirming and hissing but it looked like there were six or eight pretty large rattlers crawling on and around Rundell's twitching form. I could see at least two sets of puncture wounds on his arms.

"You go in there, you're gonna get bitten," Arthur said.

"What about him?" I pointed at Rundell.

"What about him?" Arthur raised one eyebrow.

"Good point."

Rundell began to shake. His arms were swollen to twice their regular size. The snakes hissed. The smallest one lunged at his thigh and bit.

"Ouch." I lowered the gun.

"He was not a nice man." Arthur crossed himself.

A manila envelope was lying in the corner. "Is that it?"

"Yeah." He grabbed a cane leaning against the wall. "I'll get it."

"You don't have to—" I stopped when he dashed into the room, shaking the cane at the snakes. He grabbed the file and hopped back to the relative safety of the entrance to the living room.

I took the file and sat down on the chintz-covered chair. I pulled out a series of dental X-rays. The name across the bottom of each strip of film was Lucas L. Carmichael, DDS.

"You switched his X-rays. Both of them were your patients at one time." I looked at the man. "Your *middle* name is Linville."

"I didn't switch nothing." The old man shook his head. "They came to me after the body turned up. Asked for the records."

"What are you talking about?" Nolan stood up, keeping her gun pointed at Tess.

"I closed my practice in Waco years ago." Lucas ignored her and spoke to me. "Told them I would get the records out of storage. Called my sister and asked her to see to it; she lives closer."

"Charity Carmichael." I held the X-ray up to the light.

"They got the X-rays and said it was Billy in the car, Billy that burned up. Charity was still out there, running from the law." The old man's eyes filled with tears. "But my boy would have called if he was alive."

"How did you know?" I asked.

The old man was sobbing now. After a few moments he continued. "They told me it was an easy ID, what with Billy missing his eye-tooth."

"Billy had perfect teeth." I stood up and tucked the film under my arm.

"Just couldn't figure it out. How they did it." Lucas shook his head slowly as tears trickled down his cheeks. "H-h-had three children. F-f-faith, Hope. And Charity."

"I'm sorry for what you've gone through." I looked out the window.

"W-w-why does one go bad," Linville said, "and not the others?"

The first police car pulled up outside.

The Spenser Police Department proved remarkably efficient and professional, given the circumstances.

How often do small-town law enforcement agencies come across third-rate mobsters killed by rattlesnakes? Or dead Eritrean nationals such as the man found in the trunk of the Dallas taxicab? He had a bullet hole in the back of his head that appeared to be from the same-caliber revolver carried by Tess McPherson.

Maybe their efficiency had something to do with the navy blue Chevy pickup that idled at the end of the block, the windows cracked a little to let the smoke from Clayton Barringer's cigarette escape.

The police interviewed Nolan and me and seemed satisfied by our answers. After all, we'd done nothing wrong. Neither of us mentioned the file. I rolled it up and stuck it in my back pocket.

A professional snake wrangler was called. Lucas Linville watched him carry them away without saying anything.

An hour after the first police arrived, a pair of crime scene investigators from the Department of Public Safety showed up, followed a few minutes later by two men in a government-issued sedan.

I asked the deputy who they were. He told me they were from the FBI office in Austin, part of the Organized Crime Task Force. A few minutes later he told us we could leave.

I watched for a moment as the CSI techs took pictures of Jesus Rundell's body. One pulled aside the bloody bandages on his head and said the .22-caliber bullet had failed to penetrate the skull, instead furrowing along the bone underneath the skin.

Nolan said that maybe it was time for us to leave. I nodded and looked at Lucas Linville sitting in the corner in his wheelchair, largely unnoticed by the crew of people moving in and out of the house. His mouth had sagged open and his skin was waxy and the color of milk. There was no discernible movement in his chest.

Arthur was outside, ear buds in place, jamming out. I glanced once more at Linville and wondered what his last thoughts were. Was he with his son now? Was he in the presence of Charity?

"Let's go." I touched Nolan on the elbow and we left. Once outside I approached Arthur. The Filipino man pressed a button on his music player and flashed me the peace sign.

"How did it happen?" I said.

"When he wanted to hide the file on his son, he stuffed it in one close by." Arthur pulled the earpieces out. "Carmichael to Cunningham."

I nodded and looked at the wood-framed house next door where Billy Barringer's mother lived.

A curtain in the front window twitched.

We walked in without knocking and headed to the kitchen. Billy was sitting at the oilcloth-covered table, eating a bowl of blackberry cobbler and ice cream. His hair was dyed a chestnut brown and he was wearing an ill-fitting business suit.

"How did you get here?" I said.

"Does it matter?" He put down his spoon and looked at Nolan. "We haven't actually met. My name is Billy Reynolds." He stuck out his hand and gave her the megawatt smile.

Nolan blushed a little and returned the shake.

I pulled out the file. "My guess is that this is the last link to Billy Barringer."

My friend nodded. "That goes, I'm one hundred percent clear."

Vivian Barringer banged a spoon against a pot and fiddled with the temperature on the stove.

I moved to where she could see me and said, "You did the switch."

Vivian stirred the contents of a cast-iron pot.

"Your brother calls from Dallas. Asks for you to arrange for somebody to get the police the two files out of storage in Waco." I turned to Billy. "How did your cousin die?"

He shook his head. "Rundell's gone. The matter's taken care of."

"You knew where the file was." I looked at Vivian Carmichael. "Why didn't you destroy it?"

Neither mother nor son responded, Billy suddenly interested in his bowl of cobbler, Vivian pouring a measure of salt into a pot on the stove.

"My God." I slapped my forehead. "You were saving the file to keep Billy on the straight and narrow."

"Hank, let it go." Billy spoke softly.

Vivian opened her mouth for the first time. "What are you going to do with it?"

I picked up a book of matches lying on the table and walked out the back door. There was an empty concrete birdbath near the house. I lit a match and held it to the bottom of the file. The photographic paper ignited, billowing out black, chemical-smelling smoke. I held on to one end until the flames nipped at my hand, then let it drop into the dry birdbath.

Billy was standing beside me. "Thanks, Hank."

"Stay clean, Billy. Or I'll come looking."

CHAPTER FIFTY-ONE

The local Starbucks might have been a good location to play office if you were a Web designer or aspiring novelist or drug rep, but it wasn't the greatest place for a homeless private investigator.

I set up shop in a bar near Love Field called the Time Out Tavern. They opened at eleven every morning, about the time I rolled off the lumpy bed at the extended-stay hotel on Stemmons Freeway.

On the third day back from my last trip to East Texas, I walked in at about noon carrying the *Dallas Morning News* and two sausage-and-egg burritos. I nodded hello to the small group of day drinkers clustered at the end of the bar by the pool table.

The day promised to be hot and bright, no relief forecast for the September heat wave. Inside, the only illumination came from neon. No windows disturbed the cool, cavelike atmosphere. The bar ran along the left side, running perpendicular to a big-screen televison at the far end of the room.

The bartender had a diet Coke waiting for me. I ate and drank and read the paper. On the second page of the metro section there were a couple of paragraphs about three men from out of town who'd been found killed execution-style in the back room of a gentlemen's club on the west side of town. Two were Hispanic and thought to be involved in the drug trade, so the incident didn't rate more prominent placement.

At noon the bartender flipped the satellite from coverage of the Nova Scotian curling championship to the local news.

The lead story was about the new interstate called the Trans Texas Corridor, designed to relieve the pressure on I-35 by running through East Texas. They'd broken ground on another section. A map appeared onscreen. I put down my paper and stared at the television.

"You okay, Hank?" The bartender looked up from his sports page.

"Huh?"

"You were muttering to yourself."

"Uh . . . just remembered something, that's all." I tossed money on the bar and threw away the remains of my lunch before bolting outside.

I got in the Tahoe and headed toward the jail. Tess was in the Dallas County lockup, awaiting arraignment on the murder of the cabdriver. Ten minutes later I parked across the street between a bail bondsman's office and a liquor store and walked to the visitor entrance.

I pulled a card out of my wallet that said, SANDY MCCORMICK, ATTORNEY AT LAW. The check-in room was all tile and harsh lights and family members milling about. I waited in line patiently and then told the sheriff's deputy that I was the new court-appointed counsel for inmate Contessa McPherson. I handed him the card, and he tapped the information into his computer.

Thirty minutes later another deputy led me to a room with a table and two chairs, both bolted to the floor. Tess was sitting in one of the chairs, looking small and lost and vulnerable in handcuffs and jail whites.

She looked up when I walked in and said, "Shit."

I thanked the deputy and shut the door behind him.

"What do you want?" Tess said.

"I think I've got it figured out."

She didn't reply.

"Vernon Black wanted your parents' place because that was where the interstate was coming." I sat down in the other chair.

Tess's eyes narrowed.

"He got Rundell to threaten them, maybe using you, to sell out."

No reply.

"Then Rundell turns on him, probably asking for more money, and that's when Black called me."

"When I was twelve, my mother went to Austin for the weekend to see her sister." Tess smiled once, a look that made my blood chill. "It was about midnight when Daddy came into my room."

I didn't say anything.

"I told my mom when she got back." Tess leaned across the table. "She said I was a liar, always had been, and how could I say that about a man that was such a good provider."

"Tess, I'm sorr—"

"Shut the hell up, Hank. I don't want pity from anybody, you hear me?"

"Vernon Black's not gonna get away with it." I stood up.

"Shit." Tess laughed. "You couldn't even take out Billy, a convicted murderer. What the hell you think you're gonna do to a state senator?"

I moved to the door.

"One thing, Hank." Tess stood up. "Did you really think Billy is out of the life?"

Vernon Black's waiting area was vacant except for the same reception-ist. Her smile turned to a frown as I ignored her and made my way into the inner sanctum.

"Hey, wait a minute." She ran after me. "You can't go in there."

I pushed open the door to Black's private office. He was on the phone staring out his window toward downtown. He turned, a surprised look on his face.

I ripped the phone off his desk and threw it across the room.

"What the hell?" He looked bewildered.

"I'm sorry, Senator." The receptionist stood in the doorway. "I tried to—"

I shut the door in her face.

"Hank, have you lost your mind?" Black stood up, hands on his hips.

"You got in bed with Rundell and Tess just to get her family's place."

No reply.

"For a few pieces of silver. All this pain and suffering." I shook my head. "You've got enough money for ten lifetimes."

"You've heard the saying, haven't you, Hank?" He sat down, the barest trace of a smile on his lips. "Can't be too rich or too thin."

I tried to control my breathing.

He laughed. "You can't prove a thing."

"You're right."

"So get the hell out of here before I call security."

"It's a law of physics." I moved to the door. "For every action, there's a reaction."

I drove around Dallas for a while, thinking. I called Nolan. She had hooked up the night we got back with an aluminum-siding salesman twenty years her senior. They'd spent the last two days in his double-wide lake house, where he promised her he was gonna leave his wife just as soon as the last kid got out of high school. She'd come back to town to get clothes. I asked her to meet me.

A Realtor called and asked if I wanted to go look at houses. I told her no, I didn't know if I'd be staying in Dallas. Finally I drove to Delmar and Olson's.

Delmar was in the backyard, drinking beer and staring at dirt. He looked like I felt, unshaven and tired and empty. He'd been concentrating the last few days on what to do to Larry for shooting up his Bentley. That was better than thinking about other things.

The current plan involved honeybees, piano wire, and raw jalapeños. I wrote down Vernon Black's name on a scrap of paper and handed it to him. He asked a few questions. I answered. He got excited. I went inside to visit Olson. They had put him in a hospital bed in a room downstairs. The TV was on when I walked in, a nurse sitting by the window, knitting.

I nodded hello. She smiled and said she was going to get some coffee and did I want any. I shook my head and sat down by my friend. I talked to him for a long time, explaining it all. I think he understood. He closed his eyes every now and again, so it was hard to tell.

After a while, I went back outside. Nolan was there, sitting in a lawn chair one down from Delmar.

I sat between them in the big canvas recliner usually occupied by Olson.

"Senator or not," Delmar said, "he's going down."

I shrugged without replying.

"Nolan explained it to me," he said. "Billy's mother did the switch."

"Yep." I nodded. "Rundell breaks Billy and Charity out, in exchange for Billy's help in taking over North Texas."

"Got it so far." Delmar tilted the beer can back, draining the last drop.

"Billy and Charity were cousins," I said. "Charity's dad was Lucas Linville Carmichael, Vivian Carmichael Barringer's brother. And also a preacher wannabe, a drunk, and a dentist who had treated both of them as children. Lucas calls his sister when the police arrive. He's worried that his boy might be dead."

Delmar crushed the empty can in one hand and dropped it on the ground.

Nolan continued my train of thought. "Never occurs to Linville that his sister might be upset or worried that her son might have checked out. The booze had done a number on him by this point."

"The records are archived in Waco." Delmar opened another Miller Genuine Draft. "So before the investigators can get there, Billy's mother switches them."

"And everything would have been cool," I said, "except that one of the investigators happened to mention how easy an ID it was since Billy was missing a tooth. Only problem was that Billy had perfect teeth and Charity didn't."

"Why didn't Linville say something?" Delmar asked.

"He was drunk most of the time." I raised one eyebrow and looked at the pile of crushed cans sitting next to his chair.

"But he knew something was off, so he mentions it to his sister," Nolan said. "And he tells her he's kept an extra set of X-rays for his son, like he does for all his kids and he's sure that it was Charity that died in the fire."

"I get it now." Delmar waved me off before I could speak again. "She's trying to save her baby boy and sees the plan start to come apart because of her brother, so she tells Billy, who tells Jesus Rundell that if his cover gets blown, then there goes the Barringers' help in taking over."

"That's right," I said. "So Rundell gets his hooks into Carlos, a guy with a gambling problem and also Linville's assistant at the soup kitchen. He has him steal the file from Linville's office. Only problem is that Carlos decides to get tricky and hides it at his mother's apartment."

We were all silent. After a few minutes Delmar said, "What about the girl? Tess McPherson?"

"Hank gets to sleep with another client." Nolan spoke before I could. "I never trusted her."

"She had a thing for bad boys," I said. "Turns out she was playing me and Billy."

Nolan turned to Delmar. "What about Olson? Is he gonna be okay."

"Y'all better hope so." He got up and went inside. Nolan and I sat for a while without speaking. After a while, she left, too.

An hour later, Delmar came back. He was wearing different clothes now, a dark shirt and pants, nondescript. He carried a duffel bag that clanked when he walked. He asked if I wanted to go with him.

I said yes.